Behind these walls, a darkness lives

HOUSE OF DESIRE

Suzi Wieland

Twisted Path Press

Copyright ©2019 by Suzi Wieland
All rights reserved. The reproduction or utilization of this work in whole or in part, by any means, is forbidden without written permission from the author.
This book is a work of fiction. Names, characters, places, and incidents are products of the author's imagination or are used fictitiously. Any resemblance to actual events, locations, or persons, living or dead is entirely coincidental.
Cover design by Amanda Walker PA & Design Services
Published by Twisted Path Press
First edition April 2019, Second edition October 2023

Part I

Chapter One
House of Desire

The flashing and beeping slot machine stole another hard-earned dollar from my pocket. The noise, the blaring lights, the young people drinking and having fun. Vegas was not meant for an old woman like me. I hated it.

And I hated that I hated it.

A cheer erupted from a few slots down, and a neon yellow sign above the machine shouted *Jackpot!* A young vixen in a way-too-tight dress threw her hands in the air and bounced in her seat, her breasts bobbing. She ran her manicured fingers through her impeccable hair and smiled coyly at the man at her side. A second guy squeezed her shoulders in an overly friendly way and exchanged looks with the first guy. I'd give anything to be her, and not because she won a bunch of money. Those two fine men could make a tired woman happy, although I'd take the girl too. Maybe a foursome—three sexy twenty-year-olds and an elderly woman.

How absurd. I slumped on my chair. I just wanted to go back to the hotel room, slip into my pajamas, and go to bed. Sixty-two years shouldn't make me feel so ancient, but I'd arrived at senior citizenry in my fifties, unlike my friend Jackie, who at fifty-four was never offered the senior discount.

"Hey, Lillian, did you see that?" Jackie waved to the woman who won, and I nodded. She sat next to me on her own winning streak. Not a quit-my-job type of winning streak but more like an I-can-buy-a-new-recliner winning streak. She'd return to Indiana with a smile on her face as long as she didn't lose it all before then. And she wouldn't because she was practical like me. Stick to a pre-planned budget, and you won't go home crying.

"I'm not doing so well," I said, unwilling to fix my droopy face. My money was draining away too quickly, and it'd be gone before our vacation was up. Five hundred dollars I'd allotted myself for gambling and entertainment.

"Let's go get some food." She jumped to her feet before I commented about how my chubby body didn't need more junk. It was nine o'clock at night, and all the fat would add another layer to my hips. Jackie raised her brows and grinned. "Deep-fried pickles? I'm pretty sure they were on the menu when I checked earlier."

My mouth watered, and I finally smiled. "Only if they have ranch sauce."

She linked her arm through mine. "I'm sure they will. Let's go."

I slid off my chair and groaned, rubbing my aching hip.

"Sitting too long?" Jackie asked.

"I'm heading toward another hip replacement." Being off my feet for so long would be depressing, but I inherited bad hips from my father.

"But you got a new one eight years ago."

We passed by the jackpot girl, who was breathlessly telling her story to the small crowd surrounding her.

"It should've lasted longer. I might get through the next year. We'll see." I didn't want to talk about my hip issues or the arthritis in my hands. At least all the slots were touchscreen, so I didn't have to grasp that stupid lever and pull it down just to lose my money. I'd imagined Vegas to be such a fun place, but it was a lot of work too. "Oh, you forgot to tell me the story about Macy."

Jackie's eyes lit up, and we headed toward the restaurant. She loved talking about her grandkids, and I loved hearing the stories. I'd been a stupid career woman who only thought kids would get in the way, so now I had to live vicariously through my friends.

We devoured deep-fried pickles and cheese-smothered nachos, drank a few cheap glasses of wine, and Jackie talked me into hitting the slots one more time. My sore feet screamed at me from all the sightseeing we did today, but I faked my enthusiasm for her benefit. I promised her a good time, and I would deliver. She was one of my closest friends, after all, and in a few days we'd be back home, back at our jobs, back to the monotony of our lives.

Somewhere along the way I'd become old.

"Let's check out how the other people live." She winked and dragged me away and out of the building, down the street to one of the posh casinos. We didn't fit in among the modelesque women with their Coach purses, Jimmy Choos, and fine jewelry, but I wouldn't let my insecurities bother me. We had every right to be here too.

"What about roulette?" Jackie motioned to the tables on our right. "We should give it a try."

If I was lucky, I could win a few bucks like I did yesterday.

"Let's do it." I peered around one of the watchers to find the minimum bet sign. A snort escaped my nose before I could stop it. All sorts of colored chips covered the table.

"Not these tables. These are the hundred-dollar tables." And that was the minimum bet.

Jackie bounced on her feet, her eyes wide. "Let's watch. Maybe some of their good fortune will rub off."

I laughed, and we stepped closer. A number of men and women lined the table, drinking and chatting as if it meant nothing to throw away thousands of dollars without a thought.

My head snapped to a giggling woman with flawless skin, perfectly styled hair, and bright eyes. Her radiant smile showed off her straight white teeth. She was the type of woman I would've chased after in my younger years.

She leaned forward and set her arms on the table, effectively pressing her breasts together. If her dress dipped any lower, she'd be flashing us. She touched her fingers to the platinum crown pendant on her neck. It was pretty, but it belonged on an eight-year-old, not a grown woman.

Jackie was busy watching the play on the table, and I took in the man who wore the lovely woman on his arm. I gasped, heat filling my cheeks. Jackie looked over to me, and I covered my mouth like I'd coughed. The noise from the table and the room buzzed in my ears as my stomach flip-flopped.

His gray eyes and thick chestnut hair were so familiar. The strong chin and those full lips. I knew him. I knew that boy. An almost exact copy of his father. Walter Marceline the II was the son of Walt Marceline, a man I'd once loved and lost but never forgot.

"What's got into you?" Jackie laughed and then turned in the direction of my stare. "Oh wow. It's what's-his-name. The hotel guy with the castle of whores."

Prostitutes, yes. Walt Senior created an empire and was most known for the House of Desire, the brothel he owned in southern Nevada. His life was a far cry from the boy I grew up with in a small town outside of Fort Wayne. He had been socially awkward but was gifted with a sense of humor he didn't show to many.

"I knew his dad. Before he was famous." We were both nerds in high school. "We went to college together too."

"Didn't he die years ago?"

I quit ogling Walt's son and nodded. Another scantily clad gorgeous woman sat on his other side, not to mention all the people crowding behind him, his entourage.

"Twenty years ago or so. I'm not sure."

"So you knew his dad well?" Jackie asked.

The brilliant and handsome Walt Senior was a fascinating study, and I'd followed his career. For many of his adult years, he surrounded himself with the most beautiful women in the world. Hookers, maybe, but high class. We'd lost touch after college, but I read the stories about him in the business magazines long before the internet was around.

"Yes. He was a quiet, shy kid back then. It's why we connected. We grew apart in college, and I didn't see him as much. Although our senior year, we slept together a few times."

"Lillian, were you a wild girl in college?" She pretended to chide me with a wag of her finger. Then she laughed. She wouldn't judge me for my past indiscretions, but I wasn't that woman anymore. I hadn't been that woman for a long time.

"You should go say hi. Tell him you knew his dad."

"Millions of people *knew* his dad."

"Yes, but you knew him in the early years."

I glanced back at a smiling Walter Junior, probably charming the women like his father. Walt had started some successful shows at the casinos, built several hotels, and then delved into the brothel business. His House of Desire made him a household name.

"No, I can't." I wasn't even sure I'd approach *my* Walt if I saw him now, if he was still alive. Not the way I'd aged. An invisible hand squeezed my heart. Walt had been a sweet boy who turned into a sexy, virile man. He died too young in a stupid car accident.

Jackie nudged my shoulder. "Live a little. We're in Vegas. What's the worst that'll happen? He'll smile politely, talk to you for a few minutes, and go back to his game."

I sighed, looking back to Walter Junior. "Okay. I'll go introduce myself, but then we're going somewhere else. Because I can't stay around here if he tells me to skedaddle."

Every step I took toward Walter Junior raised my body temperature. I could be his damn mother, with as old as I was. I tried not to pay attention to the stunning girls at his side who would make Miss America feel like dog food.

I concentrated on the young man, so handsome in his dress shirt and pants. He swiped his hand across his scruffy chin and rested his arm on the woman next to him as he laughed with her.

Walter Junior's smile was just like his father's.

Somehow during those years of college, I didn't notice Walt changing. He acted the same, hardly had any friends, and did way too much studying, but in our last semester before we graduated, I finally saw what most others did.

A mature man with amazing brains. I had realized how deep my feelings ran for him, but shamefully, I never told him.

I stopped across the table from Walter Junior, a stalker in the shadows. This was preposterous. I couldn't talk to this guy—the son of a man I hadn't seen forever. I was about to turn around and run, but he shifted to the left and stared at me.

His gray eyes widened, and his mouth dropped. My throat dried up, taking away my voice. He held my gaze, and my cheeks warmed again.

I should've never listened to Jackie. I had to get out of there, but she was a wall behind me, not allowing me to back up.

Walter Junior stood from his seat and skirted the table with a few quick strides of his long legs. I couldn't move under his penetrating gaze. He towered over me, a good six inches taller than his father, and a whiff of his clean woodsy scent sent a shot of déjà vu through me. He wasn't an exact replica of his father, but he was damn close. I swallowed my nerves down.

"Hello. Walter Junior, right? I knew your dad. We grew up together. Then we went to college together." The words spewed out, and my face flushed with embarrassment.

Walter Junior opened his mouth, but mine was in overdrive. "I'm sorry about your father. I didn't get to the funeral. I was working, but I wanted to be there, and I know there were a lot of people there. I'm so sorry. He was an amazing man. I really should've sent a card."

His nose wrinkled up, his eyes scrutinizing me, and I waited for him to say *Hit the road*, but his lips twitched into a warm and bright smile. He stuck out his hand, and his head tilted to the side just like his father did when he was studying something... or someone.

"And you are?" His deep voice made me feel at ease, but the others in his entourage circled around us, scrutinizing me like I was on a dissection tray. I clutched my purse to my side and tried to straighten up.

"Lillian," I choked out.

He grasped my hand firmly. "Nice to meet you, Lil."

The way he said my name sent flutters through my chest, a feeling I hadn't experienced in a long time. Nobody called me Lil anymore. Not since college.

He continued to hold my hand, clasping it between both of his. "I'd love to speak with you more and hear about my father and his younger years, but my friends and I were about to leave for a show."

"Oh. Okay." I stepped back. At least he was polite. That was the one thing the media always said about Walt Senior. Despite his fortunes and glory, he always remained gentlemanly and modest, values he must've taught his son.

He reached into his back pocket. Out of his wallet he pulled a business card and handed it to me. I scanned it and looked up at him for an explanation.

"Can we meet tomorrow?" he asked. "I'll send my driver to pick you up in the evening if you're free. We have dinner plans set, but I'd love for you to join us."

This man was a business icon, a celebrity, and he was taking the time to meet with me. I forced my jaw to work. "Yes, that would be lovely."

More than lovely. It would be amazing.

"Great." He took his phone out. "If you can give me your number, I'll message you about what time my driver will be by."

I spit out my number, and he tapped it into his phone.

"Oh wait." My stomach sunk. Tomorrow night was my last night with Jackie. I couldn't abandon her no matter how much I wanted to talk to Walt's son. "My friend and I are only here for one more night." I motioned toward her but spoke in a lowered voice so she didn't hear me and encourage me to go. "I'm afraid that won't work."

"Do you two have plans?" he asked.

"Nothing specific. But I won't leave her on our last night." The disappointment grew stronger. It'd been so long since I'd even thought about Walt, and so many memories were swirling through my mind as I spoke to his son.

"We'd love to have you both if she is agreeable to that?" He raised his brows and peered over my shoulder. "Dinner tomorrow evening?" he said to Jackie.

I spun around to find her looking like a bobblehead with all that nodding. I laughed before turning back to Walter Junior.

"We'd like that, thank you."

"I'll get a hold of you tomorrow. It was nice to meet you, Lil. I look forward to seeing you again." He stuck out his hand, and we shook.

His group soon vacated the crowded floor, and I watched them drift away, down the main aisle and around the corner. Why hadn't I stayed in contact with Walt after college?

Life happened, I supposed. He moved far away, and once he made a name for himself, I didn't want him to think I was like all those others who just wanted to befriend him for his money and fame.

"Earth to Lillian." Jackie snapped her fingers inches from my nose, and I stepped back. "Are we really going to go to dinner with Walter Marceline Junior and his people?" She beamed.

"I guess so." This couldn't have just happened. I didn't just run into Walt's son in a Vegas casino. How was it possible that he invited me to dinner? Jackie's exuberant face pushed through the muck. We were dining with Walt's son.

She clutched my arm and shook it. "Oh my goodness, we have to go shopping. Neither of us have any clothes to wear. This is Walter Marceline Junior. I mean, it's not like we can compete with those women, but I'd rather not go to dinner like this." She swiped her hand to highlight the brown cardigan over her teal shirt. She dressed stylishly for her age, but I'd given up trying to look good years ago. Most of the clothes in my closet were at least a decade or so old.

The loose-fitting button-up shirt I was wearing over black slacks was boring, and I had no desire to spend hours at the mall anymore. But I needed something more sophisticated for dinner out with Walter Junior.

I glanced up toward one of the exits that led into a mall. Chanel and Versace were the first stores I spotted. "We'll have to find another place. I can't afford the underwear at those shops."

Jackie chuckled. "Let's go see where we can find more reasonable stores."

We headed out, and over the next two hours, we shopped for something trendy to wear. By the time we finished, I was exhausted, but Jackie was still too jazzed up to go to bed. I retired to our functional but boring room while Jackie ran downstairs to hit a few more slots at our hotel's casino.

Walt… Walt… Walt… He was all I thought about back in my room. They way he'd made me feel. Everybody called me Lily when I was younger, except Walt. He called me Lil, which caught on with others in college. I wasn't sure how that innocent boy grew up to build the House of Desire, the most prestigious brothel in Nevada.

So many times I wondered what sex with the manly version of Walt would be like. Our first time was awful, for me at least. His inexperience led him to finish way too fast, but three months before graduation, we hooked up again, and he blew me away. He insisted he'd only been with two other women, but I didn't believe it. He knew what to do, how to do it, and when to do it.

And we did it a few more times until we graduated. He moved far away, and I came back to Fort Wayne. Our relationship had been more than sex though, and his leaving devastated me. Maybe if I'd told him how much I cared for him, things would've turned out differently. I'd been worried he'd think it was because he'd become some suave co-ed. I could admit his looks were the catalyst that made me realize how great a guy he was, but he was so much more. I should've seen it years before, but the attention of the boys and girls who were no good had blinded me.

But college was decades ago.

For the first time in years, I touched my own body in bed, imagining how Walt had made love to me. The feelings were foreign, but I reveled in it. I might have been a shriveled-up speck of what I used to be, but I still craved loving. Wanted it, needed it.

If only I hadn't let Walt walk out of my life. He was the first man I truly loved, and I let him leave without ever telling him.

Chapter Two

House of Delights

My body was in a constant state of flux as we prepared for our night with Walter Junior. Jackie and I didn't have a chance of hell with fitting in with his entourage, even wearing the nice dresses we'd found, but I felt like a teenager getting ready for prom. *Will he like me? Will his friends welcome us? What will we talk about?* Well, that one should be obvious.

We rushed downstairs five minutes early to wait for Walter Junior's car.

"This will be so much fun. I wonder where we're eating." Jackie nudged me as a black town car arrived, but a couple got out.

"He never said." Undoubtedly, some place with cloth napkins and unnecessary pieces of silverware and fancy desserts too pretty to eat.

A few minutes after seven, a black limo pulled into the drive. A chauffeur got out and opened the door to let out Walter Junior. I released the breath I was holding.

"Holy crap!" Jackie whispered. "I've never been in a limo before."

I was shocked although I shouldn't be. Walt Marceline had passed down a fortune to his son when he died. "I've been in one a few times. Mostly weddings years ago."

"Come on." Jackie tugged on my arm, and we met Walter Junior outside the door.

"Lil." He threw his arms up and hugged me like we were old friends. "So wonderful to see you."

I peeked at Jackie to see if she noticed, and she wore the same expression as me. Walter Junior was a friendly guy.

He released me and turned to Jackie. "I'm afraid we didn't properly meet yesterday. I'm Walt Marceline." He held out his hand, and they shook.

"Jackie," she said, stars glittering in her eyes. Walter Junior was the closest either of us had come to a celebrity. "Jackie O'Connor."

"So you go by Walt too?" I asked.

"Yes." He chuckled. "It created a few problems when my father was alive, but that's how it goes for any father and son with the same name." Walt Junior patted the back of my shoulder, and we headed to the limo, where the chauffeur opened the door for us.

I let Jackie crawl in first and then went in. She stared around in awe at the decked-out limo, but all I saw was the handsome man in front of me dressed in a dark gray suit with a royal blue shirt. A matching blue handkerchief peeked out of his pocket. My Walt had often used them when we were younger, and I teased him about how awful he was for making his mom wash his snotty handkerchiefs.

"So where are we going?" Jackie asked, turning her focus on Walt Junior as we drove away from the hotel.

"One of my favorites in town. Crawford's Steakhouse. Their steaks are the best."

"I'm sure it'll be delicious. Thank you for inviting us," I said.

Walt Junior touched my arm, and a tingly jolt of electricity shot through me. "No," he said, "thank *you* for coming. You've made my night."

I wasn't quite sure how to respond, and he laughed. "I don't see too many people from my father's past, and I look forward to hearing your memories."

We made small talk on the drive, discussing everything Jackie and I had seen and done in Vegas.

At the restaurant, the driver jumped out to get the door for us. Walter Junior waited for us to crawl out and then thanked the driver.

A man in a tuxedo waited at the door. "Good evening, Mr. Marceline. Your guests are waiting in the Prime Room. I can show you the way."

"Great, thank you. After you, ladies." Walter Junior placed his hand on my back to urge me forward to follow Jackie and the maître d'.

"You'll enjoy Crawford's," he said. "I'm fond of the prime rib, but you might also like the filet mignon."

My stomach rumbled, silently at least. Filet mignon was my favorite cut, but I rarely got one unless it was a special dinner out.

We paraded past the hostess and through the main dining room. Waiters in black pants and shirts with a burst of color from their bright red ties bustled around the dining room. Crisp white linens covered the tables surrounded by the fashionable diners, not one pair of jeans or shorts in sight.

At least twenty people filled the back room, all standing around talking with drinks in their hands. Someone shut the doors behind us, and the chatter lessened.

"It's about time," one man stepped up and slapped Walt Junior on the back with a smile. "Your poor guests are withering away with no food. I tried to get them to bring the appetizers out, but they said something about having to wait for the guy who's paying."

Walt Junior threw back his head and laughed. A leggy blonde waltzed up to him and flung her arms around his neck. "I missed you, Walt," she said. The girl, who'd been with him last night, was perfect from her long, silky hair to the makeup on her face to the strapless black dress that hugged every curve of her body.

"Of course you did, my dear. We hit traffic on our drive." He slid in between me and Jackie and put his arms around both of us. "This is Lillian Dray and Jackie O'Connor. Lil was a friend of my father's when they were growing up."

The doors slid open, and a few waiters strode in with trays of appetizers. In seconds the men disappeared, and the doors shut.

"Ladies," Walt Junior said, "this is one of my oldest friends, Diego Garcia, and this is Cindie, one of my D-girls."

"Nice to meet you." Diego offered his hand.

I was about to step forward to shake Cindie's hand, but she folded her arms. A waiter approached us from the side. "Can I get you something to drink, Mr. Marceline?"

"Yes, thank you. I'd like a cabernet. Ladies, can I tempt you with a glass of wine or a mixed drink? We have a fully-stocked bar, including beer and wine coolers."

I laughed. I'd drank a lot of wine coolers in college but grew up to adult drinks after that.

"Chardonnay for me, please," I said. Jackie put her order in, and the waiter rushed off. Within a few minutes, he was back, and in the shuffle to get our drinks, I noticed how Cindie scooted her way next to Walt Junior. She didn't speak to us, but Diego was friendly.

A woman sauntered up with a small plate of food, her low-cut emerald dress showing off her fiery red hair. "I thought you would like some appetizers," she said with a silky voice.

"Thank you, my dear." Walt Junior smiled broadly. Cindie huffed quietly off to the side. "Lil, Jackie?" Walt Junior pointed to the delicious pieces of bruschetta.

After we'd all helped ourselves, Walt Junior wrapped his arm around the redhead's bare shoulders. "This is Ari. And Jaslyn." He nodded to another beauty who approached us.

Cindie. Ari. Jaslyn. I'd forgotten that his House of Desire had a princess theme. Jaslyn had the most stunning dark skin and deep green eyes, and I imagined Walt's three ladies in sparkly princess costumes. They probably dressed like that at the brothel.

"It's a pleasure." Ari smiled softly and offered her hand to me and then Jackie. She brushed her hair out of her face, and the gleam of her ring caught my eyes. All these girls were decked out in jewelry and fancy clothes, and I felt like the old church lady next to them.

"Mr. Marceline." A waiter asked to speak with Walt, and he excused himself and stepped away, leaving us alone with these people we just met.

What should I say? I'd never been around people like this, and my brain wasn't able to convey one single sentence to my mouth.

"So is this a girl's trip?" Ari asked. "Did you leave your husbands at home?"

"I'm not married," I said. "Jackie is though."

"Yes, and he was about to sneak into my bag, but Lillian told him no." Jackie chuckled.

"She needed a weekend away," I added. After all her years in marriage, Jackie was still lucky in love with her husband. She'd found a keeper, a hard-working, decent guy who made her laugh.

"Hell, I need a month away." She sighed dramatically and laughed, all talk. She was having an awesome time, but she missed him too.

"Then Vegas is the place to go." Ari's bright eyes sparkled. "I didn't hear where you were from."

"Indiana," both Jackie and I said and then exchanged grins.

"Indiana, exciting." Cindie rolled her pale blue eyes and slipped away. I should defend my home state. Sometimes I hated living in Podunk, USA, but it wasn't fair for others to make fun of Indiana.

"Good riddance," Ari muttered, shaking her head as she stared at Cindie's retreating figure. She looked back up to find me and Jackie gawking at her. Jaslyn chuckled, and Ari grinned. "Sorry. Cindie's awesome. I love her. We're like sisters." She said the words in a monotone voice, and Jaslyn let out a burst of laughter.

"So don't let Walt know you know the truth." Jaslyn nudged me, and both Jackie and I laughed along. We'd looked up the House of Desire earlier today, and so many articles talked about how close the girls were, all best friends.

"Here's your drink." A man held out a glass of wine to Jaslyn as he butted between the two girls. She thanked him and introduced him to me and Jackie.

"Brian is the entertainment director at Eden," Jaslyn said.

"That big new hotel?" We hadn't even ventured into that one. Too little time and too many sights.

"Yes." Brian's gaze remained only on Jaslyn, or her breasts to be exact. "We've got some big shows coming up. I'm not at liberty to announce." He smiled, licking his lips.

One part of me was jealous of the desire he had for Jaslyn, but the other part was disgusted. Did Walt's girls get tired of being ogled all the time? They were celebrities after all.

"Ari, get your ass over here?" some guy called from across the room.

She huffed and rolled her eyes before turning to him. "In a bit." She smiled sweetly and turned back to us. "So what do you two do back in Indiana?"

I let Jackie answer as I scanned the crowd. The three D-girls seemed to be the youngest here, and the rest appeared to be closer to Walt Junior's age, maybe in their thirties or forties.

"… and Lil works for a company that runs a bunch of nursing homes."

I focused back on Ari and Jackie. Ari's eyes lit up. "Are you a nurse?"

"No. I'm in HR," I said. Her brilliant red hair was shocking but stunning.

"I used to be a nurse, once upon a time. But that was a long time ago." Her gaze dropped, and the smile fell from her face. She barely appeared to be twenty-five, and I was about to ask her when she had been a nurse, but she brightened up again. "I'm not familiar with Indiana. Do you live in a small town?"

"Fort Wayne's about half the size of Vegas, but of course it feels smaller," Jackie piped up. I soaked in the atmosphere as Ari peppered her with questions, and Jackie continued to answer. A waiter asked what we wanted to eat, and I opened my mouth to ask about a menu, but he spouted off the choices.

We ordered, and a few minutes later, Walt Junior strode over to us. "I apologize for leaving, but after the waiter left, Hagen caught me and wouldn't let me go." Walt Junior looked toward Ari. "Thank you for taking care of my girls."

I almost acknowledged his thank you, but Ari nodded as if he was talking to her. "Would you like another glass of wine, Lillian?" Ari asked.

I glanced down at the empty glass in my hand. "Oh, yes, thank you."

Ari scooted away, the eyes of several men near us following her. Walt Junior patted me on the shoulder. "I'm afraid this setting wasn't the best for us to talk, but we'll be sitting soon, and then you'll have my undivided attention."

What a charmer. He knew just what to say to the women.

Soon we sat down at the table, Walt Junior on one side and Jackie on my other. Diego was on the other side of Walt, and Cindie seemed to be fuming because Diego sort of bumped her out of that seat.

"So, tell me about yourself first. Where did life take you after college?" Walt Junior said as we started on our salads. I glanced at Jackie, relieved that she was talking with Ari.

"Well, after college I went back to Fort Wayne and have been there ever since. I'm the HR Director for a wonderful company. They own several nursing homes around the state, so I get to travel sometimes." I cringed internally. Walt Junior trekked across the globe, and I made it sound like I was lucky to travel around Indiana. Pathetic. "I considered leaving a few times, but Fort Wayne has been good to me."

"It's hard to break out of your comfort zone sometimes." He nodded, so poised and polished.

Talking with him reminded me of so many memories of his dad, things I hadn't thought about for years.

"Your father was such a smart man. I always figured he'd end up a scientist because of all his experiments. And his mom—did you know your grandparents?" They had died young too, not long after college, but I couldn't remember exactly when or if Walt Junior had been born yet.

"No. They died when I was a baby."

"They were terrific parents. She rarely complained about his messes. Baking soda volcanoes and gooey concoctions when he was younger and more serious chemistry experiments as a teenager. I often worried he might accidentally blow up his house." I laughed. He even had a white lab coat that his mom had stitched his name on, and plastic safety goggles. "He was a nerd and didn't mind being one. And he got me to love science. He was a great teacher, able to explain things well."

"And yet he ended up in business," Walt Junior said.

"Yes, I wonder why. I guess he had a knack for the business world too. And you've taken after him, I see."

"Thanks." He smiled softly. I glanced at Cindie, but she sulked in her seat, playing with her uneaten food and hardly taking part in the conversation with Diego or the others around her.

The urge to tell Walt Junior how much I cared about his father prodded me on. I didn't care that others were sitting there listening to us.

"We didn't see each other in college as much. I had my things, and he had his, but I wish I would've… that we would've stayed friends." I took a drink of my wine. Walt had worked hard his whole life, and it would've been interesting to know who he'd become as a man.

"You seem like you cared for him deeply."

"I did, and I regret not telling him how I felt."

"You should've," he said. "He might have felt the same way."

I chuckled. "But if I had, and things turned out differently, and we ended up together, you wouldn't be here today."

"Perhaps not." He nodded, staring off over my shoulder as if lost in his thoughts. A typical Walt Senior move.

"You're like him," I said. "The way you speak, your expressions. It's been almost forty years, but it feels like yesterday."

"Walt?" Cindie's voice broke into our conversation.

"That is a terrific compliment. Thank you," he said and tugged on his shirt collar.

"Walt," Cindie said again. He held my gaze for a few moments longer, his dark eyes consuming me, and my heart fluttered. God, he was sexy. He turned to her, and I drank some ice water to chill my body. Not only was I old enough to be his mother, but I'd slept with his father, and I shouldn't be thinking of Walt Junior in any sexual way.

Dinner passed in a blink, and after a few hours, the guests started to disappear until only Diego, Walt's three girls, and a few other men and women were left.

Jackie covered a yawn, but I didn't want this night to end. Walt Junior had shared so much about his life and what it was like growing up with a father who was so known and disliked solely because of his House of Desire, even though it was a legal brothel.

Diego stood and said his goodnights, and Walt Junior turned to me. "I'd like to extend our evening together. If Jackie prefers to retire, we can give her a ride back to the hotel, and I'll get you home after that."

I about jumped out of my seat to say yes, but if Jackie wanted me to go with her, I would.

"Walt, aren't you coming back with us?" Cindie frowned.

"I'm not sure of my plans. Lil?" He glanced at me, and I, in turn, glanced at Jackie.

"Only if I get to ride back in that limo."

"That can be arranged." He chuckled.

We escorted Jackie and the other girls to the waiting limo, and the two of us retired to the lounge and settled into a corner table with more drinks.

A quiet silence hung in the air, but it didn't feel uncomfortable. Maybe Walt Junior was remembering his father like I'd been doing all night long.

"How old were you when he died?" I asked.

"Twenty. His death thrust me into the business. Luckily, his legal counsel and assistant were there for me. They made the transition easier. Amira, my assistant, is retiring soon. She's been with my father since the beginning. It'll be hard to replace her."

"So you're looking to hire someone?"

"I only hire the best." He patted my hand. "It's a demanding position actually. Amira deals with the squabbles efficiently, which is something my assistant must do. I can admit that what is seen in public isn't exactly how it is at the house, but that's like any business. Overall, we have a close-knit group."

"I understand. The working with women part." I took a sip of my wine and savored the strong flavor. "There are always some difficult employees with any job. I've been with my current company for six years now, and I'm sure I'll retire with them. They're very patient with my health issues. I told my boss about my hip replacement that I'll need, and he was very supportive. And I have a wonderful assistant who can help while I'm down." The work environment was one of the best I've ever seen, a huge plus to me at my age.

"Hip replacement?" Walt Junior frowned. "You seem too young for that already."

I hated admitting how old I was. "I got it replaced years ago, but it's time again."

"You've worked hard all your life."

"I did. And my employers are willing to let me go down to part-time when I get older."

Unfortunately, older was coming sooner than later. At least I hadn't gone out at such a young age like Walt Senior. "How many years has your father been gone now?"

"Seventeen. But it doesn't seem like that long ago." He quieted for a moment, staring off over my shoulder. His gaze settled back on my face, and he leaned forward. "Lil, it's…" His eyes flitted around the lounge.

"It's what?" I asked.

He straightened up. "Can you take a few more days off work?"

"What? Why?" What was he talking about?

"It's been great catching up on things, but I feel like there's more you can share. My father's life and his younger years are a mystery to me. I know you're supposed to be leaving tomorrow, but I'd love for you to stay at our castle for a few days and share a few more stories. My father left behind a trove of photo albums I'm sure you'd love to page through. I can fly you home. You don't need to worry about the cost."

My mouth dropped. "Stay at your castle?" The House of Desire, the house with all those beautiful women.

He reached across the table and clasped my hands. "Every woman deserves to be pampered."

"I… I…" Work was no problem, but I shouldn't ditch Jackie. This was our trip together. But we only had the flight home now. "I should talk to Jackie first. I can call her."

I might get to see where Walt lived, a place that would hold reminders of the man I once knew. Although the biggest reminder of him was sitting across the table from me.

"You do that." He leaned back in his seat.

I excused myself to make the call and shuffled out of view. Talking to him tonight brought up so many memories, not only of Walt but of the crazy girl I used to be. I explored my sexuality in college, sleeping with both men and women, and now I was maybe going to a castle filled with sex. How did those women live? What was it like working in a high-class brothel? What kind of women worked at the House of Desire?

I dialed Jackie up and explained the situation, and she stunned me by telling me to go. I thanked her profusely and hustled back to Walt's table.

"I'd love to go back with you," I said.

He took my hand and squeezed. "Thank you. It means a lot to me."

Spending a couple of nights at Walt's castle was the chance of a lifetime, and Jackie was right... I couldn't pass it up.

Chapter Three
House of Discoveries

The next day we said goodbye to Jackie at the airport and drove the hour to the House of Desire. I spent most of the time babbling to Walt Junior about how different Nevada was compared to Indiana. I'd known full well Vegas was in the desert, but the mountains and sandy terrain were so foreign, not like the greenery of a flat Fort Wayne. I could get used to this heat. The temperature at home today hovered around a chilly twenty degrees.

We turned off the main highway, and my first view of the House of Desire in person rendered me speechless. The reddish-brown castle with its beautiful spires looked more in place in the hills of medieval Europe than the rocky, arid landscape of Nevada. Towers framed the castle, extending above the steep roofline with their tall spires.

"Can we go on top of the towers?" I asked. The view would be magnificent.

"Yes, of course. I'll bring you up there."

Lush-looking green grass, which was actually artificial turf, spread out in front of the castle—a contrast to the sparse grass and sandy ground everywhere else, and a driveway led up to the front entrance. But no parking lot.

"Where do all the…" How did I say this? "All the men park?"

His lips curled into a smile. "Our clients have a special parking garage. A parking lot out front would've ruined the view."

We pulled up the driveway and around the side of the castle, the walls rising up around me. "You trust them to wander the grounds?"

"No. We have our guardhouse manned twenty-four seven, and clients check in here first. We're an appointment-only place. You don't have to choose your girl right away, but we need to have a booking." Walt Junior waved to the man at the guardhouse window and passed by the first garage door to a second. "There is nowhere for them to go. All our doors are secured, and we utilize fingerprint technology and an extensive video monitoring system. I take the safety of my D-girls seriously. When a client enters the house, he is greeted and escorted to our welcoming room by our hostess."

The whole process fascinated me, and I had a million questions, but I kept quiet and let him talk. We entered the second garage, and my jaw dropped at all the luxury cars lined up in rows.

"Do all the girls get an expensive car?"

He bit back his smile. "Most no. I provide enough vehicles, so there's always one for usage. Having a pool cuts down on fighting. But a few girls have purchased their own."

Walt Junior parked in his spot and touched my hand. "Let me get the door for you, Lil."

I stayed in my seat until he came around. He brought me to a door with a fingerprint scanner, and soon we were inside, strolling down hallway after hallway, and I breathed in the light scent of vanilla. I'd never get out of here without help.

Bright lights and abstract artwork dotted the walls, and I was curious if this was Walt Senior's or his son's interest.

We arrived in an elegant room decorated with plush sofas and other seating and warmed by soft lighting. One man sat at the bar with two girls flanking him, while another was seated at a pub table with a couple of girls.

"Walt!" A woman wearing a silky black negligee ran up and kissed him on the cheek. He laid his arm on her shoulders and turned her toward me as several other girls approached.

"Lil, I'd like you to meet Briar Rose."

"Just call me Briar." She swept her long platinum blonde hair out of her eyes before offering a hand. Several other lovelies crowded around us and greeted us.

I cringed as Walt Junior introduced me to the ladies, all dressed in classy lingerie. Some had voluptuous forms, some with lessened curves, but all were perfect poised princesses that every young girl dreamed of being. His girls held a position of prestige, unlike the worn-out hookers on the street corners.

So many years ago I could've competed with these women, but not anymore, and now they were stirring up feelings inside. Their tight curves and sparkling smiles were turning me on.

I was the proverbial kid in a candy store. I would never enjoy the touch of their smooth skin or run my hands through their silky hair. My wallet didn't hold enough money to purchase their time.

We retired to the sofa, and a girl brought over a bottle of chardonnay and some glasses. Walt Junior hadn't introduced her yet, but I figured out who she was by the black bob and pouty red lips.

"Lil, this is Bianca," Walt Junior said.

"Bianca?" I asked.

Her bright eyes sparkled with laughter. "I thought going by Snow White was super cheesy, so Walt let me use Bianca"—she said the name with an Italian flair—"which is white in Italian." She grinned and touched Briar's shoulder. "You're next appointment is here."

Briar excused herself, and after kissing Walt Junior on the cheek, she sashayed to the door and waited. A guy came in, and she welcomed him with a hug before leading him to the bar and getting a drink.

Bianca seated herself next to Walt, her royal blue babydoll swishing. My old body didn't belong with these stunning women, but at least they didn't treat me like an unwelcome intruder. I checked out the guys in the room. One closer to my age and one younger.

"Do all the clients…" I glanced at Walt, glad to have a better word than john. "Do they come have drinks here first?"

"Not all," Bianca replied. "A lot do, but many want their anonymity, and they go back to the rooms right away. But the welcoming room helps some men relax, especially for newcomers. Others want to take in as much of the house and girls as they can."

A woman, the first I'd seen wearing more than lingerie, entered the room and came over to Walt. She wore a button-down blouse and pencil skirt, the type of clothes I wore to work every day. He introduced her as the hostess, and she whispered into his ear.

"What does the hostess do?" I asked Bianca.

"She checks in the clients, explains the rules, and handles the payments."

"Lil, I apologize, but I have a phone call I need to take. Perhaps Bianca can give you a tour, and I'll catch up with you shortly."

"Oh, I couldn't bother her. I can wait here." And stare at half-naked women.

"No bother." Bianca stood and offered her hand. "I'll show you my room and a few others. You can't visit the House of Desire and not experience it."

I clutched at my pearls. She didn't mean I'd have sex with any of these girls, but the thought left me breathless. I concentrated on what I'd see: some of the famous rooms Walt's girls worked in. He didn't allow photos, other than a rare special feature, so my dreams tonight would be so much more real with the vivid memories of the sex rooms.

I followed Bianca down the hall, and she stopped in front of a door and swung it open. "Here's our theater room."

I popped my head in. Despite the giant screen on the wall, it was small, with only a large leather sofa, a blanket hanging over the back.

"This is for clients. Men who want to watch the big screen. We have our own private movie room too."

"Guys pay you money to sit and watch movies?"

She raised her brows and grinned. "You'd be surprised. There are a few men who only want to talk or cuddle but not a ton." She waved to the room. "We have clients who enjoy porn. They like being up close and personal."

The actors would seem life-sized on that enormous screen, but, still, here was a brothel with a gorgeous, voluptuous woman, and it was silly that a man would prefer to watch a video instead of being with the flesh and blood.

We headed down the hallway, her heels clicking on the hardwood floor, and she pointed to the doors as we passed. "These are the studios. That's where we work. Each girl has their own private studio."

The twelve-foot ceilings and endless beige hallways reminded me more of a hospital than a brothel, not that I'd been in a brothel before.

"How do clients keep track of which room belongs to what girl?" I asked when we stopped.

"They're not out here roaming around. There's always someone accompanying them. And *we* know whose room is whose." She swung open the door, and I gasped. We stepped into a fairy tale.

The muted burgundy damask walls had a gorgeous golden floral accent. Fabric was draped from the edges of the walls to the chandelier in the middle of the room, completely covering the ceiling. The colors switched back and forth between deep burgundy, soft pink, and dusty rose.

A Queen Anne chair sat in the corner, and against the wall was a majestic bed with the same fabric leading from the ceiling down to the floor. I wandered over to the bed and ran my hand over the silky pink bedspread. It felt so good against my skin.

"Oh, look…" I rushed over to the ornate brass oval mirror on the wall.

"Yes, the evil queen's mirror." Bianca laughed.

"Is it an antique?" I'd love to have a mirror like this in my entryway at home.

"No. I bought it brand new in a shop on the strip." She motioned to the room. "Each girl has her own themed studio. Walt allows us to decorate it as we choose. Within reason."

"It's a lovely armoire." I touched the glossy dark wood, admiring the intricate carving.

"Open it."

I swung open the door to find wine glasses and bottles of red wine, plus a mini-fridge with chilled white wine. The top shelves held... I peeked closer. Vibrators and dildos and other sex toys. My face reddened, and I shut the doors. I shouldn't be embarrassed—Bianca wasn't—but it's not like I handled sex toys in front of others.

"Come on. Let's show you another room." She led me back down the hall. We visited another studio and two more lounges: the first room fit for a medieval castle and the second like a modern nightclub. Then she showed me the shower room with space to accommodate at least six or eight people. I didn't dare imagine myself in there with all these magnificent women.

Walt Junior met us in the nightclub, and Bianca excused herself. I checked out the spread of food on the bar: sandwiches and salads and trays of fruits and vegetables with ranch dip.

I took a bite of the turkey croissant'wich and sighed at the tanginess of the cranberry cream cheese. "I bet you eat well around here."

"We have a chef. Meals are usually informal. Whoever is not working at the time will often join me for dinner, and the rest eat the food prepared for them later. Or some enjoy cooking their own food."

"I'd gain fifteen pounds living here."

"I'm sure you'd take advantage of our gym and pool."

I sighed. My own private pool. Well, privately shared with the other staff.

"Your pool parties are legendary." I couldn't help my silly gushing. Celebrities and gorgeous women and men and drinks and food. Even I'd heard the rumors about the orgies that went on behind closed doors and wondered if they were true.

He raised his brows at me. "You could be a part of that someday."

"Me?" I snorted and covered my nose, my face heating. A wrinkly old grandma running around in her lingerie would drive down his business.

Walt Junior reached across the table and covered my hand with his. "You're gorgeous, and don't you ever forget it. Any man would be lucky to have you."

His intense stare ignited my face even more. The way he was eyeing me was almost… No, I shook off the feeling. It wasn't desire. It was gratitude.

He released my hand and sat back. "I wanted to show you this." He slid over an old photo album. "It's one of many left behind."

"Oh my goodness." Black and white pictures filled the album. "How old is this?"

He flipped open to a page. "Getting close to fifty years old. This…" He tapped a picture, and my heart warmed. Walt Senior and me from our sophomore year in high school.

"The sock hop." It was so long ago, but I remembered it like yesterday. The innocent times, the laughter, the music.

"Look at how adorable you were in your modest skirt and sweater. And… my father in his blue button-down shirt and black pants."

"I was so cute back then." I laughed. Cute in a nerdy way. My mother had been no help teaching me how to tame my curly hair, and I usually wore it in braids. "I believe your father got a haircut just that day. See how short his hair is."

"That was the style." He laughed.

"I don't remember much about that dance—there were so many in high school, but I think your father had fun. I'd really love to page through this album and others if you have them. It's been forever since I saw your grandparents."

"I have a few more." He patted my hand. "And after we finish eating, I'll show you my office and the rest of the grounds and tell you more about the history of the castle."

This was seriously a dream come true, and I couldn't believe I was actually here. I had to enjoy this time because it would come to an end much too quickly.

Chapter Four
House of Declarations

The day passed in a blur, and I learned so many interesting facts about the castle and about Walt Senior's life. And the girls. One stunning girl after another left me drooling all day long.

In the evening we dined with several girls, and I was grateful to have the company of Ari and Bianca again. Of all the girls I'd met that day, only a few were standoffish or snotty, which was less than I anticipated.

We were sitting around the dinner table talking with Tia and Ari when Walt Junior stood. "I have a few more things I'd like to show Lil around the castle, so we bid you ladies farewell."

"Goodnight, Walt," the girls chorused, and Tia gave him a kiss on the cheek, her black hair swishing in his face. He rubbed his nose and laughed.

"Sorry," Tia shrugged light-heartedly.

Ari gave me a hug. "Have a great evening, Lil." She stepped back and smiled softly, and I told her thank you.

"What will we see now?" I asked Walt Junior as he led me down the hallway. I hated to admit it, but I almost wanted to escape back to my room. After seeing so many stunning girls today and reviving the memories of Walt Senior, I wanted to crawl into bed and do a repeat of the other night. If I were a forward woman, I'd stop by Bianca's room and ask her where I could get a toy to help myself along. I surely wouldn't ask Walt, even though he'd told me about how they kept supplies on hand for clients to purchase.

"I want to show you the beauty surrounding us."

He said no more as we headed to the top floor, and I could tell he slowed down to wait for my lagging body. We walked all the way down the hallway, which was comprised of the private bedrooms.

"This is the north tower room, one of my favorites," he said after following me into the room.

I didn't hold back the brewing laughter. "I feel like I've stepped back in time."

My feet sunk into the lush rust-colored shag carpet, and the bright furniture almost blinded me.

Walt Junior stepped over to the blaze orange sofa. "As things grew and changed around here, I wanted to hold onto the memory of this place from its first days. It was a simpler time. It's not the original furnishing, but similar, although I'll admit I got rid of the silver foil wallpaper. Even that was too much for me."

"Good choice."

"This," he continued, "is where I go for quiet, but it's also where I go for fun." He led me over to the window and swept aside the brown curtains. The view overlooked the grounds, now bathed in the soft sunset, and the colorful sky hung over the peaceful brown Nevada hills.

"It's amazing." I inched closer to the window. A narrow walk-bridge stretched over a small ravine, and a patio and pool area lay off to the side. But the hills were what impressed me the most.

I felt his body behind me, and he set his hands on my shoulders. "This is the type of beauty you deserve once again. And I can make that happen."

His steamy breath tickled my ear, his woodsy scent strong in my nose. With him behind me, it was so easy to forget he was Walt's son. He took my hand and led me over to the oversized sofa. I stood there until he gently pressed on my shoulders, and I sat.

He caressed my skin, his gray eyes burning into me. "It's me, Lil. It's *your* Walt."

I gave an awkward laugh. The wine was getting to my head. "Of course it's you."

"No. I mean, it's really me. Walt Senior." He lifted my hand, turned it over, and ran his finger up the blue veins in my wrist, a move his father had done back then too.

His face remained sober, but I shook it off with another laugh, not sure what to say.

"It's been so much fun to go down memory lane with you," he said. "I owe you a great debt of gratitude. When you slept with me the first time, you gave me the courage to take risks."

I jerked my hand back, my chest tightening. Why would Walt tell his son about his sex life?

"I was pitiful back then, but you were always a friend. Always found time for me like nobody else did. And your body..." His gaze dropped to my sagging breasts, and he licked his lips.

This handsome man half my age, the spitting image of his father, was staring at me like he desired me. Me with all my wrinkles, age spots, and too much padding on my hips and stomach.

"You are as beautiful as ever," he whispered.

No, I wasn't.

"I appreciate your words. Your father was a brilliant man, and he'll live on forever in my memory."

"How can I convince you what I say is true? I'm your Walt." He leaned back and folded his arms, his head tilting to the side.

I forced a laugh. I could play along with his little game.

"That dance, Lil. I remember how when we showed up, I was so embarrassed. I was the only one in dress pants and a shirt. All the other boys wore jeans and t-shirts, but you told me I was the most handsome boy there. I knew then how special you were."

His shirt. When we'd talked earlier, he'd mentioned his blue shirt. He couldn't have known it was blue from the black-and-white picture.

"Make love to me," he breathed.

"You're too much. But I guess I should expect such knowing your father." My mind was spinning. Why was he saying these things? What was going on?

His steely eyes probed me, and the silence stretched on. I avoided his gaze, a mounting pressure to speak even though I had no idea what to say. This couldn't be my Walt. That was impossible.

He ran his fingers behind my ear. We were so close, and all I smelled was his scent, that of a man who had the power to make me want for nothing. All I felt was the warmth of his body and his desire, and a shiver raced from my head to my toes.

"I was serious about what I said." His voice was deep and breathy. "I want you."

His touch enflamed my tired body. I'd been sexless for four years, afraid to reveal my aging body to any man or woman, and now I exploded to life again, but this wouldn't happen.

"Please don't tease a weary woman." I tried to brush his words away. He shouldn't want a woman like me. It was some kooky fetish. His father certainly had many *things,* and maybe after growing up around all those girls, Walt Junior wanted a maturity out of his women.

He tilted my head toward his, and his lips crushed into mine, electrifying my skin. Every part of me came alive, remembering the way Walt had touched me so many years ago.

Before I understood what was happening, Walt was straddling my waist, thrusting his tongue deep inside my mouth, and I let him ravage me, wanting so badly to experience those feelings I'd once enjoyed.

"Lil, Lil, Lil," he said, unbuttoning my sweater. My droopy breast fell out, and I shrunk back, but he gathered them up in his large hands and smiled. "You are as beautiful as the last time I saw you."

He removed my pants and spread my legs open wide, stroking and kissing my bare skin. With gentle tenderness he thrust inside me. The pleasure was like nothing I'd experienced before.

No, nothing I'd felt in years.

And I knew... Everything he'd said was true. This was my Walt. The man I'd once cared for was making love to me, and I didn't want to try figure things out. I wanted to enjoy him and his magical touch.

We made wild, passionate love, and I wasn't sure my heart would ever slow down. With my body buzzing in the afterglow, we lay satisfied and naked together on the sofa.

"You were amazing." He kissed my cheek.

"How did you do it?" I rasped.

He chuckled and caressed my belly in small circles, and his gray eyes stared into mine. "I discovered a way to regain my youth. It was actually my son who died, and I took his place."

"How?" I sounded like a record on repeat.

"I met someone special who showed me the way." His smooth hands kept me warm in the cool room, and I cuddled into him. "And I can give you the gift too. I can make you young again."

I sucked in a hard breath. He couldn't make me young again. This was an elaborate joke. But the things he'd done to my body, the things he whispered in my ear. Only my old Walt could've known those secrets. What he said must be true.

"I need a good woman on my staff. My assistant is leaving soon, and I'd love to see you take her place. It's been years, but our friendship still means the world to me."

I clutched the string of pearls on my neck. There was no way I could work around all these sexy women. I'd see them prance around half-naked or even naked, knowing they'd never be with a woman like me. Even if Walt and I had sex occasionally, it wasn't the same.

"I won't fit in here." I avoided his eyes. And I couldn't forget my pending hip replacement that would leave me out for weeks.

"You don't understand. I want to make you young and beautiful again. The old Lillian will die, and a new one will be reborn. You'll be as gorgeous as the Lillian from all those years ago."

Maybe Walt was on drugs; maybe I was drugged. But no, this was real. My body recognized this man I'd once loved, and his soft smile assured me his words were true. He'd grant me shapely legs, perky breasts, and smooth, clear skin.

His face remained sober. "It's not something to take lightly. You can return home for a short time, but then you'll leave your old world behind. Your friends. The old Lillian will disappear, and we'll create a new identity for you. It's a big decision."

How would I leave all my friends behind, the life I'd built up over so many years? The bowling team, our Friday night movie gals, and all my co-workers who had become like family.

"I don't know what to say." Everybody would assume I was murdered or something if I just disappeared.

Walt rolled me over so we were face-to-face. He tucked a few strands of loose hair behind my ear. "You don't have to decide now. Sleep on it. Tomorrow morning we can talk, and I can show you what I can do." He slid his hand over my shoulder and down my side to my hips. "And, Lil, if this life isn't for you. Yes, I'll be disappointed, but I'll understand. And I'll always cherish this second chance we had together."

He kissed the top of my forehead, my temple, my cheek, my chin. His hand slipped between my legs and once again provided that pleasure I craved.

I didn't know what tomorrow would bring, but for now, I'd enjoy every second of this night.

Chapter Five
House of Dawn

I woke up in the middle of the night, an intense pressure on my bladder. Walt's arms cradled me, and I hated to crawl away from him, but nature called. The loss of warmth from his body caused the goosebumps to rise, and I threw off the fuzzy blanket and stumbled around in the dark, searching for my clothes. The nearest bathroom was down the hall in his bedroom.

"Lil?" Walt's sleepy voice called.

"I have to use the bathroom." And I would at least one more time before the sun came up. Dammit—where were my clothes? The moonlight wasn't bright enough to find them.

"I'm turning on the light," he said, and I heard him getting off the sofa too. The light flicked on, and I shaded my eyes, squinting until I got used to the light.

Walt stood across the room, grinning at me. His body was perfect. Thirty-seven years old and all muscle, not one bit of fat. "Let's go back to my room." He sauntered over and took my hand.

We were halfway to the door, and I stopped. He was insane if he thought I'd prance down the hall with no clothes on. "I can't go out there like this," I said.

"Lil," he said with a chuckle, "this is a brothel. We see naked bodies all the time. Besides, nobody is roaming the hallways up here now."

A sour tang filled my stomach. "But they're all twenty years old and gorgeous. They have none of this." I pinched the giant belly flab. I needed clothes.

Walt wrapped his arms around me and drew me closer. "I told you that you're beautiful. I wish you could see that."

His words from earlier played through my mind. *This is the type of beauty you deserve once again.* He could make that happen.

"But you said you wanted to make me young again. What if I don't want that? What if I want to stay the same way I am now? You wouldn't want me then. You wouldn't want floppy breasts and rolls of fat." The defiance had sprung out of nowhere, but Walt didn't want me. He wanted the old me.

He let out a long sigh. "I value our friendship more than anything, and I told you that if you choose to leave me, I'll honor your decision. We can remain long-distance friends and talk to each other every once in a while, or you can choose to never see me again."

Walt's grasp on me tightened, and he continued. "I want you to be by my side. If that means you remain the Lillian you are today, I am fine with that because you'll be here with me. But life is so much easier once you go through a renewal. You can do things you haven't done in years. You'll feel great and won't have any hip problems. You'll be able to keep up with me and the other ladies around the house. This decision is yours, and I'll accept whichever one you make."

"You will?" I still didn't believe it.

"Well, no." He frowned. "I'll be disappointed if you cut me out of your life completely." He let the grin slip back onto his face. I smothered my head into his chest and would've stayed put if not for the pressing urge to pee.

"I really need to use the bathroom," I said quietly.

He laughed and moved away from me to open a closet door. Out came a silky black robe that he slipped onto my shoulders. "I never want you to feel uncomfortable here," he said and opened the door.

I crept out, and he joined me, buck naked, and strode down the hallway like he owned the place. And I guess he did.

We didn't pass a soul and made it into his bedroom suite. We'd only peeked in the doorway earlier, but now I admired the splendor of his private quarters. Trendy with a charcoal gray king-sized bed and modern art, the fireplace in the wall, and the sitting room off to the side.

"The bathroom is through that door." He pointed to one of several doors in the bedroom, and I rushed in and shut the door behind me.

Oh my goodness. I leaned against the wall, the need to pee forgotten for a moment. His bathroom was bigger than my bedroom. It had a separate tub and elaborate walk-in shower, and almost every surface was made of cool marble.

I found the toilet and raced over to get relief. The shower had so many shower heads sticking out of the walls I'd never have a clue how to run it. I finished up and returned to the bedroom.

Walt was on a chair in the sitting area, and I went back to him. "I'm afraid I'm wide awake now," I said. "I'm not sure I'll be able to get back to sleep for a while."

"What are you saying, Lil." He winked and glanced over at the bed, which now had turned down covers.

"No. I didn't mean…" We had sex twice already, but thinking about earlier stirred up the feelings inside me.

Walt laughed. "Well then, I have a different idea because I am awake now." He stood and stepped over to a dresser and removed a pair of boxers. I willed him to come back, but he got dressed. "Let's go to my office."

He opened another door and flicked on a light. I couldn't believe I was following him down a private stairway to his office right below.

I gaped at the clutter before me. Papers lying willy nilly, writing utensils scattered about, and folders sprinkled here and there.

We went behind his desk, and he flicked on his computer before patting his lap for me to sit. I can't remember the last time I sat on any man's lap, and I smiled.

"I want to show you what I can do for you." He flipped through some directories and opened several files. "This is Briar Rose when we first found her. She was a drug addict living on the streets."

I gasped at the woman with sunken eyes and bad skin, her body rail-thin and covered in bruises. "This is the Briar I met?"

The current Briar was a platinum-blonde stunner with brown eyes.

"Yes. She was thirty-two years old, and she was so lost in heroin that she could barely pick up a john or two to support her habit. I cleaned her up and gave her a new life. She's healthy, and her addiction is gone." He clicked on a current picture of Briar, vivacious and healthy.

"She's a knock-out. How did you do it?"

"My special gift. And here is Jaslyn. She's only been with us about a year." He opened the before picture of her.

"She was blonde? How did she get the dark skin and hair?"

"It's a part of the process. You can choose however you want to look, but you must take care of your body because it will age as everyone else's. Jaslyn's story is similar to Briar's, which is similar to so many other D-girls around here. I found her in the Ukraine. She was an alcoholic, forced to work the streets by her pimp. She could barely speak two coherent words because she was so drunk when I met her. She has come so far this past year."

"Jaslyn's from the Ukraine?"

"Yes. Our D-girls are from all around the world. That will be one of your jobs, scouting out ladies who need to be saved."

"I've never heard about any of these stories."

Walt grinned. "Well, the world doesn't know the finer details. I can't exactly tell them what I can do."

That was stupid of me. Of course he couldn't announce what he was doing.

I never imagined the altruism behind Walt's brothel. He gave these girls a second chance at life, and he probably got no credit for it.

"That's sad that you've discovered the fountain of youth, and you can't share it with others."

He chuckled lightly. "It's not the fountain of youth, and this gift isn't meant for everybody, but we save who we can, one girl at a time."

This man was pure inside. I'd given up so much so long ago, and it wouldn't take long to fall for him again, but I wasn't sure that he'd ever be mine. It was presumptuous of me to think he wanted to be exclusively with me.

But this was Walt, and he was asking me to make a huge decision. I'd let things go unsaid years ago, and I lost out. I needed to speak my mind now, to consider everything before I made my decision.

Another picture of a third girl flashed up on the screen, but before he spoke, I laid my hand on his and considered my question. "If I choose to stay, what would that mean for you and me?"

He spun me around so I was facing him. "I learned years ago that I wasn't meant for one woman. That won't change. But you'll always have a piece of my heart, and I look forward to many more nights with you in my bed. I don't make love: I fuck. And I want to fuck you over and over." His raspy voice sent a flush that scorched every part of my body.

"I want it," I said. I'd miss my friends, my job, my home, but Walt was giving me a chance at a new life. These ladies here would be my new family.

His grin grew. "Then we will make plans for your future here and for the end of your old life. It won't happen tonight but sometime after you return to Fort Wayne."

At that time, I didn't know how Walt would do what he promised. If I'd known it meant someone else would lose their life, would I have chosen a different path?

I'd like to say yes, but deep inside that wasn't true. I would've given anything to receive his gift and to be a part of Walt's life again.

And that was exactly what I did.

Part II

Nine Years Later

Chapter Six

House of Desperation

The battered and used-up prostitute stared down the Strip in front of one of Vegas's many hotels. Years ago she might have serviced her clients there, but now she was practically begging for men. Too many drugs, too much alcohol, too much disease. Maybe all three.

My job was to provide the answer to all her afflictions. I'd been watching her a few days to vet her out, and she seemed to be the perfect woman for the job: desperate.

Today I was an employment specialist. My position at the House of Desire for Walt Marceline was many things, and this one I enjoyed. Not only did I crave his approval, but his body. When I brought home another girl, one who fit into our group well, he rewarded me immensely.

I traveled the world searching for the perfect women, but this time I stayed closer to home. Vegas had its share of lookers after all. I was regretting my decision though since the August sun was beating down on me and making my deodorant work overtime. I should've chosen to go somewhere cooler. Europe would've been lovely. Our clients would enjoy a girl with a Scandinavian accent, and Norway was at the top of my list.

Times like these made me wish for the moderate temperatures of Indiana.

I sipped some water from my bottle and tossed it into my purse before approaching the pathetic hooker. She seemed to be in her forties but was probably younger, aged by a hard life. Her pit-stained tank top clung to her saggy breasts, and the love handles protruded over her shorts. Some of our girls questioned why we didn't just pick a gorgeous woman to join us, but they didn't understand Walt's ways. Hopelessness made them grateful for the gifts they received from him.

"Excuse me." I tapped her sweat-laden bony arm and winced over the pungent BO. The thick makeup on her face failed miserably at hiding her burdens, and I was sure the men who used her services had to be hard up for sex.

She eyed me up and down and shot off a bunch of ridiculously low prices before I said another word. For Christ's sake. I could've been a cop. At least she was motivated.

"I'm in no need of your services," I said. "Well, not directly at least."

Suspicion lined her dark eyes, which told me she wasn't high.

"I'm busy." She shoved by me, hobbling on her platform heels toward a spiffy group of men who would reject her.

"I'd like to speak with you about a job."

She snorted but stopped. Slowly she turned around, her acne-scarred face curious but doubtful. "Me? Why would you want me?"

It wasn't her I wanted, but the girl she could be. I had an eye for picking out beauties, or women who used to be.

I caught up with her and pointed down the street to a high-class restaurant she could only afford in her dreams. "Let me buy you dinner, and I'll explain."

With a wrinkled brow, she eyed my Chanel jumpsuit and Manolo Blahniks, but she agreed.

Very shortly we were seated in a spectacular restaurant with a bottle of wine and appetizers on their way. She dug into the bread, cut a big piece off the loaf, and gobbled it down without butter. Her face scrunched up, her nose wrinkling. Her hand shot out to grab a glass of water, and she swallowed down several gulps. After that, she took smaller bites.

"So first of all, my name is Lillian, and your name is?"

"Dana." She offered a grimy hand to shake and nudged the plate of bread to me. We shook, but I took a pass on the bread.

"Great to meet you, Dana. I work for Walt Marceline." I waited for some acknowledgment, but she didn't give any. I reached into my purse for a small bottle of sanitizer. Under the table I rubbed my hands together. She didn't even notice, too absorbed once again in her bread. "Walt owns several hotels around the state, among other things."

Her ears perked up. Walt had his fingers in so many different business ventures, more than I could keep track, but my only concern was the house.

"I work at the House of Desire, the most exclusive brothel in Nevada, with the finest women in the world." I took out my cell phone to show her pictures of our grounds. She let out a big gasp, and I squelched the urge to plug my nose.

"Walt's father built the castle, a replica from the Middle Ages. Two hundred private acres nestled in the hills. Our clientele is top-notch, and we require appointments. No walk-ins there."

I paged through the pictures of our girls.

"They're all princesses." She leaned way too close to the screen. Eye issues, a good thing for us. The more problems she had, the more likely she'd want a new body.

"Yes, Walt's thing. Our theme. All men want to have sex with a princess, and at the House of Desire, we provide that fantasy to the fullest extent." I smiled at Dana. Her brown hair would shine once more, her green eyes would sparkle, and those long, skinny legs would be envied by the other girls. For their first renewal, we sometimes stayed with their original looks, but the following renewals required a readjustment to their appearance. Otherwise someone might recognize her. Some of the girls didn't like changing their appearances, but they had no choice. We couldn't pass off their youngness as plastic surgery forever.

"Are you hiring maids?" She unconsciously folded and unfolded her napkin while she spoke.

I chuckled. Most women didn't believe my offer right away. "I want you to play the part of Belle."

"But—"

I flung my hand up to stop her before she argued with me about how she wouldn't fit in. "Walt has these special abilities. He can take any ordinary woman and turn her into a desirous vixen."

I'd been sixty-two when Walt found me and made me into a stunning twenty-four-year-old. Nine years had passed since then, and I still looked damn hot at thirty-three.

She snorted again, a bad habit she'd have to break if she was to become Belle. Walt's renewals made the girls young and gorgeous again but unfortunately couldn't change their habits or personalities.

"Let me show you." I skipped ahead to some other pictures. "This is Jaslyn before and after. And this is Briar before and after."

Dana squinted, then stole my phone to go back and forth between pictures. "No way it's the same girl."

"But it is. Look at the structure of her face. The shape of her nose."

She stared, and soon her eyes got wider. "For real? How's he do that?"

"Saying magic is so cliché, but really, it's a special ability he has. You'll have to leave your friends and family behind and start fresh. No contact at all with your previous life."

Walt's ability came with a high price, but the girls never thought about what they'd lose beforehand. I, too, missed my old friends, my old life, but I'd gotten so much in return, and with the internet, I kept tabs on everybody. I saw Jackie's grandchildren grow up, but I also heard the news of former friends' passings.

She blinked back the tears. "So you… you can make me gorgeous again?"

None of them ever questioned how or why.

"Oh yes. But that's not it. You'll be paid handsomely for working at the House of Desire. Walt has the best clients. Sometimes celebrities and politicians, people with power. You'll have your own themed studio and your own bedroom and bath. We have a chef on staff, several maids for laundry and cleaning, and many other employees."

Dana finished her second glass of wine and poured herself a third, her gaze darting around me and the table. "It sounds too good to be true."

"In addition to working with our clients, Walt often has parties he requires our girls to attend. Sometimes pool parties or dinners at the castle and sometimes at other facilities. Every once in a while, he'll invite a girl or two to accompany him to an event, although it's your choice."

The prospects never asked about payment, health insurance, and days off, which always surprised me after my previous years working in HR. Walt was generous, but they were more enthralled by the parties and other affairs.

"There are a few conditions," I continued. "Privacy is one. You are not allowed to share anything about your clients with the public or what goes on inside the house. We have rules about pictures you post on social media, and there is a contract to sign."

"I'm in." She grinned, ear to ear.

I leaned back in my chair. "Can I answer any questions for you?"

"Nope. I'm in." She sipped her wine as she stared off into the distance, and I almost saw the dream playing in her head. To be stunning again, to be rich. It was hard for most desperate women to turn such an opportunity down. And unlike with my predecessor, no girls I picked had ever backed out of the job, and I was proud of my record.

"Well then, let's finish dinner. You may return home to pack if you'd like, but everything will be provided for you."

"Got nothing I wanna take."

Exactly what I wanted to hear. I took another drink and messaged my driver about when we'd be returning.

Everything was working out perfectly this time, and I knew Walt would be happy with my new find. Transitioning a new girl in always came with some headaches, but nothing I couldn't handle.

Chapter Seven
House of Displacement

A haggard Dana stepped onto the balcony and surveyed the rocky landscape underneath a blue sky. All our prospective girls were enthralled with the medieval castle. Probably part of the reason they ignored what they were getting into. An opulent castle, parties with the rich and famous, and jewels fit for a real princess always clouded their judgment.

Beyond the green castle grounds lay the typical sandy and rocky ground of the Nevada hills, and she peered off toward the peaks of the larger hills in the distance. I waited for her to finish so we could go back inside to the cool comfort of sixty-eight degrees. After nine years here, I still wasn't used to the scorching summers.

"The view is spectacular." Dana stepped toward the edge of the balcony, her worn stilettos clicking. She leaned forward, resting her arms on the railing. If she bent over any farther, I'd see her saggy buttcheeks.

"Thank you so much for this opportunity, Lillian," she said as I envisioned how the new-and-improved Dana would look as Belle. Perky breasts, full lips, and shapely long legs.

"Call me, Lil. All the girls do." I laid my hand on her shoulder and squeezed. I didn't want the girls to think of me as their madam. I wanted to be one of them.

I wasn't, and they all knew it, but I treated them with respect and love, and most of them returned it back.

Dana smiled gratefully. "Is that one of the johns?" She pointed to a car at our front drive.

"Clients," I said. "Yes, that's one of our drivers. We provide free transportation from Vegas to—"

"Free? It doesn't cost anything?" She gaped at me.

"No." I chuckled. It was well worth the cost. In fact, not many men used the service, which had always surprised me. "Why don't we head back inside, and if you're still ready to move forward—"

"Oh, I am. This is where I want to work." She threw her hands in the air and bounced, her boobs jiggling. Not a pretty sight.

"Great. Let's get you in to meet Walt, and we can proceed to the next stage."

Her mouth never stopped jabbering on the way to his office, talking about the authenticity of the reddish-gray castle walls and the matching old European charm. At least she appeared to have brains.

We turned a corner and just about slammed into somebody.

"Lil." Cindie waved a blue silk shirt in my face. "You've got to talk to Judith."

I slapped her hand away. "Why don't you talk to her yourself."

"Because," she huffed. "She doesn't listen to me."

Maybe because you treat her like a low-class maid.

"What happened?"

"Check this out." She held the shirt up again and showed me a spot. "She ruined it."

"What is it?"

"Wine. But do you think she's going to buy me a new shirt?" Cindie pinched her lips together. "No way. You need to talk to her."

"Did you tell her it was there?"

I'll bet a hundred dollars the answer is no.

"She should know to look over fine silk before it's cleaned." She folded her arms, and I rolled my eyes.

"And you should know that you need to tell her." I crossed my own arms.

Cindie glared. Then her eyes flicked to Dana, who was standing next to me. Cindie sniffed a few times, and her nose wrinkled as she gave Dana a once-over.

"Hi," Dana said.

"Yeah, hi." Cindie spun around. "Just talk to Judith," she called as she stalked down the hall.

"Well, she seems nice," Dana said once Cindie disappeared, her voice dripping with sarcasm.

I chuckled. Cindie was Walt's pampered princess. "Let's go meet Walt now."

We entered Walt's office, and Dana stood tall. He set down the paper he was reading and came around his cluttered desk. Dana's mouth dropped, her eyes taking in the whole man. I couldn't blame her. He was handsome as hell with his scruffy face and striking gray eyes. Intelligence and drive got him here, and his experience kept him at the top. Walt appeared to be forty-six, but his actual age was seventy-one. Not even all of the D-girls were aware of who he really was.

I glanced at the beverage contract in his inbox and refrained from reminding him to finish it. We still had two days to return the paperwork.

We did the standard introductions. Dana's low-class look was a huge contrast to Walt's navy pants and coat, with the baby blue shirt unbuttoned at the top and silk handkerchief in his front pocket.

"Lil, why don't you prepare the room, and I'll take care of the paperwork with this beautiful lady." He winked at Dana, and a flush filled her face.

I retreated downstairs to the renewal room to find it almost set up. This was the worst part of my job, one I'd prefer not to see, but it was necessary.

Renewals differed per girl. We could sometimes pass the first renewal off as plastic surgery, but the second usually required a new name and appearance. No girl stayed young and pretty forever. I was on my ninth year here and didn't plan on doing my renewal for a few more years since I'd have to change my identity again. I'd kept my first name nine years ago and gotten a different last name, but I couldn't remain Lil after my next renewal.

I checked the wrist of the naked man sleeping on the velvet sofa, his body propped into a sitting position, and he didn't move. His pulse was still strong. Walt was the one who procured the sacrifices, but they were always the dregs of society. Repeat criminals who continued to hurt women and children, men who got away with heinous crimes. Walt was doing society a favor by exterminating them.

The man was never aware of what was happening to him since Walt sedated them. It was a peaceful, easy death for someone who didn't deserve to live.

I sniffed the air for a sign of stench. We cleaned them up, but sometimes their smell lingered. He smelled okay now.

Several mirrors surrounded the sofa. We needed the girl to see the changes immediately, as it took away from the harshness of the situation. One of the mirrors had some fingerprints, and I retrieved a bottle of cleaner to wipe them off.

The room was so peaceful now, and I enjoyed the solitude. Things would be hectic these next few weeks as the new Belle adjusted to life with us; we'd be getting her studio changed to fit her personality and having her coming out party. Walt always presented his new girls to the world in big fashion, and it took us time to prepare all the documents we had to submit to the sheriff's office to license our new employee. Getting her in for a health check was never a worry because after Walt's renewal, her body would be clean.

An hour later, Dana and Walt arrived, her wet hair pulled back, and she wore a cute skirt and a sequined top that didn't fit well.

"What's going on?" Dana's head whipped around between me, Walt, and the unconscious guy.

Walt laid an arm across his shoulder. "A test, my dear. We need to see that you're qualified to do your job as you complete your renewal."

"Is he alive?" She wrinkled her nose and crept closer to the body.

"Of course he is." Walt chuckled as Dana poked the man in the arm. "To be honest, we have clients into kinky things. Fetishes you'd never believe. It's always your choice how far you'd like to go with them. Jackson here," he said, pointing to the man, "likes to have sex when he's knocked out or sleeping."

Dana's brows raised, and she almost looked intrigued.

I stepped forward. "Guys like Jackson come here, and we administer sleeping pills to knock them out. Then one of our girls has sex with them, and when they wake, they watch the video and get off again."

But there would be no waking for Jackson. I'd scanned his file earlier in the week, horrified at the crimes he'd committed over and over again.

"Where's the cameras?" Dana twisted her head, peering around the shadowy room.

"In the corner?" I pointed to the non-existent camera. Our house had plenty of cameras but not down here.

"Okay." She pursed her lips. "He's kinda ugly though."

I almost laughed, doubtful she'd turned down jobs from ugly men on the street. Funny how walking into a castle raised her standards so quickly.

"We don't discriminate here at the House of Desire," Walt said gruffly, and Dana flinched. "Wealth doesn't guarantee good looks and a fit body. Many of our clients may be physically repulsive to you, and you'll have the choice to accept which clients you take, but if you don't entertain a man because he's ugly or fat, you won't make as much money."

Dana stared at the floor, biting her lip.

"If this job isn't for you, then it's time to leave. But if you'd like to stay, go ahead and get started. Show us what you can do and pretend we're not here." Walt motioned for her to get moving.

"I can do that." She strode over to the naked guy and got down on her knees between his legs. He was already hard, thanks to the erectile dysfunction pill we gave him.

"Don't hold back." I nudged her and then explained what she had to do. She mumbled back a reply that it was no problem and took hold of the man's penis.

Walt took his place behind the sofa as Dana began to do the job, her head bobbing between the man's legs.

"Make sure you take it all in your mouth," Walt demanded.

She garbled what sounded like a yes and kept working, not noticing that Walt no longer looked like himself. His skin was a mottled gray, rough and scaly like a lizard. His eyes glowed green.

The oppressive heat smothered me, and I took deep breaths. Dana didn't see the ceremonial dagger Walt had in his other hand, how the light glinted off the long steel blade. I glanced up at Walt, whose body didn't scare me anymore. Not as much as it used to, at least.

He smiled and nodded as Dana mouthed the guy, touching and teasing him in a way that'd drive any guy wild. Well, any conscious guy. I held my breath; it was almost time.

The guy shot his load into Dana's mouth, and Walt slid the dagger across his neck. His deep baritone voice filled the room with Latin, and chills erupted through my body.

Bright red blood poured out of the man's neck and down his bare chest, and the metallic tang filled the room. Dana raised her wet head and gasped.

She shrunk back, her eyes not straying from the bloody gash. Her hands trembled.

I sprung forward with a large mirror in my hands. "Dana," I yelled and stuck it between her and the dead guy. She focused on the image being reflected back.

"No way." She tenderly touched the now-flawless skin on her cheeks. Her lustrous brown hair shined under the lights, and she rose to her feet. The off-the-shoulder silver sequined top proudly sported perfect pointy breasts, and she stared at her long and lean legs.

"What do you think?" I asked, hauling her back to the other mirrors so she wasn't facing the grisly corpse. I hit a button hidden on the wall, and the scent of gardenia covered the pungent odor of death.

"I look amazing." She sighed.

Now I had to get her out of there before she saw the body and freaked out.

Chapter Eight
House of Duality

I accompanied Dana down the hall to the bathroom to clean the blood off her body. She stripped off her shirt and wiped the spatter from her face before removing her denim skirt. She stood in front of the full-length mirror on the back of the bathroom door and stared.

One minute passed without a word. Two minutes. Sometimes the girls were in shock over what happened, and I let them have a few quiet moments.

Dana brought her fingers to her unblemished skin and ran her hands down her cheeks and neck. A small smile graced her face, and she fingered her thick brown hair.

The smile grew brighter as she gazed upon herself.

My skin prickled. She seemed so entranced with what she was seeing. She arched her chest and spun around on her stilettos to check out her ass. Her eyes grew wide, and she patted her perfect backside.

"What do you think?" I asked. I loved seeing the girls see themselves for the first time after a renewal, their wonder and amazement, but for some reason I was picking up another vibe, an uncomfortable one I couldn't explain.

"Oh. My. Fucking. God. How?" She twirled around to admire every part of her new-and-improved body. "I am absolutely incredible," she gushed.

"I told you Walt had special abilities."

"Does he ever." She grinned. "I can't wait to fuck Walt. Where is he? Did he see me?"

Some girls were troubled by the whole situation and needed time to let things sink in. But Dana… the death didn't even seem to bother her.

She wasn't one of our girls yet, technically, but the confidence oozed out of her. I bet she was a happy hooker in her day. I motioned to the shower. "Why don't you get cleaned up. There's a bathrobe on the hook, and I'll bring you back to Walt's room after this."

I left her alone and waited in the hall. I wanted to see Ari and tell her how things went. Dana took forever, but soon I led her up to Walt's bedroom for her christening.

He welcomed each girl into the fold with an all-night sexfest, and the new girl got to stay in his room until hers was ready.

I did my fingerprint scan at his door, and it unlocked.

"Welcome to the family." I gave Dana a quick squeeze of her shoulders and then held Walt's door open for her. Once she came out of this room, she'd be Belle, and Dana would be forever forgotten.

After I filled Walt in on a few details, I took off down the hall. I wanted to find my special girl.

I slipped inside Ari's studio, and the aquamarine room welcomed me. Of all the themed rooms, hers was my favorite. Her sandy-colored carpet, soft pink bed, and shell décor always soothed me. Of course, the vivacious beauty swayed my opinion too. She looked so different now than the first time I met her, but she'd always been the same sweet girl inside.

A baseball game was playing in the background, most likely San Francisco, as she lay hunched over on her bed, her long, thick amber hair covering her back and her journal under her hand. Her t-shirt rode up her back, revealing even more pale skin since she only wore lacey purple panties. My heart skipped a few beats.

"Are you done?" Her voice held a slight trepidation, her brown eyes blinking at me. She never liked the renewals. She'd gone through it twice herself, the last time during my seventh year here.

She tossed the journal on her nightstand and propped herself up on all her pillows. I made my way to her bed and sat down, swishing the soft strands away from her face.

"Yes. She seems like a nice girl. Walt will love her, and I'm pretty sure you guys will too. You okay?"

"Including you?" Her dejected voice killed me. Her insecurity had never annoyed me though. She and her husband were high school sweethearts who married right after graduation, and I was the only other relationship she'd had besides him. Her parents were dead, her son died of cancer, and her husband committed suicide. Opening her heart to someone new was a huge step.

"Don't be silly. You're the only one for me." I meant it with all my heart. Walt might have been a part of my life too, but she was the only woman I wanted to be with. I scooted up behind her, breathed in the smell of oceans and beaches, and nuzzled the back of her neck.

We'd been close friends prior to her last renewal, but after she'd changed into a new look, I fell for her. Hard. It took over a year for Walt to give us the okay to date—well, in private only, but a relationship in private was better than none at all.

"She doesn't compare to you." I laid my head next to her shoulder and wrapped my arm over her waist. Being this close to her was revving me up inside. I kissed along the line of freckles at the nape of her neck, but the tension didn't fall away from her body like it usually did. "Everything go okay with your last client?" I asked.

"Yeah. But I was thinking about the renewal thing. I wish we didn't have to do it. What happens when I have to change again?" She wound one of my curls around her finger and let it spring loose. Then did it again.

Walt had made her change her look this last time, and she'd accepted it then, but now we were together, and she worried I wouldn't be attracted to her anymore.

"That's a lot of years off. Don't worry about it now."

She sighed, and I stroked her arm.

"I love you and will continue to love you no matter what you look like." Her bone size and shape would change again, not to mention her face. Sometimes he'd allowed girls to switch princess personas if another one was open, but Ari loved her character. She grew up in California close to the beach and missed the salty fresh air and laid-back lifestyles.

She sucked in her lip and nodded, not quite satisfied. I thumped her heart. "Even if you look different, it's still you in here. And here." I gave her a noogie, and she smiled.

"I know, but it'll be weird at first."

"It might be." I shrugged. More so than I'd admit to her, but no matter what her appearance, she'd still be my Ari. "But it'll pass, and you'll learn to love your new body too. Besides, it's years away." Anywhere from five to ten.

"He'd better give me way bigger breasts this time." She arched her back and shook her chest, a laugh spilling from her mouth. Her 34Bs were the smallest in the house, but I loved them.

I laughed with her, and when her smile faded, I reached under her shirt and touched her bare skin. "These would be fine because you're perfect the way you are."

She smiled gratefully, and I leaned in to kiss her. I loved this woman, and now was the time to think about her and not all the chaos that'd come with Belle's addition into our home.

Chapter Nine
House of Drama

A loud knocking slammed into my head, and I squeezed my eyes tight. It was too early. I didn't want to get up and out of this warm bed.

"Lil," Ari said, nudging me awake.

"Lil, are you in there?" Cindie squawked from outside Ari's door. "Get out here."

"Just a second," I yelled back and turned to Ari. "The queen has summoned me," I said quietly. I only blamed Walt because Cindie was his creation, his favorite for so many years.

"Her Majesty is waiting." Ari put her hands on her hips and straightened her shoulders in a perfect mimic of Cindie. I sighed and threw on my clothes. It was too early in the morning for this.

I opened the door to find Cindie with her arms crossed and her eyes blazing. The red stain on her ragged t-shirt jumped out at me.

"What are you doing?" I huffed, jerking her into Ari's room and shutting the door. What was with this girl and stained clothes? "You can't be walking around like this with clients here."

We were a twenty-four seven brothel, and if she wanted to strut around in ratty clothes, she needed to stay in our private areas. We had a fantasy we needed to present. In and out of the house.

"Check out my shirt. Tia spilled her drink on me." Cindie stamped her foot, her golden-blonde locks swaying. "On purpose. She goes, 'Whoopsie, I'm sorry, Cindie,' in her fake sugary voice.

What a crock of shit. She's been pissed ever since Robert dumped her for me. It's not my fault he couldn't stand her infernal racket."

Robert Gillian. An idiot client of ours and one of many. Most men knew not to pit the girls against one another, but he reveled in doing so.

I had no energy for this, but handling their disputes was my job. Cindie and Tia acted like children sometimes, fought like sisters, always in competition.

"It's funny how Robert decided to switch to you not long after Walt suggested Tia work with you at the Literacy Center."

Cindie rested her hands on her hips and shook her head. "It has nothing to do with that."

Ari laughed, and Cindie scowled. "Maybe if you weren't so busy fucking your little mermaid, then you'd see what kind of crap Tia was pulling."

My face heated. I wasn't running a preschool. "That's enough. I'm so tired of your crap. And you know who else is?"

I don't give a damn." She lifted her chin, defiance in her voice. "

My eyes flared, and she stepped backwards.

"You will care. Because Walt's this close," I said, pinching my fingers together in her face, "to booting your Botox-filled butt out of here, and you'll end up on the corner getting paid nothing for a blow job as your beauty drains away."

She shrank back, her face drooping. "Like he did to Belle?" Her voice was quiet.

"What are you talking about?" The old Belle had been cheating Walt, stealing money from the house, and she was about to sell his story to the tabloids for big bucks. She betrayed him… she betrayed us. She got what she deserved.

"She made her choices," I said. "And you make yours."

Cindie stared, her gaze flicking between me and Ari. "Yeah, she was dumb."

Belle had been the oldest girl around here until she died. Now the spot belonged to Bianca.

"Get Ari's bathrobe on and get out of my face." I took the robe off the hook and tossed it at her.

When a girl first arrived at the House of Desire, they always dressed the part of a princess. Not the fairy tale one, but the spoiled one. They never left their rooms until fully make-uped and wearing the cute and stylish outfits they bought with Walt's money.

But after a few years, reality set in, and they realized being the princess wasn't as glamorous as they once thought. Most of the girls dropped the act, behind the scenes at least.

Even my Ari, although she'd never acted like a diva. It was one of the things I loved her for.

Walt had never gotten used to us lounging around in sweats and t-shirts, but he carefully chose his battles. He could force them, but he was a good guy and cared about his girls. He wanted them happy.

After slipping the robe on, Cindie opened the door. She muttered "bitch" under her breath, but I let it go. It wasn't worth the fight.

Cindie slammed the door, and I leaned against the wall and closed my eyes.

"Why did Tia go to the Literacy Center with Cindie? I didn't hear about that."

Even Ari knew the Center was Cindie's turf.

"I don't really know. Walt should've known better." I rubbed my tight forehead.

Tia had been trying different volunteering opportunities, unable to find a place where she fit, and when Walt told her to go with Cindie, I tried to talk him out of it. Cindie loved working at the Center, helping adults who'd slipped through the system as kids. She herself had been one of them, graduating high school with the reading skills of a fourth grader.

"Sorry about your robe," I said. "I'll have Judith wash it. Get the Cindie stench out of it." Ari had several robes, and I went to her closet and took out the silky teal one I'd bought her. "This one will do for a while." I grinned. "Not that I want to see you cover up."

She smiled seductively and patted her bed. "You want to sit down so I can return the favor from last night."

The desire welled up inside me, but I couldn't. Actually, she shouldn't.

"I wish, but you have an appointment soon, and you need to get ready."

I preferred seeing Ari natural, but this job required a ton of makeup. When she wore a ball gown and was all dressed up, my knees went weak, but today's client was seeing mermaid Ari.

Her sequined tail lay over the edge of the bed. How guys got turned on by the mermaid thing, I didn't know. Of course they loved watching her bare breasts jiggle about.

"Rain check, then," she said.

"Rain check," I agreed and slipped out the door.

I dreaded my next big job, so luckily I had a few things to take care before I headed to the old Belle's room. First, I needed to discuss a few things with our hostess in the welcoming room.

Several men were already here, and I stopped when I saw who was sitting in between Meri and Mulan. Walt's son. Junior was twenty-two years old and went back and forth between living here at the castle and at his apartment in Vegas. He should've been finishing his last years in college, but he'd partied too hard and flunked too many classes. He beckoned me over with a wave.

"Lil, hey. I've got something for you." His honey-brown hair was so much lighter than Walt's dark brown, and other than their matching noses, they looked nothing alike.

"What's that?" I stepped closer to the threesome, hoping he wasn't planning on asking for one of the girls. Although it was their money lost if they missed out on a client because they were having sex with him.

He reached behind Meri and brought out a paper bag with Louis Vuitton emblazoned on the side.

"What's this?" I took the bag.

"Just a little sorry from a few weeks ago."

Wow, a pair of sunglasses to replace the ones he'd crushed. They weren't the same color as my old ones, but the style was the same.

"Thanks, Junior."

"You're welcome. It's the least I can do."

"Lil?" Our hostess called from across the room. "You ready to talk?"

"Yes," I said and turned back to Junior. "Thanks again, I appreciate it."

But he was already whispering sweet nothings into Meri's ear. She giggled. I turned to head to the front office where our hostess worked. Junior's gift stunned me. Not because of the cost—Walt's credit card paid for the sunglasses—but the gesture was a surprise. He rarely thought of anyone but himself.

Usually Junior would disappear for a few weeks and then show up and stay here a week or so until he got tired of his father. I knew he'd share his plans with us later, and he'd be interested in the new Belle for sure.

I left the welcoming room behind and found our hostess behind her desk. "We've got a few things to cover. First though, can you send a message to Walt that his son is here." Let her break the bad news to him.

Junior had never been crazy about me. I'd arrived at the house when he was thirteen, during those awkward years, and he seemed to resent me like an unwanted step-mom even though I'd never tried to be his "mom." I never knew why he disliked me, and finally I figured out it was him. Walt's second child was a jerk, a brat, unlike his first son, whose body Walt now inhabited.

And him returning would make the hectic transition with Belle even worse.

Chapter Ten
House of Decay

I tried to prepare my stomach for the revolting task as I unlocked the door.

The skunk-like stench hit me as soon as I slipped into the old Belle's room, and I slammed the door shut so the offensive odor didn't escape into the hallway. I skirted around the pile of ash and to the heavy royal blue curtains. Belle had been a big part of the house, and I never would have thought she'd betray Walt like she did.

Lugging them to the side allowed in the bright light, and for a few moments I enjoyed the majestic blue room. Belle's studio.

The painter who'd created the grand staircase on the wall was a genius. The red-carpeted platform and red steps up to a small balcony gave Belle and her clients the illusion of the real thing. But the life-sized candlestick, cup, and other characters freaked me out.

The old Belle always pretended they were real, talking to them like friends. Walt didn't have the magic to bring them to life, but the former Belle always made me feel like they were alive.

I tiptoed to the large closet and shook my head at myself. There was no need to sneak. As I took inventory of the closet, the bedroom door clicked shut.

"Lillian?" Judith's voice boomed through the door.

"In here. Be out in a second." I examined one of the yellow ball gowns. Luckily new Belle was the same size as old Belle.

Judith stood over old Belle's ash with a pained look on her face and a couple laundry baskets in her arms. "That smell is awful. He should have taken care of her somewhere else."

I shrugged. "That would have been wise, but another day, and it should be okay."

We needed to get the contractors going on the room, and somehow I knew this Belle would make big changes.

"Shall we start in the closet?" I waved Judith toward me, and we sorted clothes. The formal ball gowns would be kept, and Walt had already sent the other girls in to see if they wanted any of old Belle's clothes. Sometimes they would lay claim to the former girl's cute dresses, but basically, we ended up donating a ton of clothes to the women's shelters.

Even in the closet, the putrid smell scorched my nose. Her body went through the same process that the bodies of the renewal men did. In less than a week, it turned to mush. Then the corpse dried up into a pile of bones. Then ash. Then nothing. Walt had perfected the process. The ingredients of his special powder he sprinkled over their bodies were unknown, but in a short time, Belle went from a dead woman to ash that eventually disappeared into thin air. And the remains could not be touched until the process was finished.

Walt let her choose if she wanted to turn herself in to the police or lose her life, and the vain Belle couldn't imagine going to prison and dying unknown and ugly. She'd made some bad choices, and even though it had been hard to understand why she stole from Walt, I'd miss her.

With two baskets full of clothes, we hefted them out into the main room, and Judith sat on the bed. "I need some new shoes." She took off her shoe and rubbed her foot. Poor Judith was getting up there in age, her fifty-seven-year-old body slowing down. She'd worked for Walt for almost forty years, longer than anybody else.

She sauntered over to the windows and opened them up, letting the fresh breeze into the room. She eyed the ash with sad eyes.

"You've known them all, haven't you? Do you miss the girls who leave?"

Judith had come to work for Walt the year before he realized his dreams with this castle, and she'd been here ever since. My nine years didn't seem all that long.

Every once in a while, a girl chose to leave the house instead of doing their renewal ceremony. Walt gave them a bonus before they left, but part of their agreement was to disappear from the public eye. He worried all the time about people finding out his secrets, but so far he'd been lucky. We never heard from the girls who left us.

Right after I arrived, the previous Jaslyn had left. Walt showed us her postcards at first, but then those tapered off. I couldn't blame them for starting a new life.

"I do." Judith nodded. "Some more than others."

"Have you thought about retirement at all?" Judith lived on site, and Walt would buy her a condo if she chose to retire, but she loved her work.

"No, I'm not ready to…" She glanced at the pile on the floor. "Be done. I still have a lot of life left in me." Judith grinned; she was the hardest working woman I knew.

She chatted about her bowling league as we continued working. She often asked me to fill in when one of their regulars was gone, and we always had fun together.

It was tougher for me to have real, true friends outside of the House of Desire. Everybody wanted to be my friend, but it was the lure of money and excitement, the chance to meet Walt and other celebrities. I'd learned to trust no one.

Judith tucked a gray hair behind her ear, and we stripped the bed all the way down to the bed skirt. She effortlessly folded the sheets, even though they'd be washed. Judith's energy never waned, and she was Walt's faithful servant. She never renewed herself and just preferred to live a life that ended in natural death, no matter what age she was.

Not me. I'd signed the deal with the devil, and there was no backing out now. Well, unless I wanted to get old again and return to my arthritis and bad hips.

"Judith, did you ever regret dedicating your life to Walt?" Like everyone else, I'd had a doubt or two but always pushed them away. We all worked so very hard, but Walt provided well for us too. And although Ari and I couldn't live a life outside the castle, we could here.

"No. You're aware of the story, aren't you?" she said, and I nodded. She'd grown up with an abusive father, moved on to an abusive boyfriend, and then another. Walt had rescued her from a horrid life. "I honestly believe I would've died if I'd stayed with Lyle. And Walt's always given me everything I need."

They'd never had a sexual relationship, but Walt was like the father she'd never had. Sometimes I thought being around Judith helped restore the humanity in Walt. It would be easy for him to lose sight of what's important. His family.

She wiped her brow and frowned. "Lil, are you—"

"Of course not." I knew what she was about to say, but I'd never leave. "I have everything I want right here."

"Good." She sighed. "What's this?" she said with a frown and nudged the mattress over. A hole was cut inside the top of the fabric covering the bed frame. She reached inside. "Newspaper clippings."

We sat down on the bed and skimmed the stories. Missing girl stories. "Why in the world would she have this?" I asked. Some of them were so old, from way before my time.

Judith studied an article but then shrugged and crumpled the paper up. "Belle was an odd one."

No disagreements there.

We finished going through the armoire and bedside tables, removing all papers, photographs, and personal effects. Pretty soon the room was bare of anything except furniture and ashes.

Judith lugged one of the clothes baskets onto her hip and disappeared from the room. I stood at the door, staring at the mess on the carpet. Old Belle had been here so long, but we never became friends. She was ... different. Not very personable and she'd been cold with her housemates despite being warm and friendly with clients.

Maybe her distance made it easier to betray us, to steal from us and to tell the world the inner-workings of this grand home, but she'd paid for her choice by taking the easy way out.

I shut the door. Time to report to my boss.

Chapter Eleven
House of Debauchery

I knocked on the ornately carved door at Walt's office on the third floor of the castle.

No answer. But he'd told me to report immediately after the room was cleaned, so I opened the door and peeked inside. The room was empty; well, of people, not things. His enormous desk held piles of paperwork and two computer screens. Golf memorabilia lined the shelves on the wall, and a TV hung on the wall across from the sofa.

Walt might have been a genius, but his workspace was a mess. Filing cabinets lay partially open with forms to be filed stacked on top, and the latest revenue reports, printed because he preferred paper copies, lay unread within the chaos on his desk. Yet, he always found what he needed.

"Ohhhh god." Muted squeals wafted into the room from the door to his stairwell, and I headed up his private steps to his bedroom. No Walt or Belle here either.

A scream again. I rubbed my hands together as little twitters of excitement ran through my body, and I hurried out the door to the balcony, stepping over the two wet bath towels on the floor.

A sprawling canyon lay beyond the walls of the castle, but I focused on the two people going at it on the chaise lounge. Belle held her legs up in the air while Walt leaned over her. They rocked together in one motion.

She didn't notice me sneak in across from them, but Walt did, and his eyes lit up. Walt loved sex. Doing it. Watching it. Having others watching him do it. And I had to admit, I enjoyed the voyeurism too; he instilled in me the penchant for peeping years ago.

We used to sit in front of the video monitors as the girls screwed their clients, me in his lap while he touched me. Then we'd have sex. Then we'd watch, and we'd have sex again.

Now I spent more time with Ari.

Belle grunted with every thrust, sweat beading on her head. Those squeals had to be an act; they didn't sound real. I didn't need to fake it with Walt. He brought me to heaven every time, but sometimes the girls wanted him to think he was faster than he was.

I didn't understand why they pretended to orgasm. Walt knew how to satisfy a woman.

Belle's grunts grew louder, as did the slapping sound of skin against skin.

"Oh Walt, oh Walt, Waaaalt," Belle screamed so loud, anyone outside on the castle grounds would've heard her.

Definitely an over-exaggeration from the girl who didn't realize her lover was busy watching me. He sported a sexy smile that made me feel like I was the only one he cared about.

They soon finished, and he wiped a hand through his short, dark hair, the roots graying. He'd never go out in public until he got a dye job but didn't mind us seeing him real. Other than the grays, he hadn't changed at all over the last nine years.

His finger traced a circle around Belle's belly. "If you please your clients like that, it won't take long to build your list."

She beamed until she spotted me in the loveseat. Something flashed on her face, not anger or annoyance. Maybe curiosity. Walt slowly stood and strutted over to my seat. I admired his sculpted chest, created from an hour-long workout every day.

Walt's fears over his toned body not being good enough were unwarranted. Sexy, hot, distinguished. Those were all the words to describe Walt. His body might have been forty-six years old, but his brain was seventy-one, and that brain worried about his body catching up in age.

He sat down, his body pressing into mine. A lean finger ran up and down my arm, leaving behind a trail of sparks. He provided a great life for me, almost anything I wanted, plus sizzling sex.

"Belle is... wow," he whispered, searing my ear with his steamy breath. "You must fuck her if you get a chance."

"Ari wouldn't appreciate that." And he knew I'd never cheat on her.

He chuckled. "You girls and your monogamy."

His words made me laugh inside. Ari was with other men all the time, and I had sex with Walt, but our hearts were true to each other.

"You've done well this time, my dear Lil." He kissed my cheek, his hand on my thigh. Then another kiss, and another... all the way down my jawline. Both hands held my face, and he gently turned my lips to his.

My senses alighted, the heat radiating out from his touch. Every square centimeter of my body came alive. My heart pounded, wanting him, needing him, and I didn't give a damn that Belle sat there with folded arms and a frown on her face.

His strong lips took control, feeding the frenzy inside me. Life with Walt only got better with each passing day. I used to be more like the other girls, there to pleasure him, but now we were sexual equals. He knew every intimate spot on my body and what drove me wild, and he often gave me pleasure without expecting anything in return. This time he was rewarding me for a job well done.

We collapsed on the loveseat, sweaty with tangled limbs, and remained still, his arm wrapped around me.

Like most girls, I vied for Walt's love, but none ever came. But lying here with him, the time he spent with me, it was the closest I'd ever get, and I considered myself lucky.

His breathing slowed, and he nuzzled his face into my back. "What would I do without you?"

I peeked through my half-closed eyes to see the jealousy on Belle's face. I'd seen it often with the other girls. Walt played his favorites, but none of them, even Cindie, got the respect he bestowed on me.

I closed my eyes again and soaked up his attention. Rare was the day when I enjoyed both the woman I loved and the man I could never truly have.

And I wanted to savor every second of it.

Fifteen minutes later, the three of us were sitting, all dressed, at a table to discuss Belle's ideas for decorating her studio.

"I have to paint over those horrid characters on the wall. This is what I'd like. Something similar." She showed us pictures from the internet, and Walt nodded in agreement. Although the room would be mostly blues and golds, her décor didn't really follow the Beauty and the Beast story. Not like the old Belle.

"That's doable," Walt said.

"I still want to be Cinderella." She leaned back with a little pout, and Walt chuckled.

"I told you that position is filled."

I hid my sigh, hoping she wouldn't be another Cindie.

"I like the mural you want to paint on the wall," I said. The tree filled with branches of glittering lights would fit well with her elegant décor.

Walt folded his hands behind his head. "Since we're doing Belle's room, I'd like you to get estimates on the basement. Three more client rooms. Put a proposal together with five of your best ideas, and I'll pick my top three."

"Which rooms were you thinking?" We had many empty, unfinished rooms down there.

"The two across from the dungeon and the one next to it."

"Dungeon?" Belle's eyes opened wide, and her eyes flicked from me to Walt.

He laughed at her expression. "The dungeon is the name of our BDSM room. You'll get the full tour later."

Belle's shoulders relaxed. "I'd like to see that," she said in a flirtatious voice, fluttering her eyelashes at him.

"You do?" He studied her with his gray eyes.

"I do," she rasped and pressed her lips into his.

They were in the middle of their deep, sensuous kiss, and I stood. "If there's nothing else then, I'll schedule the contractors for Belle's room." I waited for Walt's approval.

He broke away from Belle. "Oh, check in with Kyle, please. Belle chose to have lobster at dinner and—"

"And caviar," she piped up. Walt laughed at my wrinkled nose. I loved most seafood, sushi included, but not caviar. I never acquired a taste for it.

"What did you need me to ask Kyle about?" I asked.

"Yes, the caviar. He didn't have much in stock when I spoke with him earlier, so please make sure he got some."

"I will." I was sure he did. When Walt requested something, the House of Desire employees got it.

"I want dinner for my Belle tonight to be perfect." He patted her hand, and she blinked her long dark lashes up at him.

"You are the best, Walt." Her sultry voice made him smile, and before I knew it, her hand was sliding up his thigh and down into his pants. He let out a deep groan, and she was on him, mauling him once again.

"I'll get on that," I said, but nobody was listening.

I headed to my office. All I wanted was a quiet half hour to unwind. Cleaning the old Belle's room and sex with Walt had left me drained. I wanted to grab my fuzzy blanket and curl up to watch a show.

Cindie was sitting there waiting for me, one of my coffee mugs in her hand. I glanced over to the almost empty pot and the uncapped bottle of French vanilla flavoring and brushed away my annoyance.

"What can I do for you?"

"What's she like?" Cindie had the best posture of all our girls, always sitting straight and tall. She carried herself like a princess. "She was pretty nasty."

"You all are when you first arrive at the house. But Belle will be fine. A good addition. I got the feeling she's into the whole bondage thing."

Cindie rolled her eyes. "That'll please Walt."

Only a few of our girls at the house enjoyed that type of sex, and he didn't allow anything that left marks. I couldn't get into it either, but to each their own.

"So what did you need?" I said.

"Have you talked to Jaslyn lately? She seems a bit off. Hasn't had much enthusiasm."

Sometimes Cindie's annoyed me, but she was a good source to keep track of what was going on around the house, especially when it involved a girl's job performance.

"What do you mean?" I'd have to study some of her latest tapes, but not with Cindie here. Walt didn't allow any of the girls in his video room. They were all aware he taped them in their studios, but letting one girl watch another caused problems.

"We had a threesome, and I knew she was faking. I mean, it was blatantly obvious." Cindie pursed her plump red lips, all indignant.

"Could the client tell?" Walt wouldn't like this.

"No, I don't think so. He was new, but if he'd been a regular, he would've. But I've noticed it in other places too. In the welcoming room—she hides out in the corner like she doesn't want any jobs. I even saw her pass off a guy to Mulan."

As if I don't have enough to do. It was my fault really. I should've been paying more attention, but Belle had taken most of my time this last week. I clicked on my calendar on the computer and checked the schedule.

"Thanks for coming in and talking to me. I appreciate it. Don't forget dinner is seven p.m. Sharp."

She lived on her Cindie time, which was at least fifteen minutes behind the real world. At least she didn't show up late to client appointments.

Tonight was important. Walt had cleared the schedule so the employees could welcome Belle. Groundskeepers, kitchen staff, housekeepers, and the others who made this castle run.

"I know." Cindie huffed and stalked out, leaving the dirty coffee cup behind. I ignored the cup, dug out my blanket, and curled up on my loveseat. I flicked the TV on and started my show.

The door swung open, and I jumped.

"I forgot—" Cindie stared at my TV and rolled her eyes. "Really, Lil? Are you living back in the eighties?"

That was why nobody except Ari knew about my love for these shows. I'd gone through all the seasons of the shows like *Dallas and Knot's Landing,* and now I was watching them a second or third time. TV was just so much better back then.

"What do you want?" I asked.

"I…" She frowned at the TV and huffed. "I don't remember now. I'll be back if I do though." She spun around and slammed the door behind her.

I'm sure you will. I shook my head and rewound the show to the beginning again.

Chapter Twelve
House of Disharmony

"Why isn't she in her own room yet?" Cindie's icy-blue eyes narrowed on me, as if I had anything to do with the contractors working on Belle's room. Belle had been in Walt's room for the last five days, which meant Walt wasn't spending as much time with Cindie.

"Worried you're gonna lose the top spot?" Tia smirked. We were sitting in the kitchen eating a late breakfast. I swallowed down my last bite of syrup-drenched pancake.

"Relax," I said. "Her coming out party is in ten days." I didn't let on how nervous I was about everything. It wasn't just this party but also Jaslyn's renewal. I'd reviewed some of her tapes, including the one Cindie told me about, and she'd been right. Jaslyn was holding back. I hoped Walt hadn't noticed yet because I wanted to talk to her myself first.

"More cakes, ladies?" Kyle brought over another stack and held out the plate to Tia. "Birthday girl?"

"Yes, please." She stabbed two more pancakes.

"Slow down. This isn't a trough." Cindie huffed.

Tia glared at her. "It's my birthday. I'm allowed to enjoy the day. Besides, I don't see you in the gym." She grabbed the syrup bottle.

Cindie pouted. "I swim."

I hated Cindie for being the girl who didn't have to work out to stay in shape. I spent at least an hour every day keeping my body trim. Some of us weren't as lucky as her.

"No, you don't," Tia said with a laugh and squeezed the syrup bottle. "You fuck Walt in the pool. That's not swimming."

"Not lately," Cindie muttered, staring down at the growing pool of syrup on Tia's plate. Finally, Tia flipped the bottle upright and tossed it on the counter. I capped it for her.

"It's been a while since we've had a new girl," I reminded Cindie. There's always a few weeks' transition."

"Whatever." Cindie swirled her leftover piece of pancake around in the syrup but didn't eat it. "Where are we going for dinner tonight?"

Walt always made a big deal out of the girls' birthdays. They got the choice to take the night off to go into Vegas for the celebration.

"Samosa," Tia said.

Cindie rolled her eyes. "Weren't you there a few weeks ago?"

"It's my birthday. Deal with it." Tia shook her head. I wasn't sure why Cindie was making a big deal. She loved Indian food.

"Is Meri still sick?" Cindie let out a long, low sigh. "I don't want her sneezing all over me. I can't afford to get a cold. I've got my sights on a new pair of shoes."

She always had her sights on something spendy, usually clothes.

"She's better. She'll be back to work tomorrow, I'm sure," I said. Ari had been taking care of Meri on her off-time, feeding her chicken noodle soup and keeping her supplied with Sudafed. Even though Ari had been out of nursing for years, everyone went to her with their minor aches and pains.

My growing to-do list was waiting, so I cleared my dishes, poured one more cup of coffee, and excused myself.

A short time later, Walt popped into my office. His freshly shaven face smiled at me, and I breathed in the strong scent of his aftershave.

"We all set for tonight?" He set his coffee mug on my desk on top of some papers. I slid them out from under the cup.

"Yes. Reservations confirmed for seven. We'll be in the car by five-thirty." I opened my drawer, grabbed the remote to turn down the twangy country music on the stereo, and set it back in place. In all my years here, I couldn't talk Walt into being a country music fan.

He picked up the contracts stacked in the corner. I refrained from slapping his hand as he scanned the contents. He tossed them back to the desk, and I shuffled them together.

I motioned toward the papers. "You'll be happy to know Belle's room came in under budget. The numbers the contractor sent for the new rooms look pretty good too."

"I loved the jungle-themed room." Walt grinned. "It'll be a big hit."

"I still think you should put a pool down there too."

"Lil." He chuckled. "We live in Nevada, must I remind you. Not to mention the heated pool outside."

I laughed along. I was a bit of a baby when it came to swimming in cooler weather.

"Oh, and do you plan on mentioning Belle during the interview on Tuesday?" I still had coffee in my pot, so I refilled his half-empty cup, then handed him the packets of sugar and creamer.

"Most likely. She's itching to get working. I like to see that desire in my girls." He grew silent and stared off over my shoulder.

"Is something else on your mind?" I said.

"Junior wrecked his Porsche, and I had to find out about it from the paper. He's been here for several days and failed to mention what happened." Walt rubbed his temples roughly.

"Why was it in the paper?"

"Apparently the police found the wrecked vehicle, but they didn't find him until the next afternoon. Thank god nobody was hurt, except for the car and the light pole. And he insists he wasn't drunk."

"But there's plenty of pictures and witnesses that put him out at the clubs," I finished. "Did the police give him a breathalyzer or anything?"

"Yes. Just a breathalyzer. Nothing registered, but it was over twelve hours later."

Good thing they didn't test his blood. Walt forbade Junior from bringing drugs into the castle, but he often showed up here high. Marijuana was his drug of choice, but the word was he dabbled in harder drugs.

"What will you do?" I asked. Walt needed to make that kid realize he couldn't pull this crap, but Walt was too much of a softie. Whenever talk of punishing Junior came up, he got all defensive, so it was a topic I avoided. Walt needed to take away his credit cards and refuse to fix the car.

"I'll think of something." He took out his phone and checked his calendar before standing. "You know, I'm still waiting for the report I asked you for yesterday."

I folded my arms and leaned forward on my elbows. "You know," I mimicked him, "you'd have it by now if you hadn't been sitting here wasting my time."

He grinned and disappeared out the door. I jumped on my email and sent out the report. It'd be at his computer before he got back.

*

A half hour before we were set to leave, Junior texted and asked me to stop by his room. He stood inside the door holding his blue silk tie in the air with a sheepish grin on his face. "Can you tie this for me?"

"How many years have you been wearing ties?"

He shrugged. "Not my fault the old man requires it. It's not the Stone Age."

"Gentlemen wear ties." I stood in front of him and tied it.

"I guess I'm not a gentleman." Junior laughed. I wouldn't disagree. At twenty-two he had a lot of growing up to do.

"There you go." I patted him on the chest, and he stepped back to admire himself in the mirror, running a hand through his light brown hair. "You clean up nice."

He chuckled again. "Thanks, Lil."

"By the way, I heard you got into an accident the other day."

"Yeah." He picked at an invisible speck on his pants. "A light pole jumped out at me. No big deal. Insurance is handling it."

No big deal. Only a ninety-thousand-dollar car. Only people's lives he put in danger.

"Be warned. Your father isn't happy."

"He's never happy. What?" He flung his hands in the air. "I wasn't drunk. It's like he never made one fucking mistake. Maybe if he'd give me a full-time driver. You should talk—"

"Nope. Don't involve me," I said. Junior didn't deserve such an extravagance. "Let's go. It's almost time to leave."

He followed me down to the waiting limo. Several of the girls were already inside, including the birthday girl.

"Happy Birthday, gorgeous." Junior gave Tia a kiss on the cheek, and she laughed. He butted between the girls, and they scooted to make room. I waited outside the car. For the hour's drive, we'd be sardines in the limo.

Ari strode out of the house in a glittery purple dress. "You're stunning," I said and kissed her. Although we would sit by each other tonight, we wouldn't show any affection. We'd be in public, and social media would buzz with pictures of our night out.

"Thank you. You look terrific too. Red is such a wonderful color on you." She put her hands under my hair and sort of bounced the curls on her palms. "Did I ever tell you about the time I permed my hair when I was a teenager? Fried it bad." She laughed. "I'll have to tell you the story later." She peeked in the car. "Walt said to do a check and make sure everybody is here. He'll be down with Belle in a couple of minutes."

I did a head count. "We're missing Jaslyn." I took out my cell phone to call her, but Ari grabbed my hand.

"Oh, she's not coming. I talked to her a bit ago."

"That's weird." She loved nights out.

"She's not in the mood. But when Walt asks, she's not feeling well. Stomach issues."

"Yeah, okay." I didn't mind lying for Jaslyn. She was one of the girls I'd do anything for around here, but this was unusual, and I was curious why she didn't want to go.

"Oh, there's Walt and Belle." Ari pointed to the couple, and I put Jaslyn out of my mind. Tonight would be a fun night: good food, good company, and once we got back home, smoking hot sex.

I just hoped Walt wasn't annoyed about Jaslyn. He didn't like girls skipping out on events.

Chapter Thirteen
House of Doubt

Jaslyn shifted next to me on the leather sofa in my office, staring down at the coffee cup in her hands. We needed to talk, and I wouldn't sit at my desk and look down on her like she was some lowly employee. I wanted her to open up and trust me. Some girls believed I'd go running to Walt for any little thing, but I wasn't a snitch, and I didn't need to rat out the girls for minor infractions. I thought Jaslyn knew that.

"The tapes don't lie," I said and blew on my own fresh cup. She rubbed her forehead and stared at her lap, so I set my coffee down, took out a tablet, and brought up one of the videos from the welcoming room. "You appear bored. I don't need to tell you how it harms your business."

I gathered her stat sheets, and we reviewed her hours over the past six months. Her numbers always bounced up and down, but the last few months had been more down. I placed the papers back into the folder and set it on the corner of the desk.

"What's the deal?" I sipped my coffee, but it burned my tongue still, so I blew on it again.

She slumped and leaned her head back, her eyes closed. Her whole face was tight, and I waited.

"I tried to get Walt to wait another year before my renewal, but he said no." She seemed so small and fragile, not our usual strong and tall Jaslyn. She was still beautiful, but her age was showing, and Walt didn't want to wait any longer.

"But you don't need to worry this time. You'll still be the same. We'll say you got plastic surgery."

"This time." She sighed, the weight of the world on her face. Her gaze flew up to the corners of the rooms and the ceiling. "Are there cameras in here?" she whispered so quietly I barely heard, her hand covering her mouth.

"No, of course not." Walt allowed me full access to video, and I knew the location of each and every camera in this castle.

She lifted her head off the sofa and sat up, her face so serious. "I'm not sure I want to go through with it."

"What are you talking about? Why not?"

She couldn't be serious. Did she want to leave? Walt wouldn't keep her on much longer if she continued to age, and I didn't want another Jaslyn around here. I liked this one.

Her dark eyes stared at me. "It's just those men. The ones who make it so we're beautiful again. I feel bad because someone loses their life for me."

"But they're criminals. Men who rape and murder and escaped justice." Walt picked the worst of the worst; he did the world a favor by removing those men from society.

"I'm not so sure about that." Her voice faltered.

I scoffed. "Walt searches for these men. He checks their backgrounds and finds out who they are." Jaslyn had only been through her original renewal, but she'd been around for ten years, long enough to see how it went for the other girls.

She kneaded her hands together like I used to do with my arthritic hands before Walt renewed me. "I never told anybody about this, but after my renewal, after I'd got settled into the house, I was in Vegas with Walt for something. I don't even remember what now." She shook her head, her eyes dark. "I read an article about this missing guy. His name was Xavier Carmina. He was visiting from Mexico and disappeared. He had a family and—"

"Jaslyn." I held my hand up to stop her. "It's not your guy. He just looked similar. I can look up his name for you." Walt kept meticulous notes.

"Noah. Walt said his name was Noah."

"Oh." I set the cup down without taking a drink. How did she remember after nine years? "See. Not the same guy." I gathered up her hands in mine. "Things are so hectic at renewals; they go so fast, so it's not a surprise you didn't get a good look at Noah. That seeing a picture of a similar guy would make you think of him." It would be an easy mistake to make. "Walt loves us. He'd do anything for us, and he gives us this most wonderful gift. We need to be thankful for his generosity."

She stared at me, her face so bleak, but finally she nodded. "Walt wouldn't take an innocent man's life." She dropped my hands and stood. "Thanks, Lil. I promise I'll work harder now. You don't have to worry about me." Her voice took on a more business-like tone again, and I gave her a hug.

"Thank you for trusting me."

That went well. Jaslyn was soft-hearted, and I understood why this issue had bothered her, especially if she'd been worrying for years. Renewals were emotional events, and sometimes they created doubt in a girl's head. Sometimes the girls needed assurance that we were doing the right thing. At least this was easy to clear up before Walt got back to town.

I accompanied Jaslyn to my office door, and we hugged again. It might be too late to change tonight's plans for dinner, but I should talk to Kyle about making Chinese food for Jaslyn. Maybe that would cheer her up.

Voices drifted down the hall. Junior. I swung my door shut, hoping he'd pass by. A thought flittered through my mind. Walt would never take an innocent life. There was one exception: he took his son's life. But that situation was different. Walt would've died if he hadn't. None of these girls would be here today. I wouldn't be here.

It was an unnecessary evil, one I didn't like to think about.

My door flung open, and I jumped back.

"Lillian," Junior said, giving me the what's-up nod. He'd disappeared after Tia's birthday but had texted one of the girls that he'd be back in a week. He only stayed away for a few days though.

I skirted around my desk and sat down, opening a folder and removing the papers so I appeared busy. "Back again?" I asked.

"I haven't run into the old man yet. Where's he?" Junior plopped down into the chair in front of my desk, like his father so often had.

I shrugged. "He's in Houston. He'll be back tomorrow."

Junior nabbed a pen out of my marble pencil holder. I sucked in a hard breath as he clicked it in and out. My pen would walk out the door with him like a hundred times before.

"Oh yeah, I didn't know."

Everything in his voice told me he did.

"I thought you weren't coming back for a bit," I said.

"Figured no time like now. Always like to spend time with my father." He got up and strutted past me to the balcony. I followed. He ran his hands through his hair as he stared down at the pool. "We're going swimming tonight."

"We?" I asked.

He spun around and grinned. "Yeah, we. I brought a few friends."

"How many friends?"

Walt wouldn't be happy about this impromptu party. I glanced down at the pool. Walt proudly shared with everyone how he designed the layout of the waterfall. Three tiers of cascading water over boulders. The slide, which was always a big hit at the pool parties, sat off to the side.

"Only two." He huffed like it wasn't inconceivable he'd bring twenty friends over. He'd done it before.

But two we could handle. I wouldn't need to call Walt, but I had to talk to Kyle to prepare more food.

"Check and see which girls are free tonight?" he said.

"Can you say please?" I wished Walt would keep Junior in line better, but who was I to say Walt was a bad parent?

"Please?" He slapped his hands together like he was begging.

I took out my phone and checked my schedule. Bianca was done at eight, but she'd have no interest in hanging with Junior. Neither would Ari, but she was working the night anyway, which meant I'd be on my own watching my shows from the 80s. A few girls were free though.

"Invite that new girl. What's her name?" he said.

"Belle."

He'd met her before, but I didn't remind him of that.

"Is she into girls?"

"You need to ask her." Belle was definitely into girls, but he was being so damn lazy. "Do you remember which room the old Belle was in? She might be there."

"Yeah." He gave me a smarmy grin. "Maybe I can get some pre-party action. Later, Lil." He saluted me and shot out of my office.

My pen went with him.

Chapter Fourteen
House of Dishonor

Hours later, I dropped in to check on Junior's party. Surprisingly, he'd only brought along one other guy, and his second guest was a woman.

Every light shined brightly, including the lights strung along the fake palm trees lining the pool area, and the rock music blared from the speakers. I froze at the top of the steps and stared down at the left side of the pool. Belle was sitting with her legs and arms wrapped around Junior's friend, Paris, their mouths moving and their hands roaming over each other's naked bodies. Junior stretched out a few feet away from them, his hand on his lap. I looked away from him before I caught sight of something I had no desire to see.

Belle brushed the hair away from Paris's neck and kissed her. Her boldness surprised me. Most new girls were more timid, not knowing the rules or how they fit in. I scanned the pool. Junior's buddy, Kaleb, was swimming with Tia, no clothing in sight.

I proceeded down the steps and over to the naked couple, keeping my eyes away from Junior. At least he tugged a towel over his lap, but Belle didn't let go of the girl until I spoke.

"Kyle said he'd bring the pizza out soon."

"Okay," he huffed.

"I'm going for a swim." Paris tore away from Belle's arms and sauntered toward the pool, her butt swaying. I turned to Junior again.

"Did Meri leave?" She'd been here earlier, but I didn't see her anymore.

"She was jealous." Belle smirked. First, she tried to rile things up with Cindie, and now Meri, who I doubted was jealous. This girl was trouble. She got off the seat and crawled onto the chaise lounge with Junior. She nudged his legs off the edges of the chair and scooted up between them.

Junior licked his lips as he eyed her naked body.

I shook my head in disgust.

"I'll see you in the morning. Your father should be home by eleven. Don't stay—"

I was thirty-three years old and almost told them not to stay up too late. Junior had reduced me to the old maid, going to bed while the party was raging. Not that I had any desire to be a part of this party.

Maybe being with Ari was slowing me down, which I liked sometimes, but then again, it could be my real age showing through. I'd be seventy-one if I hadn't run into Walt all those years ago.

Junior barely got a goodbye out before Belle was on his lips.

Ari was free at the moment, and so I'd stop in and give her a quick kiss goodnight, but she had a client showing up soon, so I couldn't stay long.

I left the partiers to their fun.

*

My phone rang, waking me up in the darkness. Three a.m. Dammit. I answered the call from security at the same time David burst into the room. Gram was speaking into my ear as David blabbered in front of me. I rubbed my eyes.

"Lil," David called, his face red.

"Hold up." I flashed my palm at David and focused on Gram's voice.

"Just get down to the pool now!" Gram said and clicked off. I hung up, rushed to get my robe, and followed David out the door.

"What happened?"

"I don't know," David huffed. "Tia called Gram saying something was wrong with Paris. He couldn't wake her. Tried for five minutes. She puked before she passed out."

"Is she alive?" Oh crap. What did Junior do? Drugs... it had to be drugs.

"Yeah. She had a pulse and everything, but damn, Lil. It's like she was a fucking rag doll."

"Did you call an ambulance?"

Pahrump wasn't far away, although it might be better to drive ourselves.

"No. She's breathing; she has a pulse. But I told Kyle to get a car ready so we can bring her to the hospital."

"Did you call Ari too?" She could help.

He gave me a sheepish look. "I... um... She was with a client."

"Next time get her. We can give them free hours, and if it's something she can help with, I'd rather have her there."

"I will."

We rounded the corner at the pool to find Paris sitting up in her chair, Gram next to her. Paris's white face was bobbing as I knelt down in front of her, forcing Junior aside. *Oh, thank god.*

"Are you okay?" I asked. Her bloodshot eyes blinked at me over and over. The smell of vomit hit me then, and I stepped back.

"She's fine, Lil," Junior snapped.

"She's not fine. She... she..." I looked back to Paris. "How do you feel?"

"I'm okay. My head is throbbing, and I feel like I'm going to puke again."

I glared at Junior and sat next to her. "What did you take?"

"She didn't take—"

I spun around and shoved the little asshole away. "Get out of here. Now!"

David yanked Junior back, and I returned to Paris. "What did you take?" I said firmly.

Her lip quivered. "Ecstasy. A little pot. But I think it was laced with something. I felt different."

I gritted my teeth. I was going to kill Junior. Walt would kill him.

"Okay," I said. "We'll bring you to town to get you checked out."

"No, I'm fine."

"I'd rather—"

"No, please. I'm queasy, but that's it. Really. Whatever it was, wasn't that bad." Her eyes were focused, so maybe she'd been drowsy when she woke up.

Against my better judgment, I let it go. We sent her and Kaleb off with one of our drivers, under strict orders to bring her straight to a hospital if something changed on the way home.

An hour and a half later, during my lecture with Junior, I got a phone call saying they'd picked up food and dropped her off at home. Sometimes the drama at the house was worse than those 80s nighttime soaps. God forbid Walt ever considered doing a reality show; that would be a nightmare.

Junior slumped in front of me. He was no longer a child by age, but by his maturity, he was. Walt would be awake soon, and I'd call him later since everything turned out okay.

I was done with Junior. His father could deal with him now.

Chapter Fifteen
House of Denial

Junior slept in his room while the rest of us were hard at work. We had a bachelor party coming in tonight, and I finalized all the details. It was a small party, only four men, but they wanted six girls for five hours, drinks and apps, and the groom-to-be requested use of the shower room for an hour. The House of Desire was no place to be celebrating your pending nuptials, but it wasn't my place to tell these men such a thing.

We also had Belle's coming out party in less than a week and Jaslyn's renewal the week later. Too many things were happening at once. At least Walt didn't schedule any special parties during these few weeks, and he even delayed his monthly pool party, which helped me immensely.

I checked over the schedule, spoke with our hostess on duty, and returned a few emails. My office door slammed, and Walt stalked in, fists clenched and jaw tight.

"Is he still here?" he spat before I asked him about his golf trip. Good thing he'd had fun before returning to this mess.

"Yes, he'd wanted to go, but we made him stay."

Junior didn't want to face his father and take responsibility. He never did.

Walt pounded his fist in his palm. "I'm so tired of his shenanigans. If that girl had died, the police would've brought our home under scrutiny."

"Yes, but *he* brought those drugs here. Nobody else here has any."

Walt stared at me, his gray eyes dark.

"I don't like it. We deal with enough inspectors," he growled. "He worries me, Lil. The way he fills his body with drugs. He's slowly destroying it. He might OD someday. Then what will I do?"

Years from now, Walt would take over Junior's body when his started slowing down. Walt's current body was only forty-six, so he had a lot of time left.

"Have you ever considered having another child?"

"That's an idea. By the time he's an adult, this body will be almost seventy, but it'd be good to have a backup. But you're aware how babies complicate things. They severely change the dynamic of the house. Remember when Junior was a teenager."

Yeah, he walked around with a perpetual boner. He'd been so mad that Walt forbade the girls from touching him until he was eighteen. Not that they wanted to, but he sure thought they had.

"I'll do it right this time. I learned my lesson with Junior and won't make those same mistakes." His face softened. "Maybe you want to be my baby momma." He winked, and I laughed.

"I don't think so. But it would be an honor." Another time, another place, I would've jumped at the chance to be the mother to Walt's son, but not the way my life was going now. "I know some spectacular girls who would make great mothers though."

"One in particular?" He smirked. "Perhaps an amber-haired beauty?"

Definitely an amber-haired beauty. The loss of Ari's son years ago had devastated her, and she'd be a wonderful mother if she had another chance.

"It's something to think about." His unfocused gaze stared over my shoulder at nothing.

"Walt…" I said, and his attention snapped back. "Just not Cindie."

He barked out a laugh. "You know I love her, but she wouldn't make a good mother."

Whew. Glad we are on the same page.

His face clouded over. "We've got my current son to deal with now. Come with me." He stood and headed for the door, and I ran after him.

Walt marched to the third floor and barged into the room to find Junior splayed out on his bed, not a stitch of clothing on.

"Get up!" Walt boomed. Junior shot up in bed and stared at his father. He blinked and wiped the drool off his mouth. "What the hell were you thinking?" Walt shouted.

Junior tugged the sheet over his naked body. "It's no big deal. Nothing happened. She's fine."

"Do you think I give a damn about that girl?" Walt snarled. "We talked about this months ago. You promised you'd shape up, but you put a spotlight on our house. The police would've been crawling all over here if she had died."

"She didn't die." Junior's strong voice betrayed the panic in his eyes.

"That's not the point!" Walt slammed his fist into the wall, leaving a dent.

"It wasn't me. It was Kaleb. He brought the marijuana with. And the ecstasy. I didn't touch the stuff. I wouldn't—"

"Do you think I'm stupid?" Walt yelled, the veins in his neck bulging. "You were smoking pot in my home. When I specifically told you not to."

It had always struck me how opposed Walt was to drugs. No smoking either. With everything going on around here, all the illicit sex and the renewals, he didn't allow any drugs. He'd even kicked girls out of the house who'd been using. It's how my Ari ended up at the house, when the previous one refused to give up her addiction to drugs.

"It was a one-time thing. I mean, I cut back, but then I got together with Kaleb and Paris. We hadn't hung out in a while. I told him not to, but I lapsed. I'm sorry." Junior's mouth was running a mile a minute.

A thick and heavy silence filled the room, a pressure about to blow out the windows. Under Walt's intense stare, Junior backed up into the corner of his bed. Walt clenched his fists, his back a mess of tension. The room seemed to dim, and I glanced at the open window to see the thick, dark clouds covering the sun.

Walt closed his eyes and took deep breaths. His skin had lost its luminescent tan and was turning gray, his nails black as coal. His lids opened to reveal scorching green eyes. The pungent air choked me like I'd fallen into a dumpster full of rotting corpses. Walt rarely lost control, rarely turned into… his other self. The hackles on my neck raised, and I fought the urge to flee. He wasn't angry with me. He wouldn't do anything to me.

Junior quivered on his bed under the sheet, which was no protection against his father's raging fury.

"You are lying, even now." Walt's baritone voice resonated through the room as he stormed to Junior's bed. I remained frozen off to the side. This was his son. He wouldn't hurt Junior. Walt loved him. He needed the boy.

Walt towered over the bed, the only sound his deep breaths.

I waited.

Junior's chin trembled.

Walt spun around and stalked over to the window. He grasped the frame with his mottled gray hands and stood there, his chest heaving for air.

Two minutes passed. Maybe three. Junior didn't tear his eyes away from his father.

The usual color returned to Walt's skin, and he dropped his hand into his suit coat pocket and took out his phone. For a few moments, he clicked away at the screen. When he looked back up, his eyes had returned to their normal gray, the demonic green gone.

Voices spilled out of the phone, laughter and fun. Walt strode over to his son and shoved the phone in front of his face. I couldn't see the screen, but I caught Junior's voice among the others. I strained to hear what was being said.

"You're smoking heroin," Walt said, his voice flat. "I have proof."

"You had me followed?" Junior whispered.

"You have been smoking heroin, and you will do so no more. This is your last warning. If caught again, you'll attend rehab. If that doesn't solve the problem, then I'll have to figure out another solution." Walt crossed his arms and glared at his son. "Do not disappoint me."

The venom in his voice sent chills across my body.

Junior mumbled a response, and Walt turned around and charged toward the door. I scrambled after him and shut the door behind me.

"Lil, I need you." He headed toward my bedroom door.

I wasn't in the mood for sex, but Walt needed me, and I'd do anything for him.

Chapter Sixteen
House of Disbelief

The next night all the girls relaxed in one of the lounges, enjoying drinks on family night. Whether it was swimming, a pool tournament, or make-your-own ice cream sundae night—my favorite, there were only two requirements. Every girl had to attend. And only Walt, his girls, and I were there. Well, and sometimes Junior, except Walt had banished him from attending any activities for the time being.

Ari and Jaslyn were talking their second language: baseball. I watched games with Ari sometimes but didn't get excited about it like her, so I zoned out, ignoring their discussion of San Francisco and Atlanta.

Briar stared off into her drink while Tia and Bianca chatted in the corner. Cindie was monopolizing the conversation with Walt, but every time he scanned the room and found Belle, she frowned.

I noticed black streaks on the south wall behind Ari and took out my phone to make a note to send a message to the maintenance crew. I finished my reminder and stuck my phone back into my pocket.

The funny thing with family night was that the majority of the girls would've preferred to be in their worn sweats and t-shirts, but we had an image to promote, which meant sexy lingerie. The only girl allowed to be on her phone was Bianca since she updated our social media accounts. The other girls would've complained if they knew she got paid extra for her postings, and they all would've wanted to have the job, not realizing all the work it took. Bianca was an awesome photographer and always had good quips to post along with our pictures.

Walt clapped his hands. "Let's head to the theater room in a few minutes. Refresh your drinks and get ready to cuddle."

"I have a great idea for a movie," Cindie said. "You'll love it."

"Belle already picked the movie." He glanced toward the door, but Belle was wandering out, and he looked back in time to witness Cindie's pouting. "This is her first family night. Her choice."

He followed the other girls out the door, leaving only Cindie, Ari, and me.

"I bet she gets priority seating," Cindie mumbled before she shot out of the room.

I shook my head at her jealousy. "What did she expect? Belle's the new girl."

Ari laughed. "We have a new queen ascending the throne, and somebody is a bit resentful."

I chuckled and lowered my voice. "If I had any choice in the matter, I'd give my seat to Cindie and sit alone with you." Even though I was proud that Walt always wanted me by his side, it meant I sometimes cuddled with him and not Ari. But I shouldn't complain. I got to be with Ari almost any time I wanted; well, when we were both free.

The whole group gathered in the theater room. My feet sunk into the plush navy carpet, and I ran my fingers along the velvet-flocked wallpaper lining the walls. A giant sofa was situated on the first tier of the floor, with loveseats and recliners on the second and third tiers. Everything faced the front wall, where two maroon curtains flanked the giant screen.

We posed ourselves on the sofa for Bianca to take pictures. Walt had his arms around both me and Belle, and Cindie glowered off to my side, only smiling when Bianca was about to take the picture.

"How are my boobs?" Tia asked Bianca, followed by several others wondering the same question. I rolled my eyes. Bianca would never post an unflattering picture of anybody, and every single one of these girls looked spectacular on camera.

Bianca stared at her screen, checking out pictures. "Fine," she said in response to every girl. Her patience was legendary.

Walt climbed out of his seat to retrieve another drink from the bar at the back of the room, and the other girls shifted around or stood. We didn't sit quite so closely during the actual movie.

"I should've worn my fuchsia babydoll." Cindie pouted.

"You look great." I gave my standard answer.

She stepped over to Walt, who had returned, and took his arm, blocking him from Belle's view. "Do you think this one was okay? I can go change."

She arched her back and puffed out her chest.

"You, my dear, are gorgeous. Teal is a stunning color on you." He kissed her on the lips, and she held on to the kiss as long as she could, pressing her hips into his crotch.

Belle gripped her glass and took a drink, her eyes narrowed.

"Walt, are you excited for the movie? I picked it out just for you." Belle placed her hand on his back, and he shifted away from Cindie to face Belle, missing the dirty look Cindie shot her. So many stupid head games went on around here.

"Do we have enough pictures, Bianca?" Walt called, and she nodded. "Well then, let's get seated."

I took my place beside Walt, but at least Ari sat on my other side. Cindie surveyed the sofa with a grimace and settled on the other side of Belle, who snuggled into Walt's arm.

He darkened the room with the remote control, and the movie started. I took Ari's hand, and she scooted closer to me.

After an hour of the show, Ari leaned over to my ear. Her hot breath would normally turn me on, but the violence on the screen had shut those feelings down. A few girls sat back with closed eyes, and some others talked quietly.

"What sort of movie is this?" Ari muttered.

I had no clue. It had started okay, a story about a girl escaping her abusive captors, but now she was exacting her revenge in a violent, gory fashion. I cringed as she shot one of the bad guys in the eye with an arrow. Only two guys dead, three more left, and the blood was spilling everywhere.

Even Ari, who loved horror movies, flinched when the victim turned into the perpetrator.

"Belle picked it," I whispered back. Ari laid her head on my shoulder and set her warm hand on my leg. It was the most affection, other than chaste kissing, that we showed in front of the other girls. They all knew about us, but we didn't put our relationship on display.

Walt's body shifted next to me, and I turned to see him making out with Belle, his hand on her breasts, their tongues going at it like dueling snakes. She lay back on the sofa with her legs stretched out in front of her.

Cindie glared at the screen, her arms folded and about a foot of space now between her and the make-out couple.

Belle reached over and unzipped Walt's pants, releasing his stiff length. Suddenly, Walt was leaning back, and Belle's head was in his lap. Most of the girls were pretending not to notice, but Cindie stared at them, then me, open-mouthed.

I held back my gasp. A little groping sometimes went on at family movie night, but usually it was Walt's hand down one of our pajamas. It had never become a peep show. These nights were all about the family. About the girls.

Walt stared at the screen the whole time Belle pleasured him, even during the part when the main character chopped the head off some guy and laughed about it.

And his smirk never left his face.

Chapter Seventeen
House of Division

My phone beeped with a message from our hostess saying Cindie's appointment had arrived, and she hadn't shown up yet. I wanted to whip her butt. Belle's coming out party was almost here, and I had several fires to put out with that alone. I didn't need this too.

I rapped on Cindie's door and walked in when she called out. She was lying on her bed watching TV; at least she was dressed with makeup applied.

"Your client's here. What are you doing?"

She glanced up at the phone. "Oh yeah. I forgot." She shut off the TV, sauntered over to her mirror, and fluffed her hair.

"You look fine. Get going. He's probably in the welcoming room by now."

"Chill, Lil." She grinned. "You're such a pill."

I narrowed my eyes at her, but she laughed liked she'd said the funniest thing in the world.

Back at my office, I opened a file. Cindie had been late twice these last few weeks, unusual for her. We hadn't really had any issues with too many of the girls. Sometimes Walt had to talk to them, but it never went any further.

I didn't have time for Cindie and went down to the basement to check on the contractors working on the new rooms. They were coming along well.

Several hours passed, and I ignored my grumbling stomach until I had a good break. Time to grab a quick meal in the kitchen.

Walt was sitting with some of the girls finishing their lunches and gave me a head nod when I walked in. Cindie didn't even glance up from her plate, and I slid into the chair next to Briar.

"Do you have any more questions about the coming out party?" he asked Belle, who was sitting next to him.

"No, but I can't wait. It sounds amazing." Belle sighed, and Walt stood.

"Have you been to the basement yet?" I asked Walt.

"No, I'll probably head down there later this afternoon. Right now I need to make some phone calls and talk to my attorney. Which reminds me, Lil. Will you call that masseuse and see if she can come this afternoon or evening? Those knots in my shoulder are back."

"Yes, I'll check in with her."

"Walt," Belle purred. "You don't need a masseuse when you have us." She reached out and ran her hand over his crotch. My eyes about popped out of my head, someone's fork clattered on a plate, but Belle didn't take her eyes off Walt. What was she doing?

He covered her hand with his and smiled. "I'd like that. Be in my office in thirty." He gave her hand a squeeze and dropped it. Then he walked away.

Belle turned back to the table, a smug smile darkening her face. "These last two weeks have been the best in my life. Making love to Walt every day. Over and over. He—"

"You didn't make love to Walt; you fucked him," Cindie snarled. I held my breath and waited to see if this would go anywhere.

"Yeah, Walt's a lot of fun." Briar's gaze flicked back and forth between Cindie and Belle. She got a twinkle in her eye. "Did you fuck him in the pool?"

"Of course." Belle's smirk grew. "We fucked all over the castle. I've orgasmed in almost every room. Even yours." She cast a smug look toward Cindie.

Cindie threw her sandwich in the sink, the red spreading across her face. "You did not. You fucking liar."

"Jealous?" Belle wiggled her shoulders. "The silky blue sheets on your bed were the best. I told Walt I wanted them too."

"You bitch." Cindie stomped toward Belle with eyes of fire and arms outstretched like she was about to slap her. I shot in between them and shoved Cindie away.

"Get out of here." I tried to nudge her across the room, but she stood her ground, glaring at Belle. I gave her another jab, so she turned and left.

I spun around back to Belle, who still stood there like the queen of the jungle. "Crap like that will make life hard for you. I'd cut it out before you get in too deep."

Belle stared at me with the what-me face, but I took a deep breath to give me a moment to calm down. She was playing Cindie, pure and simple, and with Briar as her audience, Belle wouldn't give up.

"Put your damn dishes away," I said. "Kyle isn't your servant." I waved to the empty plate in front of Belle and left to head for Cindie's room, not even stopping to knock. She sat at her laptop, clicking away.

Being a house mom was the part of the job I hated. "What's wrong with you? You know better."

Walt would never bring another girl into a studio that wasn't hers. We had massage rooms, lounges, spa rooms, and so much more, and they were all open for anyone to use, but studios and private rooms were off-limits to other girls unless invited.

Cindie jumped to her feet, thrusting her two fingers in the air. "She's been here for two fucking weeks, and she thinks she owns the place."

I opened my mouth to interrupt with a just-like-you, but I held back, letting her continue with her arm-waving rant.

"She struts around in clothes two sizes too small, bragging about all the guys she's going to get. Just 'cause she'll do any shit. I mean, excuse me if I don't want to stick my tongue up some guy's ass."

"Now you're—"

"She thinks she's so cool because she's into bondage crap. Like Walt's gonna let her get whipped by some asshole. That shit leaves marks."

"Cindie!" I stomped my foot to get her attention. "We go through this crap every time a new girl gets here. We all know you're Walt's favorite. Nothing will change."

She slumped onto the bed, holding her face in her hands. "What if it does?"

The weakness in her voice astounded me, and I wanted to tell her *tough shit*, but I didn't. Instead, I sat next to her on the bed. "Walt wouldn't toss you aside. We've all heard him rave about his special princess." And it pissed me off to no end, but that was life.

"Don't let Belle get to you. It's the reaction she wants. She'll play the part of a good girl and make you out to be the bitch."

I'd seen it before. Cindie had provoked many of the girls in the same way.

"Belle's coming out party will be over soon," I said. "Everything will go back to normal. Wait and see."

I stood to leave. Cindie lifted her head and said a soft thanks, a real thanks. It was a word that rarely came out of her mouth.

I went back to my office to finish some things. *A few more days*, I assured myself, and then it'd be over.

The problem was I didn't believe my own words.

Chapter Eighteen
House of Disappointments

One day until Belle's coming out party; I needed some release, and my TV dramas weren't cutting it, so I crouched down in Ari's closet as she welcomed a man to her room. A repeat client. He wasn't aware of my presence, but Ari was. The door was cracked open enough for me to see, and a black sheer drape covered me so he wouldn't spy the whites of my eyes.

Clandestine. Silly maybe, but it made both me and Ari hot. Walt didn't like me being in her room, but watching my girlfriend screwing men on the TVs in Walt's viewing room was not the same as hiding in the closet, which was why we took the chance of angering Walt. But even if he found out, I'd take the brunt of his ire and say Ari didn't know I'd snuck into her room.

Max stripped out of his clothes in two seconds flat. He'd had sex with Ari enough times that the princess act wasn't necessary. She patted his face and stepped over to her oyster shell chair. I loved climbing into that thing, pulling down the cover, and shutting away the world.

Luckily they didn't go inside, and instead Ari stood next to the hard pearl top. She shimmied out of her silky teal chemise and tossed it to the side. They rolled around on the bed, limbs tangling together. She moaned, and my body burned for her touch.

One part of me wanted to blow our cover, to see what he'd do, but the repercussion of that move kept me staying still.

Not long after, Max's ammo was spent, and he fell back onto his butt, muttering something unintelligible. I knew how he felt; Ari made me feel the same way.

She slowly crawled to her feet. "Time's up, Max. You said an hour today."

"Oh, come on. Just a few more minutes."

"No can do. I got another appointment, and I can't cancel. You should've scheduled for something longer."

My heart sunk. I thought she was free after him. They finished dressing, and Ari led him to the door, but before she slipped out, she motioned for me to wait.

I stayed under my black sheer drape. It took forever, but finally the door creaked open. She came in alone. The door clicked shut, and Ari hung her robe on the hook.

"Don't you have another appointment?" I tossed my disguise aside and exited the closet, yanking down my bunched-up skirt and slipping my heels back on.

Arial grabbed my head and hauled me in for a kiss. "I do. My favorite person ever." She laid her lips on mine, and I took in her greedy mouth. Her kiss wasn't as long and passionate as usual, and she pulled away. "Geez, that guy wiped me out. All I want to do is take a nap." She covered a small yawn.

That was so not what I wanted, but her slouching body told me she was exhausted.

"Hop into the shell." I slapped her bare butt, and she smiled wearily. "You want me to go get ice cream? I'll even get vanilla—plain, no toppings or anything. Just for you."

She laughed but said no, so I followed her into the shell chair and lowered the top. We lay back with my arms wrapped around her. Even though she didn't want sex, I slid aside the lacey material and fondled her breasts. The warm, dark cocoon might actually put her to sleep.

"I talked to Walt about going with you into town next week," I said. "He was hesitant, but I mean, seriously, it's not like we'll be making out. We'll be in a cancer ward."

Ari had invited me to volunteer with her at the Children's Cancer Center at the hospital. In her old life, she'd been a nurse, at least until her son Timmy died, and then her partner committed suicide, unable to accept their loss. A cruel twist of fate, a cancer nurse who lost her son to leukemia.

"I know. And I'm so excited for you to meet Melanie. Did I tell you how smart she is?"

"Tell me again," I said, even though she'd told me a ton of times. Melanie reminded Ari of her own son, the fighting attitude, of never giving up. Talking about the kids helped her open up about Timmy, and she eventually reached the point where saying his name no longer brought the onslaught of tears.

I'd been the one to suggest volunteering. After she'd cleaned up her life and gotten off the alcohol, thanks to Walt, she was still floundering and unable to move forward. I hadn't known if it'd work, but she decided to go, and she never looked back. Walt knew Ari loved helping those kids; she understood them and their lives and cared for them, unlike some of the other girls who only did charity events to please Walt.

I listened to her talk, and after a bit, her voice dropped off. With Ari asleep, I shut off my own mind and drifted off.

*

"Lil, get your ass out here." The oyster shell shook.

Oh crap. I didn't want to face Walt, but we'd have to leave the shell sometime, the whole working, eating, and peeing thing.

Ari opened the cover, and I scooted out first. His trim, dark hair didn't cover his wrinkled forehead, and he tapped his foot on the ground.

"I don't need this shit now," he said. "We have less than a day until the party, and my assistant is holed away fucking her girlfriend."

I wiped my brow, glad this wasn't about me spying on Ari and her client. "Everybody needs a break," I said with a smile.

He shook his head. "A two-hour break?"

Ari crawled out of the shell. "Um, we're sorry, Walt. There's no clock in there or anything."

He raised a skeptical brow and peered over at my phone, which was still in the shell.

Then he pointed his finger at Ari. "You, I expect this out of, but not you." He waved at me, and I apologized again.

"You've got five minutes to meet me in the kitchen. Be presentable," he ordered.

Wait, five minutes? That wasn't much time, but I didn't move. Before he stepped out the door, he turned and scowled at me. "And by the way. I catch you hiding in this room again while she fucks a client… your ass is mine."

"It's already yours, Walt." I curtsied, trying to lighten his mood, but he didn't drop his glare. Then he sighed and plodded out the door, muttering something to himself.

As soon as I shut the door, I scrambled to straighten my clothes.

"I hate that he treats me like a baby." Ari let out a huff, crossing her arms. "Don't you get tired of it?"

"I'm used to it." I shrugged. That was Walt. "He's got a lot going on, and besides, we did break the rules."

She stared at me with a furrowed brow.

I tried again. "You know he's been having a hard time with Junior. And Belle and Cindie. We're making it worse."

"I know." But the intensity on her face didn't lessen.

"I'd better go see what he wants. Probably something to do with catering tomorrow." I gave her a quick kiss and slipped out the door to go find Walt.

In the kitchen, he was talking with Kyle about Belle's party and the extra crew who'd be around to help. I ran through my checklist with Kyle, and just as always, Walt threw in a couple of extra requests. Good thing Kyle and I were prepared.

Walt's phone rang, and he glanced at his screen and scowled. "Okay, that's all, Kyle. Lil, stick around a minute." He put the phone to his ear. "You were supposed to call me earlier."

Kyle made an oh-oh face and scurried out of the room.

"I don't give a damn about your shit-ass excuses," Walt growled.

I was pretty sure it was Junior.

Walt listened for a few moments, his face darkening. "No, you will be there. This is Belle's coming out party, and you don't have a choice. You be here by three. Check in with Lil."

Great, now I'm his babysitter.

Walt swiped off his phone and stuck it in his pocket. He leaned against the counter and rubbed his temples. "That kid will be the death of me."

"He'll kill himself long before you ever go." I was half-joking, but then again… I could imagine Junior ODing in a swanky hotel room or crashing his car into something bigger than a light pole.

Walt sighed and stared off toward the windows. "Did you make reservations for Bianca's birthday dinner?"

"Of course. Next Tuesday at Alessia's. Did you buy her a present yet?"

"Of course," he mimicked me and returned my smile. "And what did you get her?"

"Are you sure you got her gift? I wouldn't want you to copy mine." I was in charge of buying the house gift for the girls, but Walt always bought them something too.

He laughed. "I got her a fishing trip. She can take a friend on an all-day trip on Lake Mead. Everything is included. Even the guide."

"Oh my god, that's awesome. She'll love that." She often talked about missing Montana and all the terrific fishing. "I've got to admit you did well." Probably even better than mine.

"And yours?" He raised his brows, all smugly.

"Remember Fred died a month ago?" I waited for him to nod. "So I wanted to get another crayfish. This one is called a blue lobster. It's bright blue. They're lovely." Bianca had an awesome hundred-gallon fish tank in her bedroom filled with exotic fish.

"Sounds like you have everything under control. Inform me when Junior arrives tomorrow."

"Will do." I saluted him. He shook his head, and his lips twitched before he headed off.

Chapter Nineteen
House of Decadence

The room swarmed with princesses in ball gowns the night of Belle's coming out party. No appointments for today, which allowed the girls all day to get ready for the party. And Walt brought in a traveling spa: pedicures, manicures, massages, hair stylists, and makeup artists. Even I got the celebrity treatment.

The coming out parties were the only time Walt required the girls to dress in stereotypical princess dresses. They were grand performances, and Walt put on one helluva show.

We had a suitable blend of celebrities, local and national, along with preferred clients, and *friends* of the house.

The center of attention swept across the room on Walt's arm, schmoozing with the guests. Belle's ruffled off-the-shoulder yellow dress glimmered under the lights, not a hair out of place in her up-do, her smile luminescent. Everyone seemed to be having fun, but I was wishing to be with my own girl.

Bianca glided up with a handsome guy on her arm. Aaric Staus, an up-and-coming Canadian actor. She introduced him, and I asked if he was having a good time.

"Phenomenal." He gave Bianca an appreciative but respectful glance. "I have a terrific hostess."

Bianca beamed. I'd paired them up once I heard he was coming because she had a crush on him. Our girls were in high demand, and every man dreamed of having ten minutes with them, and yet they had their own dream men too.

"Can I get you a drink, Lil?" He motioned toward my empty wine glass.

"Yes, thank you."

As soon as he was out of earshot, I grasped Bianca's arm. "So what's he like?"

"He's such a gentleman."

The girls here understood what their jobs meant, but getting treated like a piece of meat got old.

I reached up and adjusted the red headband on her black hair before straightening her collar. "You look terrific tonight. You'll blow Aaric away."

She grinned. Then her eyes flickered. "Check that out." She pointed across the room to where Junior was talking to Cindie, her blue dress shimmering. She usually avoided him at all costs.

"How can she stand to be around him?" Bianca said.

Aaric arrived back with my wine, and I thanked him. Just as I was about to ask about his latest movie, Belle sauntered up.

"Aaric Staus," she said in her sexy voice. "I love your work. I heard you were coming tonight and couldn't wait to meet you. I'm Belle. Thee Belle." She waved her hands in the air as if presenting herself to him. "And this is *my* party." Ever so slightly, she nudged her way between Bianca and Aaric. Bianca stepped away, and we exchanged glances.

"Well, thank you. I'm glad to be a part of the big night."

"Oh, you're so sweet." She giggled and ran her hand down his arm. I about rolled my eyes. "How are you enjoying Nevada?"

"It's interesting country. And even more interesting women." He glanced over at Bianca and grinned. Her cheeks burned the same color as her headband.

Belle latched onto Aaric's arm. "I heard you haven't been to our house before. I'd love to be the one to show you *around*."

"Oh, I…" His face now matched Bianca's from a few moments ago, and he stuffed his hands in his pockets. Bianca winced, casting her face toward the floor.

"Yes," I said. "We'd love to give you a *tour* of the house. There's so—"

"The white room," Belle said. "You'll love the white room. It's like being in a polar paradise. White walls, white pillows, white everything. It's one of our new rooms, and it's delightful. We can christen it."

Aaric swallowed hard. "Um, that sounds nice, thanks." But the way he said it sounded like anything but nice.

"Oh, Belle." I tapped her arm. "Walt's looking for you."

"He is?" Her face lit up. "I better go find him. I'll see you later, Aaric." She did the standard curtsey and shot off across the floor, her head sweeping back and forth in her search of Walt.

"I'm sorry about that," I said to Aaric. "She's new and doesn't realize that not everybody wants to sleep with her."

Aaric laughed uncomfortably. "Um, I guess, um… what should I expect? This is The House of Desire."

"Belle thinks everybody desires her." Bianca sighed. Aaric laughed again, sounding more relaxed this time. "Maybe we should talk about your work instead."

"I can definitely say I've encountered my fair share of Belles in my line of work." He started talking about his latest project, and I excused myself.

"Lil," Belle called from behind me. "I can't find Walt."

I turned around to face her. "I'm not sure where he is now. He was over here. I'll help you try to find him."

He should be here. Walt rarely left a girl's side at coming out night. This party was to introduce her to his clients and friends, and he would be the only one screwing her tonight. Tomorrow he'd share her with the world, but for one last time, she'd be his alone.

We waded through the room filled with over three hundred guests. Nobody wanted to miss Walt's parties: free drinks and food and the chance to hob-knob with other rich and famous people. I spotted him across the crowd, so handsome in his black tux and yellow bow tie that matched Belle's dress. I led Belle to him and the others.

"Hello, Lil." Leonard Wilkins nodded, and I returned the greeting.

"I thought I'd lost you, my dear." Walt wrapped his arm around Belle. She giggled, a sound that was getting to be like nails on a chalkboard. "I'd like you to meet my special girl, Belle." He introduced her to the three men and two ladies. "Leonard is the head of the Animal Network."

"Oh, you're the one who's building the animal sanctuary. It's such a worthwhile cause. I'm really interested in learning more about it," she purred.

"Thanks to Walt's generosity, we'll be able to open a full three months ahead of schedule."

Walt smiled. "I'm just the money. You're the one behind the scenes doing everything. Many animals will have another chance at life thanks to you."

"What kind of animals will be at the sanctuary?" Belle fluttered her lashes at the men.

Leonard started sharing the plan with Belle, but something caught Walt's eye from across the room, and I followed his gaze to Cindie in her sparkling blue dress.

A frown grew on Belle's face. "That should've been my dress," she muttered so quietly that I was the only one who heard it. She forced a smile and returned her focus to Leonard.

"I'll have another update when we meet for golf next week," Leonard said to Walt.

"Golf?" Belle perked up.

"Another golfer?" Walt's friend Diego laughed. "It's about time."

Belle beamed at the men. "I love to golf. It's been a few years though."

"We'll have to try her out." Walt chuckled. With all the girls here, none of us enjoyed golf. Not one, and Walt often guilted us for that.

"Maybe we can get you out again, Lil," Diego said.

"Sorry, I sold my clubs." I shrugged and laughed. I'd been halfway decent at golfing, but I just didn't like it.

"She did," Walt said all seriously. "I bought her a fancy set of Callaways, and she sold them for five bucks at the flea market." He winked at me and smiled.

"I did not." I jabbed him in the side playfully.

"I can't wait to get on the links with you, Walt." Belle grasped his arm. "We'll have so much fun." She continued to babble on about golf, and I wandered away.

I made my rounds, talking to so many people until I decided it was time to find my Ari. She sent her date off to retrieve some food, and we had a few quiet moments together. Well, as quiet as could get in a room filled with hundreds of people.

"You look terrific," she said. "I want to rip that dress off and do you right here." She tugged on one of my ringlets and let it spring back.

I jutted out my chest, put my hands on my hips, and swayed to the music. The slit in my long red dress rose all the way up to my thigh. All of the D-girls were wearing the flouffy princess dresses, which in some ways made me feel even sexier because I wore one of the latest styles.

Ari's stare followed my uncovered leg up to the tight fabric on my waist and then to my cleavage about to pop out of the halter-top.

"Don't do that to me." She laughed.

She'd paid me a wonderful compliment, but she was the most stunning princess of them all with her flowing sea-green dress with its puffy sheer shoulders and the small purple shell pendant on her neck that I'd bought for her.

"Break it up, girls." Bianca sidled up, putting her arm on Ari's shoulder. "Pretty sure your date won't think much of your girlfriend."

"Probably not." Ari chuckled. "But sometimes I want to say, screw it!"

"You're right there, girl." Both ladies laughed.

"Where's Aaric?" I asked Bianca.

"Well, he's a famous actor, so there's tons of people who want to talk to him. We've had several dances though." She grinned.

"And will he get a private dance later? Or did Belle scare him off?"

"Attention, attention, everyone!" The voice echoed over the speaker system, interrupting our conversation, and I whirled around to see Junior up on the stage, a glass of beer in his hand.

"What's he doing?" Ari gasped.

"I don't know." I scanned the crowd for Walt, who was staring up at his son. I headed toward the stage where Walt had introduced Belle to the crowd earlier.

"I'd like to make an announcement. No, I mean a toast." Junior spoke loudly, his voice barely audible over the background music.

Walt met me at the stage, fists clenched, but his face seemingly calm.

"Hey, Father." Junior raised his glass in the air. "Everyone, this is my dad. Walter Marceline the II."

Walt smiled graciously, then whispered to Junior to get off the stage, the smile remaining on his face. Junior ran a hand through his disheveled hair, his eyes bloodshot and his tie missing. He shook his head with a smirk.

The music died.

"Thank you, everybody, for coming. And thank you to the new girl, um…" His head swung lazily, looking around the room until his gaze fell on the girl in yellow. "Belle. Thank you, everybody, for coming to meet Belle. Isn't she wonderful?"

All eyes turned toward her, and the crowd clapped, a few men letting out whistles. She curtseyed, holding the skirt of her dress like a lady. Walt took that moment to try to seize Junior, but he backed away from the edge.

The crowd was once again gawking at the stage, and Junior continued. "So have a good night, everybody." He smiled down at me. "Oh wait, I forgot the toast. Everybody raise your glasses to my old man. The king of the castle. Cheers."

Several shouts of cheers rang out, and Walt's smile broadened. He held out his arms for his son to descend the steps, and Walt jerked him in a hug. Only I saw the smoldering anger in his eyes.

"You're high," Walt growled, his face hidden in Junior's shoulder. The music started back up again, hiding our conversation from the crowd.

"No. I would never." Junior straightened up. "Oh, hey, Lil. Looking hot tonight." He held his hand up in the air for a high-five. "Where's your little mermaid?"

"She's around."

He pulled down his hand when I didn't slap his, and Walt swung his arm over Junior's shoulder and led him away. Some guests stopped them, and they stood there for a bit. Junior babbled on until Walt excused himself. He gave me the head motion to follow him, and we went across the hall and into the nearest room. Walt slammed the door, shutting the music out.

"What the fuck is wrong with him?" He started pacing. "I told him. I warned him."

"What will you do?"

He stared over my shoulder toward the wall, his mind working. "First thing tomorrow, I want you to call some suitable rehabs and see which one he can get into. I don't care where he goes. He's going."

"What if he doesn't?"

Walt clenched his hands.

"He won't refuse." His voice was flat, emotionless.

The door swung open, and Belle rushed in. "Walt, what's wrong?"

He leaned against the wall, arms crossed but face calm. "Nothing, my dear. Nothing is wrong anymore."

"But you look tense," she said in a quiet voice as she slithered up next to him, her hands at his waist. I heard the unmistakable sound of a zipper. "I can help you relax before you go back to the party."

She dropped to her knees and lugged Walt's dick out. Even in this house of whores, I was beginning to think that Belle was the biggest one of them all.

Walt smiled. "Belle and I will be out shortly, Lil. Please make sure all is well at the party."

"Yes, sir." I turned around and shuffled out. Walt had never left a party like that, never skipped out on his guests to have sex. He was acting as weird as Junior. I headed back into the party and almost ran into Thomas, a trusted friend.

"Lil, you okay?" He squeezed my shoulder.

Everyone was acting crazy around here. I steadied my voice. "Yes, fine. Walt should be back soon."

"I gotta admit. He handled that better than I would have." Thomas snorted. "Sometimes I wonder if that asshole is really his son."

"He definitely didn't inherit his father's brains." Or control or tact. Not to mention Walt's finesse or charm. I'd never met his mother, the previous Briar, but maybe that's where he got his attitude from.

"So I don't suppose you can get an in with me. Maybe Bianca."

"At a coming out party?" I laughed. I'd gladly set him up with Bianca, but it'd never happen tonight. The girls here often dated men outside the house, but their relationships never lasted long. "She's with Aaric Staus, and they seem to be getting along quite nicely."

"Hey, it was worth asking." He grinned, and I forgot about everything that had gone on earlier. Even though we rarely saw each other, being around Thomas was comfortable and easy.

"Let's go dance a song or two," I suggested. After that, I'd have to go back to roaming the room, but Thomas deserved more than a two-minute chat.

"Lead the way, my dear." He grinned, bowing down to take my hand. I got three whole songs with him before Walt returned, hand in hand with Belle. I spotted Cindie scowling in the corner. Things would only get worse between those two girls, and I didn't look forward to dealing with their drama.

Chapter Twenty
House of Deceit

Georges couldn't believe his luck. First his job, then a chance to get some clean clothes and possibly move out of the fleabag motel he'd been living in for the last six months.

Now, sitting across from him were two D-girls, as hot as he'd ever imagined. Well, one wasn't a princess—she just worked there, but still, he'd seen enough of Walter Marceline in the news to know that she was his right-hand woman. She, Lillian, was the one who was talking so much. Jaslyn was kinda quiet.

He had returned from the pisser, and Lillian got them their second round of drinks. He took a sip. This was the spendy shit.

"So, Georges." Jaslyn scooted her chair closer to his. "Lillian's been telling you all about our lives, but you haven't talked about yourself. What do you do?"

Well, I got the old pink slip for drinking on the job, and pretty soon I'll be starting a new one sucking shit at the porta-potty company.

Heck no, he couldn't tell them the truth. That wouldn't impress them too much anyway. He had to think of something else.

"I'm an accountant. I work with numbers and shit."

"What sort of accountant? I mean, what do you do?" Jaslyn blinked her pretty eyes at him.

Better to keep his mouth shut since he didn't really know what they actually did, other than taxes. "I do everything."

Lillian smiled at him. "I like working with numbers too. Who do you work for?"

"Um…" Damn. He should've said he worked for the shit-sucker. "It's a small company in Vegas. You probably haven't heard of it."

"Probably not," Lillian said. "We don't keep up with what's happening in Vegas. Do we, Jaslyn?"

She chuckled. "No. What do you like to do in your off-time?"

Easy question. Georges talked about his love for horse racing. He'd actually grown up around them, so he knew about horses.

"I don't know much about horses," Jaslyn said, "but I'd love to go riding again someday. It's been a few years since the last time."

She had hardly said a few words to him before he went to the pisser, but now the whiskey was loosening her up. Or she liked horses.

He wanted to get back to the House of Desire though.

"So is it true you girls all sleep in bed with Walter each night?" What he wouldn't give to trade places with that guy for just one day. Be king of the castle. Screw any and all the women he wanted.

The last sex he'd had was from a two-bit whore, a blow job in the alley that emptied out his wallet.

Jaslyn giggled and took a sip of her drink. Good thing they were buying 'cause Georges's wallet was a bit light. He'd snuck into the club in hopes of finding some drunk college girl to lay him, but these two had actually came up to him.

"Well, not all of us, every night. We'd never sleep." Jaslyn wiped her black hair away from her shocking green eyes. "We all have our own rooms and our own beds, but sometimes we have fun with Walt."

"And I heard you guys walk around in lingerie. Like all the time. Even when you're not working." Georges figured he'd have a constant boner if he ever got to go to the house. How much money would one hour with a girl like Jaslyn cost?

Over a thousand? Way more than he'd ever have.

Lillian glanced down at her cell phone, then gave Georges a look like he was stupid. He hated when women did that.

Jaslyn, though, her smile was real. Her dark eyelashes and those pouty lips were calling to him.

"Yes, we do. Walt keeps the temperature set high so we're comfortable. I got a new teddy. Red and gold. It's the silkiest fabric I've ever worn. Of course," she said, covering her mouth, "it doesn't stay on too long."

Whoa, boy, he said silently to Big Joe, worried they might see his hard dick. These girls screwed rich men, celebrities, and they probably expected a certain amount of restraint.

Unfortunately, Big Joe didn't care about what it should or shouldn't do.

"And what about you?" He turned to Lillian. "Do you roam around half-naked too?"

She raised her brows and motioned to herself. "I dress like this. I'm always on duty."

Lillian probably stuck out like a sore thumb around those hot girls. Her skirt and dress shirt showed a business girl, but sexy—no.

"Gawd. I'd give anything to see the place. I've heard the castle is sweet." He didn't really give a damn about the castle, but he couldn't let Jaslyn think all he cared about was sex.

Jaslyn laid her hand on his arm. "Really? I'd love to give you a tour."

A tour. No way. Did that mean he'd get to screw her too? It had to 'cause why else would she offer?

Georges started to sweat, his heart racing. He wanted to tell the whole world, but after years of too much whiskey and gambling, nobody would ever believe him. Besides, he hadn't had a cell phone in a few months now, and could only connect to free wi-fi. With this new job, he'd get it back again.

"Are you for real?" he asked Jaslyn, praying this wasn't a joke.

"Totally." Her bright smile lit up his day.

"You can see my room." She licked her red lips, but Georges thought of them licking something else.

"Jaslyn's room is amazing. You'll love it. Gold velvet drapes, plush red carpet. All the finest antiquities from Egypt." Lillian spoke like she was reading off a list. Her bored voice annoyed him. "Even a magic carpet?"

"Magic? For real?"

"No, silly." Jaslyn smiled softly, her eyes on him. "But my carpet sits up on a pedestal, overlooking my room. Are you interested?"

"Heck yeah. Let's go." He jumped out of his seat to his feet, and two sets of eyes checked out the tent in his crotch. The heat spread across his face, and he slipped into his seat and stared down at the table, unable to speak.

Jaslyn set her arm on his shoulder and leaned so close to his ear he felt her breath and smelled her exotic scent.

"I think that's sexy. Now I know you want me as much as I want you."

Georges gulped, his throat tightening. She wanted to screw him. This was gonna happen. Really going to happen. *How did I get so lucky?*

Lillian smiled at him, her gaze wandering up and down his body. "Why don't we get going," she said, but her voice was cool.

He shivered in anticipation; he was ready for action with Jaslyn.

*

The castle was everything he'd ever imagined. Walter Marceline swam in money, and it showed all around his house. Georges didn't know shit about art, but he was sure the paintings on the walls cost a pretty penny.

He followed Jaslyn, and they stopped at the doorway to a large room filled with leather couches, a fancy ass bar, and a bunch of TVs. In the corner, a guy was talking to a brunette with hair that hung past her ass, and a black girl sat on some guy's lap.

"Gawd. Is that Tia?" His little niece had gotten all mooney-eyed over that princess.

The other guy ran his hand up her arm to the hair piled on her head, held in place by a tiara. Her green silk nightie bunched up to her hips.

"Yes, it is. And this is where we meet up with our clients. Usually, if it's the first visit, we hang out here for a while, getting to know each other."

First visit. After he screwed Jaslyn, she'd invite him back 'cause he had some great moves. He'd make her scream.

"What's that smile about?" Jaslyn blinked her sweet eyes at him.

Um. What the heck should he say? "Nothing. Just thinking how cool all these paintings are." Maybe she'd think he was into all that fancy shit.

"This place is like a gallery, isn't it?" She smiled softly.

He didn't answer 'cause he'd never been in a gallery. Jaslyn took his hand in hers and led him down the hall.

"Wait, aren't we hanging out here first?" He wanted to check out all them princesses.

"Nope, we can come back, and I'll introduce you to the girls, but we have other plans right now." She winked.

They were soon heading down the endless hallways again until she finally stopped.

"Welcome to my place." Jaslyn threw open her door, and Georges stepped inside, his mouth wide open.

A giant mural took up the whole wall: a window looking out over a starry night in the desert. She had a giant stuffed tiger and a golden genie standing some eight feet tall.

"If you'd like to play the part of my Aladdin…" She waved to a pile of white clothes, but he didn't need to look like some goofy ass. He just wanted to screw her.

"What. Is. That?" He gasped at the tower in the corner. A platform covered by a purple and gold carpet and a golden lamp.

A magic carpet ride.

"This is all for you, Georges." Jaslyn slid her fingers back and forth above her waistband. "I'm going to get more comfortable. I'll be out in a minute."

She walked away and into the closet. He thought about following her, but he had to search the room. He had to somehow get a picture, except he had no phone. Or better yet, he could take a souvenir.

Georges scanned the room for something small that would fit into his pocket. Some gold jewelry sat in the corner, fake probably. But then again, maybe not. Walter only provided the best for his girls. Georges got to his feet and ran to the jewelry box. He opened it and found rings, necklaces, bracelets.

"What are you wearing?" he called out.

"You'll see," she replied. Georges rummaged through the jewelry chest.

"How do I look?"

He jumped at Jaslyn's voice.

Oh. My. Gawd. Jaslyn glided back into the room, her shiny black hair flowing and her large boobs spilling out of her green bikini top. Her puffy pants hung low on her hips, exposing her belly button, and she wore pointy slippers. He couldn't keep his gaping mouth shut.

She smiled. At him. And once again Big Joe jumped to attention.

"This is a dream come true," Georges said under his breath. He reached for her boobs and yanked them out of her top.

"Oh." She frowned.

What'd I do? "Sorry," he said automatically.

"Don't worry about it. Do you like it rough?" she asked.

"Rough. Yeah. Who doesn't?" He tried to cover up his mistake, but then she smiled again. Yeah, she liked it; she was a prostitute in a whore house. She liked men touching her.

He grabbed her tits again. "If I had boobs like this, I'd never leave my bed."

She let him grope her for a short time and then moved away.

"Why don't you let me take care of things," Jaslyn purred, leading him to some giant blue pillows. Her fingers unsnapped his pants, and she yanked them down.

His worn tighty-whities slipped off, and he stepped out of his clothes. Her face sat inches away from his erect dick, and she ran her hands up and down his hips.

"I bet you drive all the women wild," she whispered, pushing him back into the pillows and straddling his waist.

"Heck yeah. They can't get enough of me."

Her body swayed. *Those hips. Damn, they move so smoothly.* Before he knew it, Jaslyn was on him, bouncing up and down.

It was over way too soon, and she lay on his chest, and he wiped his sweaty brow. She was a woman and didn't sweat. He liked screwing ladies like that.

"You'll stick around a little longer, won't you?" Jaslyn ran a finger along his receding hairline.

"You didn't get enough of me, huh?" He puffed up his chest.

"Nope. How about I get a drink, and you tell me when you're ready." She pointed to his limp dick. "I've got something special for you planned now. An exclusive room very few have access to. If you're interested in more."

Her lips were so big and full, perfect to swallow Big Joe. "You gonna suck me off? 'Cause Big Joe wants you to wrap those lips around him."

"Big Joe?" She glanced at Georges's crotch. "He does look like a Big Joe. And I've got the perfect place where you can bring him out to play."

"Maybe you should invite Tia along. She was sure checking me out while I was standing in the doorway of that room. Or Briar. She looks like she'd be into it. I mean, all you girls are lesbos too, right?"

Georges sucked in a hard breath, and Jaslyn ran her finger down his forehead to his nose. "I love women," she said, "but tonight… you're mine and only mine."

Chapter Twenty-One
House of Dread

Gawd. Maybe he'd only get to screw Jaslyn tonight, but when she invited him back, he'd get to do two of them. Or three, a screw fest. He almost felt the three hot women squeezing up against him, taking turns on Big Joe, and he'd get to stuff his face into a sea of tits.

Georges followed Jaslyn through the hall again, dressed only in a bathrobe. They'd sat in the one room for an hour and talked about his sex fantasies before his body was ready to go again.

Down one hall, then another. A maze of brightly lit corridors and grand doors.

"You're not gonna make me find my own way out of here, are you? 'Cause I'm completely lost," he said.

Jaslyn gave him a flirty smile. "Don't worry."

She led him down a staircase and through another long hallway with tons of closed doors, except one.

The chilly air gave Georges goosebumps, but Jaslyn didn't even seem to notice the drop in temperature. "You need to tell Walt to turn up the heat. It's freezing down here."

"You'll warm up once we get going." She grinned, and he got excited all over again.

Jaslyn glanced at the open door but kept moving. He stopped and almost shit his shorts.

"What the heck?" he said, unable to take his eyes off the torture chamber in front of him. Chains hung down from the ceiling and on the walls. Handcuffs. Whips and all sorts of other things he didn't ever want to experience lay on a black table.

A girl with brown hair turned around and smiled, but before she said anything, Jaslyn grabbed his hand and jerked him down the hall.

Sweat beaded on Georges's forehead. "You're not bringing me to a room like that, are you?" A black bed sat in the center of the room, shackles attached to each bedpost.

Jaslyn patted his arm. "No. That's the dungeon. It's for clients who like really kinky stuff like getting tied up. Some men like that type of thing," she added as she headed to another door.

Not me. Jaslyn wasn't gonna tie him up and whip him till he bled. He wouldn't mind trying out a few of those toys, but now he'd lost his chance to chain her to the bed and screw her. Jaslyn probably loved it. Probably wanted the man to take control and dominate.

That's okay. He'd dominate her with Big Joe. Make her moan. He didn't need any of those stupid toys.

Jaslyn did the fingerprint thing at the door again—they had a lot of security around here, and on the other side was Lillian. She wore the same clothes she'd had on earlier. She should get some of Jaslyn's clothes so then she'd look hot.

"Nice to see you again, Georges," she said all flirty.

Hot damn. It was a threesome. Georges had melted away her frigid demeanor and made her pop. But Jaslyn had said she wanted him all to herself. Maybe she was fooling him.

That was all Lillian said, and they continued down the hall, Lillian walking alongside Jaslyn and neither of them speaking. Then they stopped abruptly in front of a door and once again did the fingerprint scanner thing.

Lillian went through first, and after he entered the room, she laid a cold hand on his neck. "I'll get you some drinks and will be back," she said.

Georges took in the dark room, lit only by candlelight. There must've been at least ten candles burning. There were also several couches, one almost black with tons of gold and light purple pillows, just like in Jaslyn's room.

He relaxed as the warm air surrounded him. "That's interesting." Georges pointed to the couch. "It's purple."

"Yes, plum," Jaslyn said, her voice even like she really didn't care.

"So you bring lots of men down here then? It was kinda a pain in the butt to get here."

"No. You're the only guy. Walt gives us one pick, and you were mine."

He straightened up tall. Despite all the crap he'd been through, Georges had a lot going for him. He'd been losing a bit of money on those damn horse races, but he was gonna come back soon. He knew it.

"Lil will be back with our drinks. Then we can get busy." Her voice was quiet, almost kinda sad.

Georges frowned. She didn't seem as into him as she had been earlier, but she shouldn't be losing her steam. These girls had sex all night long.

Lillian came in with a tray with a bottle of wine and two filled glasses. She set it down and went over to Georges.

"For you, sir." She smiled. Then brought the other glass to Jaslyn, whose face darkened, probably worried Lillian was going to take things over, and she'd miss out on Big Joe again.

He took a drink from his glass. This expensive wine didn't taste any different than the shit he drank.

Lillian nudged Jaslyn, and she smiled. "Time to celebrate," Jaslyn said, but it sounded forced.

"I'll leave you two alone then. Have fun." Lillian was gone in a flash.

Georges stared at the dark wall. The light shined off it differently. He stepped over and touched the wall to find a ridge running up and down.

"Is this a door?" he asked.

Jaslyn wound her arms around his waist and squeezed, laying her chin on his shoulder. "Yes, it's a closet. Let's go sit on the couch together, and I'll give you a little massage."

She rubbed his shoulders and his back and his head. It relaxed him, but he wanted more. He wanted to see her naked tits and ass. Big Joe was standing at full attention, and he tried to catch her eye, but she kept looking back at the wall.

"So, um… You want to get started?" he asked tentatively.

"Yes, soon." Her brow crinkled.

The door creaked opened. Jaslyn's mouth dropped, and he saw another fine woman in some really skimpy lingerie parade in. Her long brown hair spread out over her shoulders and down to her boobs. Big boobs. Perky and nipping out. Hey, that was the girl in the freaky room.

"Hi, I'm Belle. I heard your name is Georges. It's nice to meet you." She held out her hand, and he shook with her.

"What are you doing here?" Jaslyn kept glancing back and forth between Belle and the wall. Was another girl going to pop out of that door? Not only would he get a threesome, but maybe a foursome. Oh gawd, Jaslyn had fooled him!

"I'm here to watch." She gazed at Georges's hard-on and grinned. "I love to watch."

"You can't—" Jaslyn started.

"Walt sent me." Belle turned to Georges. "Just for you," she said with a wink, and a tremor of excitement ran through him. Belle marched over to the corner and motioned for Jaslyn to follow. "Georges, I need to talk to Jaslyn for a moment. Walt has a special message for her and for you."

In the corner Belle put her hand up to cover her mouth as she whispered to Jaslyn. He didn't see Jaslyn's face, but Belle kept smiling at him. This must be good. His hand dropped to his dick to keep himself busy while they talked. It took forever, but Jaslyn returned, and Belle stretched out on the other couch. "Let's see Big Joe in action," Belle said.

Jaslyn didn't say anything, and Belle spoke again. "Walt said to enjoy your experience. It's a once-in-a-lifetime thing, right, Jaslyn?" Belle winked at them.

Jaslyn swallowed, staring over his shoulder. Georges turned, but nobody was there. Jaslyn gave him a large smile. "Yes, let's see Big Joe. I've been wanting to get my mouth on him since earlier."

His dick was pumped and primed, and he wanted to get on with it, but what if Walt showed up? He didn't want another guy around. Years ago, some girl tried to get him to do a threesome with her and another guy. He shot that down right away. Georges didn't touch guys. Heck, he didn't even want to see another guy's dick.

Jaslyn floated around the room, blowing out candles until there was just one lit. Soft music played, and Georges looked for the speakers. They had to have something better than elevator music. He was about to say something, but Jaslyn knelt in front of him on the floor. Her soft hands took hold of Big Joe and brought him to her lips.

Open up, baby, he thought, forgetting the music.

She got to work, and every part of him buzzed. He gasped at Belle pleasuring herself on the other couch. He was gonna get some of that too.

He wiped his forehead. It was so hot in here even though Jaslyn had blown out all but one candle. She continued sucking him off, and he closed his eyes. He grunted and panted—this chick was good. He peeked down at her bobbing black head. Jaslyn's blow job was like none he'd ever gotten. Her mouth seemed to be all over, her tongue touching everything.

He felt like he was about to erupt, and with a grunt, his hips bucked, and he spewed. A shadow passed over his face, and pressure forced his shoulders down. His eyes flew open, the terror striking every inch of his body.

Bright green eyes stared down at him, a stench worse than a thousand porta-potties on a hot day, and a gray pockmarked face glared at him. Long sharp claws held him in place. Georges couldn't understand the weird words coming out of its mouth.

It wasn't real.

It couldn't be real.

But Georges knew it was.

He tried to move, but he seemed frozen in place. A scream rose in Georges's throat, and the thing smiled, revealing his yellow, pointy teeth. The weight on Georges's shoulder released, and the light bounced off a sharp steel edge.

The dagger sliced into his neck, and Georges coughed, the blood choking off his breath. A black fog surrounded Jaslyn's body. And her face. He tried to blink the cloudiness away. She almost looked—he squinted—younger.

Georges's beating heart slowed, no longer thumping strong in his ears. Jaslyn frowned at him with a blood-splattered face.

And then Georges saw nothing more.

Chapter Twenty-Two
House of Distress

Suffocating heat and the tang of blood filled the small room, and Georges's screams echoed in my ears. Walt stood tall over Georges, blood dripping from his dagger.

This was wrong... So, so wrong.

I burst out of the closet and chased after Jaslyn to the bathroom. She stumbled onto the floor, sobbing. I wrapped my arms around her, holding her tight.

When I'd returned to the closet to join Walt, I was stunned to find Georges awake. He should've been sleeping. He should've been knocked out. I'd given him the drink with the drugs that Walt had prepared.

Nobody followed me and Jaslyn into the bathroom, and I held onto her shaking body. Finally, the sobs slowed, and she leaned against the wall, her face a mess, her eyes red... Blood soaked her matted hair and now stained my shirt.

"Why did he do this to me? Is it because I wasn't sure?" She sniffed and wiped her wet tears.

"I don't—"

"And why was Belle there? What in the world was that about?" Her head dropped like she couldn't support it anymore.

I had no answers. Walt had never invited another girl into a renewal like that. Only I was ever around. It made no sense.

"Did you see his face?" Jaslyn asked. "He knew it. He saw it. He felt everything." She stared at my shoulder, her bottom lip trembling.

Georges's terror was burned into my memory. Walt had never been so cruel; the men were always knocked out, and they never knew what was about to happen.

Jaslyn stood without another word, and I took in her whole body and all the blood. She opened the door and trudged out.

"Where are you going?" I asked. She couldn't walk the hallways to her room like that.

"To bed," she mumbled.

I jumped up and chased after her. "You need to shower."

She stopped but remained still, so I led her back into the bathroom, turned on the shower, and nudged her inside. She stood under the water, eyes closed, as the blood washed away, but she didn't move or try to wash her stained hair and didn't wipe her face.

I washed her hair and let her stay until the water flowed clear, and then I shut the shower off and led her out. She didn't say a word while I dried her body and threw on a robe, nor when I led her up to her room, and not even when we passed Bianca in the hallway.

I tucked her into bed.

All the questions raced through my head as I went back downstairs. The pungent smell of blood hit my nose as soon as I entered the renewal room, and I kept my eyes off the floor. Heavy moans spilled out of the closet Walt and I hid in before the renewal.

I flung open the door to find him and Belle going at it on the floor. My stomach turned. A dead man lay just across this wall. I was about to slam the door, but Walt called my name.

"Yes?" All I wanted was to get out of there, to go up to my room, or better yet, find Ari if she was free. I wanted to clear my head of everything. I could get my answers later.

"Lil," Walt said again. "Would you like to join us?" He eyed me from on top of Belle, and she frowned.

"No, I've promised Ari I'd find her. I'll see you later." I backed away from the door, trying my best to avoid Georges's gruesome body.

I hurried upstairs and checked the schedule. Ari was off. To her bedroom I rushed and didn't even knock on the door.

"What's wrong?" She clicked the TV off.

Walt had killed a man who was awake, who'd seen what was coming, and Georges's scream reverberated through my head.

I collapsed onto her bed into her arms, and the story spilled out of me. She had no answers to any of my *whys*, but it's not like I thought she would. Only Walt would know.

My eyes weighed as heavy as my heart, and I clung to her body as I fell asleep.

*

Ari's alarm woke us both at five a.m. Her shift was starting soon, catching the last of the all-night partiers coming from Vegas. She gave me a kiss and hug, and I fell soundly asleep again.

My phone buzzed, waking me. Damn. It was nine. I read Walt's text: *Are you coming in today?*

Yes, I'll be in soon, I replied and rolled out of bed. I didn't want to face him even though I had so many questions.

Ari's family photo caught my eye, and I picked it up. Timmy's Make-A-Wish tour of the San Francisco stadium. He'd met several of the players that day, and as weak as he'd been, he went out on the field to toss the ball around a few times. Despite his bald head and moons under his eyes, he smiled brightly. The best day of his life, he had told his mom.

I'd gone through some painful times in my life, but nothing compared to Ari's tragedies. Deep down, I knew I was causing that type of pain for others, those men who had died. Georges might have been a lowlife, but somebody somewhere would miss him.

I dragged myself back to my room, showered and dressed in a crisp suit, and paid special attention to cover the bags under my own eyes.

Walt was sitting at his desk, papers scattered everywhere. Two pencils had fallen out of his golf bag-shaped pencil holder, and I tossed them inside before slumping onto the chair.

"I figured out what happened last night," Walt started. He looked like he was waiting for me to respond, but I said nothing. "I didn't use enough Rohypnol. I measured incorrectly."

"How could you—"

"It was a mistake, Lil. A simple mistake. Anybody could do it. You've made plenty of mistakes in your life."

"Why didn't you stop it?" My voice cracked, and I took a deep breath to settle down. I'd seen men die before in renewals, but they were always unconscious. I'd never heard their screams of pain and never saw the panic on their faces.

He leaned forward, his expression softening. "Impossible. Once we're in that room, there's no coming out."

Georges's terror flashed in my head, his gut-wrenching pain.

Walt rounded his desk and sat on the front edge, taking my hand in his. "It was a mistake. One I regret. Yes, it was hard to see, but you aren't aware of this man's history. He's a convicted sex offender and has a history of molesting younger boys when he was a teenager until he finally got caught when he was in college. I know for a fact he was molesting his sister's son. He doesn't deserve our mercy."

Georges was the monster. I had to remind myself that.

Walt squeezed my hands again. "I try hard to find men like him, and as I said, I regret that things happened how they did, but I don't feel sorry for him. The world has one less pedophile in it, and Jaslyn has improved her life once again."

One less bad guy was roaming the streets. "But why did you let Belle in there?"

"Because she asked."

His short answer stunned me. "But why?"

He put his hand behind his head and leaned back. "Are you jealous I made love to her after?"

"What?" I sputtered. No... I wouldn't do that... Walt and I'd never made love after a renewal. Well, not right after with a body in the room.

He eyed me like my confusion was amusing him. "Belle wanted to see what it was like from the other side." He stood behind me and rubbed my shoulders. "I owe you many thanks for all your hard work. Finding you nine years ago was the best thing that happened to me. I mean it, Lil." He kissed the top of my head.

My cheeks warmed at his appreciation. "Belle's party went off without a hitch—well, not that any of us knew what Junior would do. But thank you for finding him a rehab so quickly."

In less than two days after Belle's party, Junior was on a plane to a spectacular rehab.

"I don't know what I'd do without you." Walt slung his arms around me from behind, his hot breath making my skin all tingly. His hands untucked my shirt and crept under to grope my breasts.

"I don't thank you enough for all you do," he whispered before coming around to the front of me and straddling my lap. He cupped my cheeks and pulled my face toward his. I already felt his hardness pressing into me.

Walt needed me.

I needed him. If just to get rid of the scene from the night before.

He took his time undressing me, paying attention to every part of my body that craved his touch, and he thanked me in the way I wanted most.

We made love on the chair, and then Walt said he had something to show me. A client video.

"You did well, Lil," Walt said, and I laughed as he led me toward the sofa.

"You already said that." We hadn't watched many client sex videos together lately, and I missed that time with him.

He ran his finger up and down my arm. "Well, but I mean something new. Belle. She's opened my eyes to new things. None of the other girls enjoy the BDSM scene as much as she does."

"Oh yeah?" I wasn't into the whole chains and whip thing but still pretended it turned me on. He leaned back onto the sofa and set his feet on the ottoman. Then he motioned for me to sit between his legs. I leaned my back into his naked chest, and he put one arm around me and flipped through the directories on the screen.

"That movie we watched on our last family night. That got me thinking." He grinned like he had a secret he couldn't hide anymore.

"We had a new client, a woman. Remember Shawna?"

"Yes." Women clients didn't show up often, and when they did, they had fewer girls to pick from since not all would have sex with a woman. So when a woman came, our hostess informed me.

"She randomly happened to pick Belle, and they talked about their mutual love of BDSM." He brought up a video from Belle's studio. Her and the client Shawna. But he didn't hit play yet.

"Did she whip Belle's butt?" I laughed. That was something I'd love to see, although I wouldn't tell Walt that.

"Oh no," he said, his voice serious. He didn't say any more and instead pressed play. The scene started with them discussing rules and safe words, and it became clear that Belle was the dominant one.

Walt started fondling my breasts as the scene heated up. Belle whipped the woman's butt with a cane while her hands were cuffed to the bed posts. Walt's hard-on pressed into my back, and he lifted my hips so I'd raise myself up onto him. I had to force myself to not cringe at the woman's red welts.

He nudged me to rock up and down while Belle lashed the woman. He grunted in my ear, and I shut my eyes, but I still heard all the noise.

"Look at the way Belle swings that cane. She knows how to inflict pain."

The woman seemed hurt, but she kept begging for more and never once used her safe word. Walt moaned into my ear and hit pause on the two women kissing. I pumped faster because he was close. I had to fake it, and I timed the orgasm so it *hit* after Walt finished.

He pulled my sweaty body back into his and wrapped his arms around me. For the first time after having sex with Walt, I felt dirty.

"Belle talked to her, and she wants to come back. We plan on bringing her downstairs."

"To the dungeon?" The room with all the toys I'd never touch.

"Yes, Shawna wants both of us, so I'll have some fun too."

I was glad my back was to Walt so he couldn't see my surprise. He never got involved with client sex, but maybe this woman was coming as a guest. Our girls all had friends outside the house, but rarely did Walt invite them or other women into his bed.

Either way, it was something I wanted no part of.

"She's damn lucky." I forced my enthusiasm, waiting for the moment when Walt would let me go.

Chapter Twenty-Three
House of Dissent

"You need to perk up a bit." Bianca gave Jaslyn a nudge on the shoulder. I was sitting with the two girls in the kitchen as Bianca chowed down on some chips. I took my last bite of ice cream and studied Jaslyn's lovely face, the age lines no longer visible, her hair thicker and shinier.

She smiled half-heartedly. "I'm tired. Fighting a cold, I think." She dropped her gaze to the bag of chips on the counter and sighed.

Bianca and I glanced at each other. I hoped Walt hadn't picked up on Jaslyn's mood and that she was able to keep up the act with her clients.

"Is this about Georges?" I asked, checking to make sure Kyle nor any of the other staff were around. I had explained to her everything about Georges's history with molestation, but this was only Jaslyn's second renewal, and she hadn't developed that thick skin yet.

She shrugged, and I studied her face. She'd lost a good ten years during her renewal last week.

Bianca leaned in on her elbows and whispered. "I know it sucks, but look at what you got in return. And he's the type of guy that nobody misses. That people are thankful are gone."

"Unlike you," I added. "Think about how we'd miss you around here." Jaslyn was a valuable employee, a girl who actively sought out clients and worked hard, and she was a terrific friend.

"Yeah." Bianca chuckled. "Who would I do my trap shooting with? None of the girls around here can handle a gun. Lil, you and Ari really should try it with us. Who do you think would be better, Jaslyn, Lil or Ari?"

"Neither." Jaslyn broke in with a laugh.

"Hey, I take offense at that. I had fun those few times we did those water gun fights." I laughed along with the two of them, but Jaslyn was right. "The next time we have a pool party and do the water fights, you know who I'm picking for my team."

"When's he planning the next pool party?" Jaslyn asked.

"I'm not sure. We have that bonfire party in three days. Didn't you see it on the calendar?"

"Morning, ladies." Kyle strutted into the kitchen, boxes of food piled high. The girls responded, and I checked my calendar.

"I see we've got spaghetti tonight for dinner. Do you think we can change that to breakfast? Maybe some French toast and pancakes." I glanced at Jaslyn and grinned.

"And bacon." She closed her eyes and let out a long breath.

"Anything for my Jaslyn." He winked. Kyle had been here for four years now, and although he flirted relentlessly with the girls, he never pressured them for sex, unlike some of the other employees we'd had. I'd had to fire a number of men who thought they were entitled to sex with the girls.

"Thanks, Kyle," I said and put my bowl in the dishwasher, gave the girls a wave, and headed out the door. I returned to my office and got back to work.

*

I'd hoped that Jaslyn would get back to normal, but later that evening she was moping around and the next morning still hadn't cheered up. It was now six days after her renewal.

I was waiting in our welcoming room for our hostess to discuss a few things. She escorted a client into the room, and he went up to

Cindie. I heard discussion of a threesome, and Belle's head popped up.

"Who do you suggest?" the guy asked.

Belle smiled at the guy, who was checking out all the girls, and she sauntered over to them. The guy looked her up and down and grinned.

Cindie didn't even glance at Belle. "I'd suggest Mulan. You'll love her," Cindie said to the guy. "Mulan," she called and waved. "There's someone I'd like you to meet."

Belle gritted her teeth and clenched her hands. These little snubs were getting under my skin, each woman doing it to the other. I'd have to talk to them, and if nothing changed, I'd talk to Walt.

My phone beeped. Speaking of the devil. *Come to my office.*

I made my way to his door, and he welcomed me in but stood. "We need to talk to Jaslyn. Her work has been affected by her attitude, as you're well aware."

I wanted to defend her, but I couldn't. Her performance had declined. "Okay, right now?" I asked.

"Now." He came around the desk, and I followed him to Jaslyn's bedroom. I wondered what it was like for Georges to see the scary Walt standing above him. Seeing Walt au natural didn't shock me anymore, not unless his anger was raging.

Walt knocked on the door, and I studied his hair. More grays were popping up. Not that it mattered since his stylist would take care of them. Walt crossed his arms, his neck and shoulders a mess of tight muscles. Jaslyn yelled to come in.

Oh. I stopped halfway in the door. Ari and Jaslyn were both on the bed, but Jaslyn was sitting up, leaning against the wall, a big space between them. I scanned the blanket underneath them, but it wasn't rumpled. I shouldn't even consider such thoughts. Ari would never do that to me.

"We have some things to discuss with Jaslyn. Goodbye, Ari," Walt said. My girlfriend crawled off the bed and clasped my hand quickly before leaving. Jaslyn remained on the bed, her face grim.

"Jaslyn honey." Walt sat on the edge of her bed and rubbed his temples. "Things haven't been going well lately. Both Lil and I have noticed."

"I'm sorry, Walt. It's just that…" She gulped hard. "It's been a while, and I didn't think the renewal would be so hard."

Walt sighed and patted the bed. "Come on over here."

Jaslyn rolled over and cuddled up next to him, keeping her eyes cast down. I took my seat in the corner at her desk, waiting for my turn to speak with her. I should've had a heart-to-heart with her earlier before Walt got involved. At this point, even though he was annoyed, he wasn't yet mad. But if she didn't reverse her attitude, I'd soon be searching for a new Jaslyn, and I didn't want to see her leave.

"Taking a life is tough sometimes, but he gave you a gift that so few are able to receive. He gave his life for you."

Jaslyn choked on a sob, the tears falling down her cheeks. This was way worse on her than I'd thought it was.

"You know the way out," Walt said softly and pulled her head to his shoulder and wrapped his arm around her.

She wiped her eyes. "Yes," she whispered.

"I love you, honey, and I don't want you to leave. And I know you don't want to leave, do you?"

"No." She sniffed.

"Then things have to change. You've never given me trouble, and I appreciate that."

I closed my eyes and leaned back into my chair, glad that this would turn out okay. Ari would miss Jaslyn as much as I would.

"I will. I promise. I'm so sorry," she choked out.

Silence filled the room, peppered only by Jaslyn's sniffs.

"Now, there are three days until the bonfire. I'll let you take two days off so you'll be ready. You go into town. Maybe have a spa day and go shopping for a new dress for the party. All on me. Will that make you feel better?"

She nodded.

"Good. Because I want you to feel better. You're one of my special girls." Walt tipped her chin up to him. "I'm glad you're not leaving us." He kissed her on the forehead and lugged her into a hug, muttering something soft into her ear. He pulled away again, keeping his gaze on her, and kissed her on the lips. "You are *my* girl."

Jaslyn slid her hand over his crotch. I couldn't see her face, but I bet she was smiling at what was coming. The jealousy flared through me. Yes, I was special to Walt, but I'd never be one of his D-girls.

"Lil, Jaslyn and I need some alone time." He didn't take his focus off her.

"Have fun," I said, wishing he was giving me his loving. I waved to Jaslyn, but she wasn't looking at me, only at Walt, her face so serious.

I slipped out of the room and shut the door.

Chapter Twenty-Four
House of Discipline

"How's it look?" Jaslyn asked me and Ari, strutting in front of us like she was on a runway. She was modeling her new Versace dress that barely covered her butt.

"Holy cleavage." Ari laughed. The slit down the middle went all the way to her belly button.

"You look stunning. You'll knock them dead tonight," I said. The bonfire was in a few hours, the pre-party starting soon.

Jaslyn grabbed Ari's hand and held tight. "Thank you for your kind words the other day. I really needed a friend."

"Any time." Ari hugged her, and something inside me twitched. Jaslyn and Ari had always been friends, but never share-your-secrets type of friends. I went over to Ari's jewelry box to avoid making it seem like I was watching them, and Jaslyn waved goodbye and left.

Ari joined me at her dresser and dug around in her jewelry. She took out a necklace and clasped it around my neck before removing the other one. "This matches your earrings better." She pulled my hair off my neck, and we peered into the mirror.

It did.

"Thank you." I fingered the platinum pendant. "What was that about? With Jaslyn."

She shrugged and played with my hair, fixing a few stray curls. "Nothing, really. We talked after the Georges thing."

I hated the resentment spiraling through me. I'd tried to be there for Jaslyn, but she hadn't opened up to me. But I should be happy she found someone to talk to. It certainly helped. I held up a necklace that would look fabulous with Ari's emerald green dress, she nodded, and I put it around her neck.

"We had this session the other night," she continued. "A three-hour with a regular of hers. He must've been going through his own rough stuff because he drank too much, we had a little sex, and then he passed out for half of the time. I wish they were all like that." She laughed lightly. "While he was sleeping, we got to talking about everything. I think she was feeling so lonely. That's one of the reasons she was having doubts, along with the whole process." She shrugged. "It's all good though."

Ari smiled, but it looked forced. I was about to open my mouth and say something, but she kissed me.

"Let's have a little fun," she whispered. "Before Walt calls for you."

The way she was touching me now had me ready to go.

"That's a good plan."

She pressed her body into mine, and in seconds, the only thing she was dressed in was the purple stone necklace I'd placed on her neck.

*

I was late. Walt would be pissed. Well, maybe he hadn't realized yet. I glanced out the window to the line of cars outside. Walt was very strict on his events and didn't start until the posted time, but that didn't stop many from showing up early, even if they had to sit in their cars and wait.

The girls were able to choose whom they spent the night with, and Walt didn't care if they had sex or if they didn't have sex, which the girls appreciated. They were never forced to have sex with any client, but a girl who turned away too many men didn't make much money.

I slipped outside to find most of the girls waiting by the pool and the staff ready to go. Undoubtedly, some drunks would find their way into the pool tonight, but this was a bonfire party and would move down to the pit once the skies darkened.

I counted heads. No Belle, no Cindie, no Walt. At least I wouldn't get in trouble for being late. Kyle approached me to discuss the food, and I talked to the head bartender. I texted our lead driver, who was sitting in his car with guests, and once I gave him the go, he'd release them, and a flood of others would enter the grounds.

A check with Gram showed that security was all set, and almost everything was a go with a half hour left. I needed to find Cindie and headed to her bedroom. She'd been here for years and knew the expectations; she should be out here with the rest of us, not making me chase after her. She was on thin ice with Walt, and her behavior didn't make sense.

I flung open her bedroom door and drew in a sharp breath. Cindie lay on her bed, her head on Junior's chest, both of them buck naked. Two empty wine glasses and several bottles lay on the floor, and the pungent smell of marijuana surrounded me.

"What are you doing?" I yelled. Somebody should have told me he'd left rehab and came here. I was going to chew Gram's butt.

"Get moving! Our guests will be here in less than half an hour."

"I don't think I'll go tonight." Cindie stretched her hands and yawned. "I'm going to hang here with Junior."

What… how… why? Cindie didn't do drugs, and she hated Junior. I felt like I'd fallen into some alternate reality.

"Get out of bed and get ready!"

"You can't make me." She wore the same smug look Junior did.

"Does your dad even know you're here?" I picked up Junior's shirt from the floor and threw it at him.

"Relax, Lil. It's all good. That rehab was shit. More like a fucking prison. I was there way too long."

One of the best rehabs in the country, and he walked away.

"Want to join us? Get your little mermaid, and we can have some fun." Junior leered at me, and my rope snapped.

I spun around to go find Walt. Neither of them would listen to me.

I clutched my cell phone on the trek to Walt's quarters, hoping I wouldn't be blamed for this. I should've retrieved Cindie earlier, and then this wouldn't have been such a problem.

Walt was in his room with Belle, enjoying a glass of wine. At least they were dressed. He saw my face and frowned, and I hung my head. "I'm sorry, Walt. Cindie is being difficult, and I should've gone looking for her long ago, but she and Junior—"

"Junior's here?" Walt's face darkened.

"He said you knew he was back." Well, implied really.

"No." Walt set down his glass and straightened.

"They're naked and smoking pot in her room. She's refusing to go."

He sighed and set his arm on Belle's shoulder. "Why don't you join the other girls, my dear. I'll be down soon." His voice was tight and controlled, but the rage boiled underneath.

After Belle left, Walt stood next to the dresser, staring down at the golf ball he rolled between his fingers. One minute passed as I kept shifting from foot to foot, waiting for his command. The clock inched forward again, and sweat beaded on my temples.

Walt's head slowly turned. "Let's go see the two lovebirds."

My skin prickled, and I followed him out the door. He didn't even pause before entering Cindie's room. She and Junior spotted us and shrunk back.

"Walt, I…" The defiance disappeared, and fear laced Cindie's eyes. She looked to Junior for help, but he was staring at the floor.

"Lil, get Cindie's dress ready." He pointed to her outfit hanging on the back of her door. I snagged the dress behind me and turned around. Cindie and Junior were cowering under Walt's gaze, his skin now a mottled gray. My heart skipped a few beats. This wasn't good.

His height remained the same, but now, instead of the lean, toned man, Walt was like a body-builder from hell. I had no clue how his clothes stretched to fit his bulging arms and shoulders, and I didn't want to know.

Junior rubbed his finger over an invisible spot on his hand, and Cindie's chin trembled.

"Thank you." Walt took the dress and laid it on the bed. His hair was gone, replaced by the bald, wrinkled gray head. "Now, please accompany my *son*," Walt growled, crossing his arms, "to his room so that he will be properly attired for the party."

Junior cringed.

"Yes, sir," I said.

Walt turned to Junior, his face pinched, and his voice low. "I'll be in to speak with *you* shortly." His words seem to suck all of the air out of the room, his long finger with its black nail pointing right at Junior.

My blood ran cold. A pale-faced Junior popped up and took off for the door, still naked, before I even said one more word.

"Walt, no. Please… I'm sorry," Cindie pleaded, her voice shaky, her face red.

I shut the door, and Junior stared at me with wide eyes. We both looked to the door. It was like they had lost every one of their brain cells. How did they think there'd be no repercussions for this?

Cindie cried out, and every part of me wanted to run, but I remained frozen to the floor, my hand on the doorknob.

She whimpered and begged him to stop, and I couldn't take it anymore. I grasped Junior's arm and jerked him down the hallway. He stumbled after me.

In his room, he got dressed in warp speed. Hair brushed, shoes on, cologne to cover the smell of pot, and a quick brush of his teeth.

"Do you think he'll…" Junior's feverish brown eyes darted back and forth between me and the door. "He wouldn't do anything serious. I mean, the party. They're expecting me."

No, they aren't. Nobody is.

Junior twisted the bottom of his shirt into a tight spiral. All the disrespect he gave me, and now he wanted my sympathy for his stupid choices.

I headed toward the door.

"Lil, please don't leave," he said, his voice trembling.

I gripped the handle, studying his tense face. "There's nothing I can do."

But I stayed in my spot, watching him pace the room and mumble to himself, and I only left when Walt showed up. Except this time, I didn't stick around behind the door to listen.

Chapter Twenty-Five
House of Distance

An hour into the party, I spotted Cindie in her blue dress in the corner. The smile stretched across her face, forced and tight, and when she caught my eye, her stare was blank, emotionless. She took a sip of her wine and grimaced, then replaced it with her fake smile.

The three people I was with were talking, and I continued to search the party until I spotted Junior. Unlike Cindie, he didn't fake any smiles. Every hair was in place, he was dressed impeccably in his shirt and dress shorts, and his face was unmarked, but he moved in slow motion.

Walt came out of nowhere, slung his arm over Junior's shoulders, and led them to Cindie and a few other guests. She winced, and Junior didn't once look at her, seeming only to concentrate on the couple in front of him.

I inched closer to listen.

Walt clapped Junior on the back, and he cringed. "Yes, he's like his father, in my younger years. Too much partying, too little sleep. I told him he's got to slow down."

Junior wrapped his arms around his waist. "Yes, I should've listened to you, Father. Won't make that mistake again. The rehab I tried wasn't for me, but we've found another."

A man laughed. "Rehabs are like therapists sometimes. It takes you a while to find the perfect one. I'm sure you'll find your way." He patted Junior on the shoulder. "Don't give up."

As the woman started in on a story about her own rehab, Junior looked my way. His pain wrenched me, and I mouthed a quiet *I'm sorry*. Junior was a complete jackass, but I wasn't sure that what he'd done warranted what Walt probably did to him.

Tears rose to Junior's eyes, and he blinked rapidly, dropping his gaze away from mine. But even though I felt for him, another part of me said he should've known better. The pot couldn't have scrambled their heads that much. It had to be heroin. I sure hoped to heaven Cindie wasn't getting into that too.

In a few hours the crowd had mostly moved down to the bonfire, where the orange flames stretched up into the sky. Nights like these were perfect for a walk under the stars, and Ari and I often went out to enjoy the peace and quiet. Once we got away from the lights of the house, we enjoyed the star-lit sky.

Sneaking away together wasn't an option, but I wanted to find her. We hadn't spoken since the party started, but first I had a few stragglers to encourage to go to the bonfire.

One guy lay passed out on a chaise lounge; he could remain where he was at. A couple of lovebirds were going at it in the corner, and I invited them to join us below once they finished.

Despite the nudity often on display at our parties, Walt didn't like people having sex in the open. Most everybody was at the bonfire though, so I didn't break this couple up. It would be so nice to enjoy my relationship with Ari in the open, not that we'd have sex in front of others, but to hold her hand or allow myself to look at her the way I wanted to.

I sighed. That wasn't our life.

I made my way back down and through the crowd, getting stopped along the way. Eventually, I found Ari deep in conversation with Jaslyn.

Again.

"What's up?" I took a seat next to Jaslyn, and they pulled apart.

"What happened with Cindie? She's been acting funny all night," Ari craned her neck, scanning the crowd.

I didn't want to talk about it, to remember the cries from Cindie's room or the tears in Junior's eyes, but I wouldn't lie to Ari either. I gave a quick rundown.

"I'm not sure what he did to them, but..." I shivered. She'd begged and pleaded with him. "I heard the pain in her voice, but they shouldn't have done what they did."

Jaslyn and Ari exchanged a look that seemed to mean something, but I didn't know what, and it bothered me.

"Junior's such an idiot, and Cindie's no better. She'll get kicked out of here if she's not careful," I added.

"Lil, she can't leave. Walt—" Jaslyn started, but Ari put a hand up to her shoulder. Once again, they exchanged a knowing look, and a heaviness filled me.

Ari couldn't... No. She wouldn't.

"Not here." Ari's head swept around as if searching for someone. "We can talk later tomorrow when we're alone." She smiled at me. It was supposed to reassure me, but it didn't.

"Come on." Ari stood and grasped my shoulder. "Let's go get drinks."

She stepped away, and I followed.

"Hey, guys." Meri patted Ari on the back. "Walt asked me to send you his way." She pointed him out, and we headed over.

"What's this about?" Ari asked, but I had no clue.

Walt was standing with several other men and women, and he smiled widely as we approached. "Two of my favorite ladies," he said with a grin and wrapped an arm around each of our waists. "I have a surprise for you, Ari. I've been waiting all evening to tell you."

She looked as bewildered as I felt.

"This is John and Etta Carson." He motioned to the couple across from us. They seemed close to their sixties, although by the obvious plastic surgery along with the expensive clothes and jewelry, they could be older.

Etta stepped forward, her hand out. "It's a pleasure to meet you, Ari. Walt has told us so much about your dedication to working with children in the cancer ward."

Ari's hand slipped back after shaking. "Um, yeah. Walt encourages us to give back to the community, and volunteering at the Children's Cancer Center is such a rewarding experience." It was the canned line she often used for media purposes. As much as she loved visiting with those sick kids, it still broke her heart, and she always needed a few hours to recover. I didn't understand how she watched those children slowly lose their lives when she'd lost her own son in the same way, but she had a strength I didn't possess.

"I've talked to many doctors at CCC, and they've told me how your energy and positivity has such a wonderful effect on the children. You are truly selfless."

"Thank you." Ari's head dipped. *My girl.*

Walt dropped his arm off me but kept his around Ari. "We've decided to start an endowment for a new foundation to support the Children's Cancer Center. We will donate two million dollars to start out. Etta will be in charge of fundraising."

"Wow, that's awesome." Ari beamed.

"But that's not the best part." Etta bounced on her feet, a grin from ear to ear. "We're naming it Timmy's Time."

Ari gasped, the tears rising to her eyes. Walt nodded at her. "We wanted to do something that honors your son and your dedication to those poor children."

"I don't know what to say. Thank you." Ari wiped the tears away.

"We'd love for you to be the face of our foundation. To represent us. It won't take away from your time at CCC, but will be in addition to that."

"I... I..." She looked to Walt again.

"That's a yes, I presume." He laughed.

"Yes, yes. Thank you."

I thought of all the pictures of that little boy hung up in Ari's room. She'd told me it took her many years before she'd put them up. She had guilt over not being able to save him. Guilt over not seeing what her husband was about to do to himself. Guilt over letting her life fall apart. Timmy's story was only one in a sea of children who had lost their lives, but he was as precious as all the others, and Ari would be a good representative.

Walt had made her night, and I loved him for it.

Chapter Twenty-Six
House of Defiance

I spent the rest of the night talking to so many people, wishing I could only be with one. Later on, Ari and I lay in her bed, sweaty from the sex, and yet, she seemed unsatisfied.

"Did you see any interesting hookups?" I asked. Sometimes we'd be surprised over who a girl hooked up with at the end of the night. A few years back, the old Belle had ended up with a girl in her bed, and she wasn't into girls. Or Mulan, who'd spent all evening stalking this sexy guy, who'd unfortunately had a date, but all three went to bed together, and Mulan had more fun with the girl than the guy. Sexy men didn't always equate to good in the sack.

"Not really."

"I can't believe what Walt's doing for you. For Timmy." I glanced over at the picture of the little boy hugging his mom. I wish I'd known him.

"It's unreal. I would—"

Someone knocked lightly on the door, and Jaslyn crept into the room quietly, checking the hallway before she shut the door.

I shot up in bed to say something, but Ari tugged me back gently. "She's not sneaking in here for a midnight rendezvous. I told her to come when Walt fell asleep."

Ari motioned Jaslyn to sit on the bed, and she shifted over to make room. Jaslyn sat cross-legged across from me and my naked girlfriend.

"He's finally out." She sighed.

"Who all was there?"

"Just Mulan, Belle, and me. Which was enough. That Belle wants to be in control. It's like she was the one directing us. The same thing happens when we're working together. Have you worked with her yet?"

Ari shook her head. "No, which I'm glad. Bianca said she was a bitch too."

"Wait, why haven't I heard all this?" Usually I was up on all the gossip. Cindie wasn't doing her job, which was funny considering she didn't like Belle.

Ari shrugged. "Too much going on. You've barely had a moment to rest this last month."

The silence lingered until Jaslyn cleared her throat. "Lil, what I was talking about before… Nobody gets out of here alive?"

Where did that come from? I laughed, but their faces remained sober.

"We don't know what we're signing up for. Walt doesn't tell us," Jaslyn said. Their accusing eyes stared at me.

"I didn't bring you here."

"No." Ari gripped my hand. "We're not blaming you. Each of us made a choice. But…" She swallowed. "We didn't have all the information, and all along I thought you knew this, but now I'm not sure."

"Know what?" All this drama was getting to me.

"Nobody leaves the House of Desire. I mean, any of us girls," Jaslyn said.

"Yes, they do. The previous Tia left to take care of her dad. He had diabetes. And Meri ran away, and Walt left her alone."

Ari sucked in her bottom lip. "They didn't leave the house. They died the same way the old Belle did. You just didn't see it."

Preposterous. "That's not true. Walt wouldn't—"

"Remember how Walt told us he found the old Meri in some drug house and sent her away to get help?" Jaslyn crossed her arms, her face tight. "It wasn't true. It was the story he told you and the world. She'd run away all right but to escape him. She only made it to San Francisco. He found her and dragged her back only to kill her."

Ari nodded in agreement.

Tears scorched my cheeks, a pit growing in my stomach. I'd only been here a few years when Meri had run away; she'd been addicted to cocaine, an addict worse than Junior.

"How could you say such a thing? Especially after what Walt did for you tonight. For your son."

"It's true," Ari said softly. "Honestly, Lil, I'm all mixed up inside. Walt's done a wonderful thing, and I'm thrilled about that, but I was friends with Tia, and she gave up. She didn't want to be here anymore, and she asked Walt if she could leave. He denied her, and soon after she ended up dead. He told everyone she went to help her dad. He did have diabetes, but she never made it to him."

Ari had been upset over old Tia's departure, and I'd always assumed it's because the transition to the uptight new Tia was hard and that she missed her friend.

Jaslyn took my free hand in hers. "That day you and Walt came to talk to me. When he promised me the new clothes and the spa day. After you left, as I was sucking him off, he reminded me of my duty and what would happen if I left." Her voice faltered. "I don't want to die."

Walt might kick her out, but that was it. She was worried about losing the money, this magnificent home, and all our parties. And expensive clothes and jewelry. Jaslyn always had a thing for diamonds.

"We thought you deserved to know too. Walt saved us all in some way, but he also damned us to this life."

They chose this life just like I had, and now they didn't want to keep their promises.

Jaslyn gave me a squeeze, but I didn't respond. There had to be a reason why they were turning against Walt.

"I'm going to take off," she said. "I'm sure you guys have more to talk about."

Jaslyn said goodnight and slipped out of the room.

Ari scooted closer, and I resisted the urge to back away.

"Haven't you ever wished we could get out of here?" she said. "Have a normal life. One where we don't have to kill an innocent man." She waved her hands, motioning to herself and her room. "For all this?"

"They're not innocent men."

"Think about it," she said. "Knowing what you do now, do you really believe Walt cares about these men? Jaslyn did a search of Georges and didn't find one thing about him molesting anybody. A couple of minor convictions. Drunk driving and bad checks, but nothing horrible. He was a guy down on his luck, and nobody would miss him. That's why Walt chose him."

I leaned back, wanting to melt into her pillows. Georges was probably a fake name; johns off the street never used their real names.

Ari pressed her body into mine. I wanted space, but I didn't say anything. She threaded her finger through my hair, and I felt her winding and unwinding a big strand.

"Meri did it wrong when she left. She was dumb and used her credit cards. We can be smart. I've done some searching online at the library, and I've found a few small towns we could live in. The mountains in Wyoming or close to the shores of Lake Michigan. Small towns but big enough we can find jobs and blend in. He'd never expect us to move north."

"I can't leave." My voice wavered, and I spun around to face her, my hair jerking out of her hands.

"I can't stay." Her chin trembled, her wet eyes shining in the dark.

The tears gathered in my eyes. She wanted to leave me. I loved her, and she wanted to abandon me when we had everything we needed here. How did she expect me to start a new life all over again?

How could she expect me to spit in Walt's face and give everything up?

"You can't leave," I choked out. This house was filled with women—it was huge—but without Ari, it'd be empty.

Ari's hand stilled on my arm. "It's not a decision you need to make today, but I think I've made my decision. Sometime in the next year or so."

I didn't want to hear it, to think about losing Ari. "I'm tired. I want to go to sleep."

She sighed long and hard behind me but didn't say another word.

Sleep didn't come, not for hours, so as Ari snoozed, I visited some of our social media sites to view the pictures Bianca had posted. There were several of Ari and Junior. Bianca had even posted a teaser attached to a picture of them saying they had some exciting news to announce in the coming days. Hopefully Walt wasn't involving Junior in the cancer center work too. Ari wouldn't appreciate that.

It was unimaginable that Walt was the man they claimed. I finally drifted off, only to be woken up by Ari's alarm a few hours later.

Chapter Twenty-Seven
House of Depression

I spent the next few days trying not to think about Ari leaving. I didn't get why she'd consider running away. If she talked to Walt, he'd let her go. The only reason she'd have to hide it from him was if she planned on stealing money or was going to reveal who the real Walt was, but she'd never betray him. He had to punish the old Belle for that. So many lives would've been ruined if the old Belle had succeeded with her plans.

And the money... Ari wasn't a thief. She'd never steal from Walt either—would she? But she spent her money as soon as it came in and had no savings.

I pushed everything out of my mind. I had other things to deal with, including several complaints about Belle. Normally I'd call it petty jealousy between the girls, but after hearing from Jaslyn too, I figured I might have to bring it up to Walt. Each of the girls talked of the same thing, about how Belle took control and got all bossy. Again, it might be stupid girl stuff, but Belle's actions had turned off one of Mulan's clients.

Walt was out of the office, so I slipped into the video room and searched through the timestamps to get to Mulan's session. The video played on the screen. Belle definitely wanted to take center stage and be director, even indiscreetly nudging Mulan out of her way.

Halfway through, the guy asked Mulan to go down on him, and Belle crawled over to him lightning-fast. "You haven't experienced anything until you've had my lips on your dick," Belle purred.

He put his hand on her shoulder to stop her. "You can take a break for a few minutes."

"Baby, I'm the best here. You don't want to miss out." Belle dropped her head and latched onto him, and he gave Mulan a what-the-hell look.

"Wait," he started, glancing at Mulan, but threw his head back and let out a deep moan. Belle continued to work on him as Mulan sat on the corner of the bed with pursed lips and folded arms.

When all was said and done, Belle left the room before he finished dressing, and neither Mulan nor the guy said a thing until he had his clothes on.

He finally glanced up at Mulan. "Well, she was…" His face wrinkled as if searching for a suitable word.

"Pushy?" Mulan shrugged. "Sorry."

"No apologies. But I won't be doing that again."

A smile crept back onto Mulan's face. This client was a repeat customer, sometimes going for threesomes, but usually only hanging with her. He'd be back again and only with Mulan.

I started the second video. Once again, Belle was bossing both the client and Tia around. The guy didn't seem to care all that much, but he gave Tia a few questioning looks.

Belle didn't understand how things worked around here, how things like seniority and hard work set a girl apart from the others. That you got respect by treating others that way.

I leaned back into the sofa and sighed. No, nothing to bring to Walt, but I'd have to have a talk with her. I looked back at the screen.

At the main directory of the folder were two new ones labeled *Renewals* and *Special*. But Walt didn't have cameras in the renewal rooms. In the renewal folder was only one video, and I opened it.

Georges.

I watched the events that happened before I slipped into the closet, and I saw Jaslyn's confusion over the drugs not taking effect and when Belle arrived. Georges's face was so clear, and I couldn't bear to watch his neck get slit again.

I heard it though, and soon after the sound of the door slamming, when I'd followed Jaslyn to the bathroom, I opened my eyes to see Belle kneeling over Georges's body, Walt behind her. She touched him gingerly and then held up his arm. She released it, and it flopped to the floor. She laughed.

I clicked the video off. She had no respect for anyone or anything. Just Walt. I tried to shake off the disgust, but it wasn't working.

Instead of leaving, I checked the other new folder called *Special*. The first video was of that Shawna girl, the one Walt had shown me. I opened two more to find the same type of video. One was Shawna down in the dungeon.

Belle flogged Shawna hard, and I flinched at every hit. This was too much. I opened the other video and found a second girl. Same room, different beating. Again, Belle took the lead, a sadistic dominatrix. She even dressed the part with her black leather corset and thigh-high boots.

I shut the screen off and sat back. A door shut, and I jumped. Walt was back. I went to the doorway, and he startled when he saw me.

"I was just in your office," he said.

"Sorry." I shrugged. "I was watching videos."

"Ari videos?" He grinned.

"Guilty. Lock me up." I held my wrists up in front of me, not sure why I lied. I was allowed to review work videos any time.

He chuckled. "Come have a seat. We have a few things to discuss."

I wasn't ready to talk to him about Belle. Not until I spoke to her first.

"I've been giving this baby thing more thought, and it's the best route to go. There are so many factors to consider. Whichever girl I choose will be taking a lot of time off work. We can get up to three months of work in, but by week twelve, we should announce."

"Who were you thinking?"

"We already took Cindie off the list, and Belle is out. She's too new, and I don't want to take her out of commission because she's making some terrific money. I'd like you to prepare a report of all the other girls from the last year."

"I can do that. Is this how you picked Junior's mom? By the numbers?" She'd died in a car accident before I joined the house.

He laughed. "Actually, she and I were pretty close, so it was much easier that time. Briar was special to me." His face grew sober. "We're lucky we didn't lose Junior too. The whole thing traumatized him badly."

"I bet. I've never heard him talk about her or the accident."

"I can't blame him. I don't like to talk about it either. It was very difficult for him. For all of us." He stared off over my shoulder, lost in thought.

"Well, I'll get working on this for you."

"Thanks, Lil." He followed me to the door and patted me on the butt. His grin made me forget about all those things the others had told me, but I remembered as soon as I shut the door. Just because those former D-girls moved on with their lives and didn't keep in touch with the current ones didn't mean they were dead. I was curious about the car accident though.

Instead of returning to my office, I headed for Cindie's bedroom, but she wasn't there. I checked the schedule, and she wasn't with a client, so I headed to the welcoming room. She was sitting talking to Meri and Bianca while Tia was off in the corner with a guy.

"Hey, girls," I said. "Slow day?"

"It's a yawner." Meri sighed.

"There'll be people coming soon. They're en route," Cindie said.

"Great. Can I talk to you for a second, Cindie?"

Her brows narrowed, but she stood without questioning me.

I didn't want them to think anything was up. "Just wanted to talk to you about the bonfire and your date and see how things worked out," I said, loud enough that the others heard, but then we hit the door and went down the hall to an empty lounge.

I shut the door behind me.

"What's with all the cloak and dagger?" She eyed me suspiciously. "I'm guessing this isn't about the party."

I took a seat at the bar, and she sat next to me. "I was curious about some stuff, and you've always got the best information."

She smiled.

"I was wondering about Junior's mom and her accident," I continued. "What exactly happened?"

"Why are you asking me?"

"Because I didn't want to press Walt on it. The whole thing seems hard for him to talk about."

She stared at me for a few more moments with pursed lips. "Briar was driving to Vegas and got into an accident. That's all I know. She and I weren't close."

It hit me then that Cindie became Walt's favorite not long after that. She'd taken Briar's place. "You don't know what happened with the car accident?"

"Not really. She crashed. Junior somehow came out unscathed. Flew out of the window and only had bruises. Briar died. Life moved on. It wasn't too different from any other time we've lost a girl."

"What was she like? Was she pretty spoiled?" I asked, and Cindie gave me a strange look. "I was curious. I mean, if Walt chose her to have his baby, I bet he lavished a lot of attention on her."

"Oh no." Cindie's head flopped down on the bar, and her next words came out muffled. "He's not going to impregnate Belle, is he?"

Dammit. Walt didn't want anyone to know about the baby yet.

"No." I forced a laugh. "I was thinking about it the other day. Since I wasn't around when Junior was born."

Cindie lifted her head, a red mark on her forehead. "Yeah, Briar thought she was pretty special shit. He had to put her in her place a few times, but it was his fault. She became his pampered princess and thought she didn't have to do shit." Cindie glanced up at the clock on the wall. "Oh crap. I'd better get back. Those guys are probably checking in now."

She jumped to her feet and hustled away.

One thing was clear now; the answer to saving my relationship with Ari was getting her to be the mother of Walt's baby. She wouldn't have to work, and we could spoil her. Ari wouldn't act like Briar, and that would keep Ari here with me. She'd never abandon her son after he was born.

Fudging the numbers wasn't an option because Walt was too smart for that, but I'd have to devise an argument on why she should be the one. That shouldn't be hard. Ari was one of the few girls here who'd had a child, and I bet she was the perfect mother: loving and attentive.

Ari would be the best choice, and I'd make sure Walt knew that.

Chapter Twenty-Eight
House of Delusions

I was signing for a delivery at the service entrance and spied Belle driving into the garage with a young woman in one of the BMWs. She escorted the girl into the house, and I intercepted them on my way back through the hall.

"Lillian," Belle said. "This is my friend Leigh. I'm giving her a tour of the place."

Leigh waved at me, bouncing on her toes. "Nice to meet you."

She had the typical deer-in-the-headlights look that all newcomers had. All they saw was the glitz and the glamour, but then again, that's what we wanted them to see.

"Lillian is Walt's assistant, and she pretty much runs things around here."

"I won't deny that." I laughed. "I do get a lot of help though. Enjoy your tour."

"Oh, I will," she gushed, and I returned to my office to get back to work.

The day passed quickly. Ari had some late appointments that night, so my bed was half-empty, and I easily fell asleep.

"Lil, wake up." Walt perched on the edge of my bed, and I rubbed my eyes before reaching for my light. It wasn't very bright, but I squinted at him.

"What are you doing in my room at two in the morning?" I yawned, hoping to get back to sleep after this. Dressed in only his pajama pants, he, on the other hand, appeared wide awake. But he didn't typically make middle-of-the-night booty calls.

"I just had the most remarkable experience. I had to talk to someone." He jumped to his feet and paced alongside my bed.

"Oh yeah, what's that?"

He stopped and raised his brows, a smirk on his face. "Belle."

All our girls were sexperts, and I didn't get why he was stuck on her.

"Did you figure out how to beat her butt without leaving red welts?" I said, thinking of those videos I'd seen. But I knew by now that Belle was the dominant one. Walt was, too, and I didn't think most people in that lifestyle slipped back and forth between the dom and sub positions.

Walt grinned. "Better than that." He started pacing again. "She found a girl who was hardcore BDSM. Leigh was her name."

"Oh, I met her earlier." I could've sworn Belle said she was a friend.

"It was amazing. Everything I ever imagined."

"Why aren't you with Belle now?" Instead of talking my ear off at two a.m.

"She went to bed, but I couldn't sleep. I can't get Leigh off my mind."

"The sex must've been spectacular." I laughed, but it was somewhat unusual for him to be so fixated on anything to do with sex.

"I've got to show you the video. Be right back." He was out the door, leaving me alone. In less than two minutes, he returned with a tablet and climbed into bed with me. "We started in the tower room for a little pre-fun."

We watched a few minutes of Belle and Leigh getting it on, then Leigh and Walt.

He fast-forwarded to the soundproofed dungeon and through the ground rules and safe word talk. He was pretty strict about how our girls ran the BDSM sessions, not wanting them to go too far with clients or have our girls get hurt.

"This girl likes it rough." His eyes gleamed, his voice light and airy. "Leigh actually had some scars on her back. They were healed, but she said they were from the best sex she'd ever had, and so I couldn't deny the challenge."

"You took part again?"

"This time?" he asked, and I mentally slapped myself. Shawna had only interacted with Belle. It was the other video with the second girl who Walt had taken part.

"Remember you told me about that Shawna. Didn't you bring her down here too?"

"Yes." He grinned. "A few times."

"You lucky guy." I patted his thigh, inches away from the bulge in his pants.

Leigh inspected all his toys and picked out a few items. The black and yellow braided whip she chose had three small tails at the end. Walt chained her hands to the posts on the bed and attached her feet to a spreader bar, which was also tethered to the bed. She could move her feet, but not too far.

Walt started working on her gently with the whip, building her up to the more violent hits. The tablet must've been sitting off to the side because I didn't see her face unless she turned and smiled at the camera. Belle stayed on the bed, sometimes watching, sometimes attending to Leigh with a kiss or other intimate touch.

I tried to cover a yawn, but Walt was engrossed in the sex on the screen. Small red lines covered Leigh's back, but she seemed to be enjoying it.

The video-Walt removed a red and black leather flogger from the wall. I'd never seen one like this, which had braided tails and tips on the ends instead of just plain leather strips. He snapped it over Leigh's back, and I cringed as larger red welts appeared. He flogged her three more times in succession, and she squealed a loud "Ouch."

Her body twitched as he worked her over, but the restraints held her tight, and Belle smiled with glee. Leigh turned her red, sweaty face back to Walt, her mouth agape as she drew in deep breaths.

"More please," she begged.

Video-Walt grinned at her, then Belle—who nodded, and Leigh seemed to brace herself.

Walt clenched the flogger handle and raised his arm. "Here it comes."

He swung the flogger, and Leigh jerked. "Too hard," she called. He swung again and a third time. Large welts covered her back and shoulders, and he kept going. Harder. Faster. A flurry of tails raining down on her.

"Trudie," she choked out.

"Walt, she's crying." I gasped. Tears were sliding down her cheeks.

He chuckled. "That's part of her act. She plays it up for the camera. Wait until she really gets going."

"Trudie," Leigh called out, trying to turn her head toward Walt. She flinched away from the hits now instead of taking them. "Trudie, Trudie, Trudie!"

My skin prickled. "Why's she yelling Trudie?" This was exactly why I didn't like the BDSM crap—it was just disturbing.

"It's a woman from her circle. Her master that she visits. She was pretending I was her."

Walt ramped up the beating even more. Whip, whip, whip—the tails slapped her upper back, her lower back, her shoulders, her skin enflamed with the deep ridges.

"Stop," she screamed in between blows. "Stop."

"Walt," I choked as Leigh squealed. "You're hurting her."

Some of those ridges were wet. He'd broken her skin.

He turned down the volume so it was low but not off.

"It's all an act. It's hard for you to understand because you don't enjoy the lifestyle, but it's all about role play with her. She's a better actress than anyone I've ever met." He laid his hand on my arm, but my muscles wouldn't relax.

This is insane. Hurting each other, causing so much pain.

He whipped her back, her legs, and her butt. No piece of her skin was safe. Every time the flogger hit her skin, I flinched.

"Is it almost done?" I asked.

"The best part's coming."

Leigh was screaming at him to stop as she yelled about Trudie and thrashed around, the flogger tails smearing blood across her back. This was too much, too real. I pulled away from Walt.

He frowned. "I told you she's an actress. She told us exactly what she'd do and how she'd react. She never once used her safe word. We would've stopped immediately. This isn't real, Lil."

I sighed, watching video-Walt whisper something into Leigh's ear.

Holy shit. I plucked the tablet from his hands. Walt had turned. He stood behind her, his skin a mottled gray. Belle zoomed in on his smirking face and glowing green eyes.

He tossed the flogger to the side and ran his hands up and down Leigh's sides. She was silent now, her damp eyes closed, but her body jerked at his touch.

"You turned in front of her? Did she see you? What if she saw you?"

Walt grasped me again. "She's a sub. She listens to what I told her. There's no way she would've seen me."

"What if she lied?"

"She didn't see me."

Walt pressed into Leigh's backside, and she let out a guttural scream that penetrated my body. He pounded into her hard and fast, and I almost closed my eyes.

It's not real. She's just playing a game.

Finally, Walt released his load into her. She howled one more time, and I slumped in his arms. Thank god it was done; my ears were ringing.

"How can you even do that with all her screaming?" It wasn't like the cheesy *oh god* sex screams some girls did.

"Ear plugs" He grinned. "She even brought them along for us."

All I could do was shake my head. There couldn't be that many people out there who enjoyed something this intense.

Belle set the tablet off to the side, still recording, but we saw nothing. Not until Walt picked it up and the screen came into focus again.

Leigh and Belle were lying on the bed, on their sides, face-to-face. I only saw Belle's head since she was blocking Leigh, but the lip-smacking sound was coming through loud and clear. Watching this scene drained me, so how Leigh had the energy to make out with Belle now was beyond me.

"Just for the record," Walt on the recording said. "Was that the best sex ever?"

"Uh huh," Leigh's dreamy voice responded, and the recording shut off.

A chill ran down my back. "That was interesting."

Walt chuckled and tossed the tablet to the side. "There's not many women who like it that rough." He rolled over on top of me and kissed my neck. "It was a bit too much, I must say. All the screaming and crying. I'm glad she brought those ear plugs."

His hand slid between my thighs in a place where it normally would elicit a soft moan, but that video was too disturbing, not to mention everything else that had happened lately. Walt was sucking on my neck, so I didn't want to push him away. I needed him to choose Ari to mother his baby, so tonight I'd have to fake it.

Chapter Twenty-Nine
House of Devotion

I should tell Ari how I was lobbying for her to be the mother of Walt's baby, but I didn't want her to be disappointed if Walt chose another girl. Best to keep quiet until he made his choice. I gave him the reports he'd requested, so now it was a waiting game.

I checked my phone. Ari was on break soon, and we were taking a short hike since it wasn't blistering hot outside.

"Lil?" Belle popped her head into my office and came in. She'd never once stopped here to chat. I closed the window on my computer, and she sat down in front of my desk and leaned back. "I heard you watched our video with Leigh. What did you think?"

"It was… disturbing." Walt had been so proud of it, and I hadn't wanted to burst his bubble, but I had no problem telling Belle what I thought. Although she'd probably mention it to him.

Belle laughed. "We worked her over pretty hard. She loved it despite what you saw. I told Walt he should open up a BDSM club in Vegas. I worked at one once, but they had too many rules."

"You need them in a place like that." The red tape involved in running a brothel was awful, and a BDSM club would be a frustrating addition. Always being scrutinized to make sure it wasn't some type of illegal sex club. Prostitution wasn't legal in Vegas.

"Rules are meant to be broken." She smirked.

I wasn't sure why Belle was here, and it was almost time to meet Ari. "I've got a few things I need to finish up. Was there something you needed?"

She stood up and crossed her arms, but at this point, I didn't care if she was mad that I was brushing her off.

"No," she said. Within seconds she was thankfully gone, and I finished what I'd been working on before she interrupted me.

Ari was waiting in back and gave me a kiss on the cheek. We crossed the bridge to the start of the hills and got to one of the paths leading up, and she started bitching about her last client. Just the normal complaints.

Walt would be deciding soon who would be his baby's mother, and Ari would be so perfect. He had to pick her.

"… and then he shit on me."

Wait, huh? I looked up at Ari, and she grinned.

"You haven't heard a word I said, have you? I just told you how this guy was slapping me and spitting on me and then pooping all over me, and you nodded and gave me an 'uh huh.'" She laughed, heading over to the shade of a rock. I swiped the wetness from my forehead. I'd thought it wouldn't be so hot, but climbing up in the hills was always work.

"Sorry." I plopped down on my butt and scooted over to make room for Ari before offering her a drink of water. She waved me off and laid her head on my shoulder with a long sigh.

"What's on your mind?" I asked.

"Nothing," she said in that voice that meant it was a big something.

I waited for her to explain, staring out at the landscape. Some people hated the sparseness of the Nevada hills, but I loved it. Especially when temperatures cooled down.

"Just work stuff," she added. "What's the deal with Walt and these women?"

My mind flashed to the BDSM video with Leigh. Did all the other girls know about that?

"What do you mean?" I asked.

"His plan to make things friendlier for women."

"Whoa—what?" I straightened up, bumping her head lightly. "What are you talking about?"

"He brought all the girls who are willing to have sex with women together. You were in town that day. He wants to start promoting a special women's night where rates are reduced."

"Why?" My head was drowning in all this new information and all these changes. First a BDSM club, although that was technically Belle. And now he wanted to get more women here. "This place is a fantasy for men. Women don't care about princesses." Nor were they the target clients for prostitutes. "That doesn't make any sense."

"No, not unless we let *them* dress up and boss us around," she said, but I didn't laugh with her. "So he didn't tell you about any of this?"

"No." I studied Ari's face. I'd never, not once, had a problem with her having sex with men, but for some reason, women were a whole different story. It was her life and her decision though.

"I told him I didn't want to participate."

I sucked in a hard breath at the conflict raging inside me. I'd just thought about how I didn't want her to sleep with other women, but I was trying to encourage Walt to choose Ari to be his baby's mother, and she was being uncooperative. She might've ruined everything.

"What did he say? When did he want to do this all?"

She shrugged. "He didn't. I was one of the few who said no thanks, and he said *we'd talk*." She emphasized the last words heavily.

Like he talked to Cindie and Junior that night of the bonfire. I shivered. No, that's not what he meant. Cindie and Junior broke some major rules, and this was way different.

"He'll put the pressure on, but I don't want to do it." She tilted my face toward hers and just stared at me. "Don't you want to be free? To be happy?"

She'd already told me she wanted to leave, but I didn't want to face it.

"I am happy." It was true. Partially. A perfect life was an illusion, and we all made sacrifices.

"Don't you want just me?"

Her expression pained me. She was the only thing I wanted, and I knew my next words were untrue even as I said them. "I do have you."

"No, you don't." Her head drooped. "Walt has me. Other men have me. Maybe women too if he forces that on me. As long as we stay here, you'll never be the one to just have me."

I sat, unable to say a word, and Ari gripped my hand tighter. "I want you to be my wife. Only mine. Only yours."

My whole life was unraveling before me. All the words she was saying. The love I had for her and the fear over losing her. We'd never talked of marriage because it never seemed realistic.

"Walt might let us get married. We could never tell anyone, but we'd know."

It was a preposterous thing to say. Especially knowing… hoping Ari would be his baby's mother.

She frowned. "I refuse to pledge my life to someone—to you—and repeatedly break those vows every day. I can't do it."

I rubbed at the knot in the back of my neck and unclenched my jaw. She was serious. Dead serious.

"It's what's in your heart that matters." My voice trembled. I could live with that as long as I had her. "I don't care if you break those vows."

"But, Lil, *I* can't. I have no choice. I have to get out of here and sooner than later. But we can go together, and we can be free." She squeezed my knee, a distant hope in her eyes.

I tried to stem my tears. This wasn't happening. She'd leave no matter what, and she didn't have any way to support herself. That meant she planned on stealing from him. Walt would hunt her down and… I swallowed hard. And do what he did to the old Belle. The only way to save her was to get her pregnant.

"I can't bear to live without you. Please don't go." I opened my eyes to plead my case. "I love you so much. Don't do it. Walt will find you."

"No, he won't. Not if we do it right." She kept saying *we*, but I'd told her I wouldn't go. "We can do it. You and me." She grasped my hands and held them together. I tossed them away.

"No, we can't. You're not getting it." My swelling throat choked me. If she stole from Walt, he'd turn her to dust. "He'll kill you if you do this." The tears exploded, and I fell back against the rock, ignoring the pain in my side. I deserved this pain. We couldn't leave. Ari couldn't leave. She had to stay here and be the next baby's mother. That would keep her safe.

"You can't leave," I begged her, my face on fire. "It's too dangerous."

Ari laid her arms on my shoulders, weighing heavier than the whole world. Her lips parted, then closed, and she gazed at the imposing castle.

The air hung thick between us, and I prayed she wouldn't go. Mere seconds passed, but it felt like a lifetime. A lifetime lonely without the woman I loved.

She finally looked back, resignation in her eyes.

"You're right. We have no choice, and I'd rather be miserable here with you than dead. It was stupid of me to even consider, and I'm sorry for making you go through this. I love you, Lil."

My body relaxed only slightly. She wasn't guaranteed the baby mother position, and I had to do what I could to keep her safe.

"I love you too." I sat up and kissed her lips. After breaking apart, I leaned back, and she set her head on my shoulder again. I stared off at the castle, its beauty reminding me of all the wonderful things I had.

"I never want to leave," I lied.

Ari wrapped her arms around me and squeezed. "Me neither."

The relief inside cleansed me. Ari would see that everything would be fine.

Chapter Thirty
House of Disgrace

I hung up the phone and leaned back to take a deep breath. One of the rehab therapists had called about Junior. Damn Walt for putting me down as an emergency contact. I'd been half-tempted to give them Walt's personal cell phone number, but he would've chewed my ass.

I felt like I was the mother of a ten-year-old. Junior was an adult, and we shouldn't have to deal with his issues at rehab, but we were. I needed to relax with Ari. Thank god she was off the rest of the night. As soon as she returned with Walt from their first Timmy's Time foundation meeting, we'd be able to hang out.

I scanned through our social media pages. The post announcing the new foundation for the Children's Cancer Center was still up, but that was a few days old. The other social media pages had posts from this evening's visit to the cancer center, standard pictures of Walt and Ari, but it also included many candids of her and some of the kids. They were lucky to have her in their lives, but if I told her that, she'd say that she was the lucky one.

I'd been so close to losing her, but thank goodness she agreed to stay.

I checked another site. It'd been a while since I'd been on there because tweeting wasn't my thing. A picture of Ari and Junior was posted three days ago, a picture taken months ago. Weird.

Walt strolled into my office with a smile on his face.

"Did it go well tonight?" I asked.

"Yes, that girl of yours knows what she's doing. Did I miss anything important around here?" He stepped closer to my desk, his gaze scrutinizing me. I realized I'd let my face fall. Might as well tell him about Junior now.

He sunk down in the chair across from me. "Tell me the bad news."

"The rehab called. Junior is having a hard time following rules. They've caught him with marijuana several times."

His hands grasped the chair, his knuckles white. His jaw set as he stared over my shoulder, and I waited for him to talk.

"I'm beginning to tire of all this drama." He released his tight grip, and his face softened. "We're going at this all wrong. I'm not sure that this rehab is the place for him, and I need to consider it further, but we have other things to discuss. My baby."

He sat there and stared at me, keeping me in suspense on purpose. Good thing he didn't see my crossed fingers under the desk. I needed this. Ari needed this.

His lips curled into a small smile. "Ari will make a great mother."

"Yeah?" I asked, afraid he didn't mean what I thought he meant.

"Yes."

Oh my god. Ari would be his baby's mother. She'd be safe here with me and not trying to escape. She'd be treated like the princess she deserved to be, and best yet, she wouldn't have to work during most of the pregnancy. The tension in my shoulders dropped.

"That's so wonderful, Walt. Ari will be ecstatic. I can't believe this is happening. You and Arial are going to have a baby." I closed my eyes to take a breath, and he leaned over my desk and kissed my forehead.

"I might need help from you."

"Why's that?"

"I want her to do a renewal before she gets pregnant, just to make sure her body is in tip-top shape."

"But she renewed a few years ago."

"Nobody will notice the change, and it'll be good for the baby. She'll be at optimum health." He gave me a big grin. "You'll play a big part in our son's life. His second mother, I'm sure."

Me… a mother. I'd never had the chance to have children, and I'd never step on Ari's toes when it came to her son, but I wanted to be in his life too. Trucks and airplanes and having all this open space to run around in. This boy would be so lucky.

"Thank you." I ran over and threw my arms around him.

Finally now, we both could be happy.

*

"That was the weirdest evening." Ari stretched on my bed in her bright green dress and took a hair band out of her pocket. "Totally weird," she muttered, staring at the band.

"Can you at least take your shoes off?" I pointed to her heels and laughed. She gave me a silly grin and kicked them to the floor. My girl would once again be a mother, a wonderful mother, and the good news was about to burst out of me.

"He brought Belle along too."

"Why?" I sat up. "I didn't see her in any of the pictures."

"She was hanging in the background and taking the pictures of me and Walt. The first few hours were so boring because it was all business stuff. Walt and Etta did all the talking, and I sat there nodding along. I wanted to get in to see the kids, but we had to do all that first, and once we got in for some visits…" She pursed her lips. "It was like somebody stuffed a sock in Walt's mouth. He hardly said a word to the kids."

"He was letting you handle things. You're the one who's great with kids. And Walt, it's probably that it's not his own kids. He'll be a great father."

My Ari would finally get the one thing she missed the most: a child. Thank goodness Walt said I could tell her. But only her.

I couldn't hold back any longer.

"Walt wants you to be the mother of his next child," I blurted.

She stared at me, mouth gaping, and her forehead crinkled.

Maybe she hadn't heard me. "I said Walt wants you to have his baby."

She swallowed hard, and her jaw worked like she was unable to spit out the words. She should be jumping up and down.

"Isn't that terrific?" I smiled, nudging her in the arm and trying to ignore the uneasy feeling in my stomach. "You can have a child. A little boy to play with and love."

"I don't want to have Walt's baby." Her flat voice turned my body cold. How could she say that? Having Walt's baby was special. He chose *her*.

"Why? Didn't you hear what I said?"

She looked at me like I was the idiot. "Why wouldn't he pick Cindie or even Belle? Why me?"

"Well, Cindie's on the outs with him, and Belle. She's been here too short of time. She hasn't proven herself. But you…" I took her hand and rubbed the back of her arm. Something told me I shouldn't admit how hard I'd lobbied for her to be the one. "You've proven your loyalty to Walt. You work hard for us here, and he probably wants to reward you for that. You're beautiful and smart, and you've been a mother already. Why wouldn't he want you?"

"I don't think so." She shook her head.

"Who cares why. He picked you. Think of everything you'll get. The time off while you're pregnant."

"But think of what I'll lose." She slumped over and eyed the picture of us on my nightstand.

I squeezed her shoulder to reassure her. "Our relationship won't change. It'll be fun going through the pregnancy and seeing life grow inside you, and I'll love you even when you have a big belly." I paused. Maybe she wasn't worried about all that. "You know that having another baby won't diminish the love you had for Timmy."

I tried smiling at her, but she didn't respond, and a heaviness settled over my soul. "What's wrong with you? Walt is giving you a special gift, and you don't want it. You're being selfish."

"I'm selfish?" She shot to her feet, her arms waving. "I'm not the selfish one. And I'm not blind either. But you are. You refuse to see him for who he is even after we told you."

I folded my arms and gritted my teeth. Walt did everything for his girls, Ari included. Despite their jobs and who they were, he treated them with respect and loved them all. She shouldn't turn on him like this.

"No, Ari, it's you who's selfish. First you want to leave us, to steal from Walt."

"I'm not—"

"Selfish. That's what you are, and I won't sit here and listen to you trash talk Walt. Get out."

I would've stomped out of there, but this was my room. I went into my bathroom and slammed the door, unable to face my ungrateful girlfriend any longer.

Chapter Thirty-One
House of Domination

I couldn't tear my eyes away from the TV screen. Ari was screwing one of her regular clients, and normally it didn't bother me, but the pain sliced through me today.

Other than official business, we hadn't spoken for a week. No hiking in the hills. No cuddling in bed. No shared lunches or stolen kisses when nobody was looking. She'd tried talking to me a few times, but I refused to listen.

Strong hands grasped my shoulders. "Don't worry. She'll come around," Walt said.

"I miss her." I missed her hugs. I missed sharing bowls of ice cream with her and snuggling beneath a blanket on the balcony under a starry night. I missed her smiling face.

He seated himself next to me and clicked off the screen. "She needs time to get used to the whole baby thing. Besides, you're torturing yourself doing this." He flicked his hand toward the dark screen. "Everything will work out. She knows you love her, and once the baby is growing inside her, those motherly instincts will kick in. You two will do a good job raising him, and Ari knows all this. We had a long talk."

I squelched the shiver inside me. Jaslyn used those same words. "So she's okay with it?"

"She knows it's meant to be. But she's probably worried about this hurting the memory of Timmy." Walt leaned over and kissed my shoulder. "Now, the two of you need to repair your relationship. Why don't you take a break and go talk to her after she's done."

He was right. I shouldn't punish her any longer. "I will, thank you."

"This is her last client for the day. I'm sure she'll be showering up and getting ready to go, but you have time before we leave."

"Go where?" I hadn't seen anything on the schedule. It was only ten a.m.

"I'm bringing her with to go get Junior. He and I had a long talk, and we decided to try something different."

"Okay." But it wasn't okay. Well, it was okay, but it was odd.

Oh. He wanted to show off his relationship with Ari because people would question her pregnancy. I didn't have the energy to press him on the Junior issue. We could talk more later.

"I'll go wait in her room."

She didn't show up for a half hour. The door opened slowly, and she shuffled in. Her eyes widened upon seeing me.

"I'm sorry," I choked out. "I miss you. And I'm sorry for calling you selfish. For ignoring you when you tried to talk to me. I know this baby thing puts a lot of pressure on you and that the other girls will be catty and jealous because Walt chose you. I should've tried to see things from your point of view."

She trudged over and sat down next to me, put her arm over my shoulder, and squeezed. "I love you, and as long as you're by my side, things will be okay." Her words were strangled, and I looked up into her wet eyes to see the raw pain.

Pain I'd caused. I didn't want to do that to her again, especially after she'd agreed to stay with me and have Walt's baby.

"Think of all the things you'll have again. You've always wanted to have another baby, and this is such an incredible opportunity. He'll have everything, and with a mother like you, he'll turn out nothing like Junior."

I got a small smile from her, but not enough to cheer me up inside. "Talk to me, please," I begged.

"I'm just..." She glanced around the room, then at her door. "I wish I could have this baby with you."

"I do too, but this is the next best thing."

"I know, but it's so overwhelming."

I gave her a giant hug, wanting to wipe away the dark circles under her eyes. "Then let me be there for you."

She teared up and sniffed.

"Everything will be fine," I said. "Just fine." I repeated those words for my benefit because as of then, I wasn't so sure myself.

*

"This is nuts," Ari whispered into the phone. She and Walt were at the rehab as she spoke to me. "Walt's talking to the driver. There's two reporters waiting. How in the world did they know?"

There'd been plenty of tabloid reports about Junior going to rehab, and Walt had bitched about each and every one.

"Hold on," she said.

I heard some muffled words, and Ari came back. "Lil, you're on speakerphone."

"There wasn't anything posted on our social media pages, was there?" Walt's gruff tone hit me through the phone.

"No. I didn't even know until you told me this morning."

"It's him," Walt spat. "He called the reporters."

"Why would he do that?" Ari asked.

"Because he's an attention hog. I won't give him the satisfaction of a picture of me and him walking out of rehab together. Ari, you can escort him back to the car."

"Me?" She sounded as surprised as I was.

"Yes, all you need to do is go to the reception desk, and they'll bring him out."

Ari was quiet for a moment but then mumbled a soft okay. "I'll talk to you when we get home," she said.

"And, Lil," Walt said before she hung up. "Clear the schedules for tonight. We're having an impromptu family night to show our support for Junior. Eight to midnight."

The phone clicked off, and I was met with nothing. He wanted me to clear the schedule, which meant canceling appointments, which meant offering a free hour or more to those clients. All to *support* Junior? I didn't understand the man sometimes, but I went into the calendar and was surprised to find there weren't a ton of appointments scheduled. That made it easier.

Lucky for me, all the reschedules went okay; freebies made any anger go away.

Two hours later, I met Ari, Walt, and Junior down at the garage. Kyle was out of popcorn, and we'd have a mutiny on our hands if we didn't have any for movie night, so I offered to go get it.

Junior lumbered past me, his arms folded and his jaw set like a pouty child.

"I'm running to the store. I didn't know you guys were getting back now. Would you like to go with, Ari?" I asked, trying to play innocent.

Walt laughed. "I know you were texting during the drive. Go ahead." He waved at me, and we took off for my car. Once safely inside, I asked her about the rehab thing.

"It sucked." She sighed. "I'm used to the cameras, but these guys were pretty aggressive. They were shouting out questions about his addiction and interrogating me. It was annoying."

"What did Junior say?" The garage door opened before we reached it, and Belle drove in with another woman in her car. She waved before we left.

"He bitched for about twenty minutes about how crappy this place was. How they mistreated him, and he wasn't going back. Walt pretty much ignored him and sat staring at his phone. That only made Junior get louder. Until he finally shut up. Is Walt going to find a new rehab? He should ship him out of the country somewhere. Maybe Thailand or something." She giggled, and I laughed along.

"No clue. I'll have to ask." I glanced back at the castle and then at Ari. "We could stop off for a quick drink before we hit the grocery store."

"I like how you think." She reached over and squeezed my arm with a smile.

*

"Thanks for stocking us up with popcorn," Walt whispered as we gathered in the theater room. "Junior is pretty depressed about this all."

I checked out Junior, who was sitting there staring at the dark screen. Meri nudged him on the arm and said something. Mulan laughed at it, but nothing registered on Junior's face.

"Picture time." Walt clapped his hands, and Junior flinched. His face twisted like he was in pain. I hoped he wasn't on something again already.

Walt set himself in the middle, with Junior off to his side. There was a big space between them until Walt said to move over. Junior did… slowly. Then Ari. I got to sit next to her again, and he placed the others.

Bianca stood in front of us. "Cindie, scoot six inches over. Mulan, get the hair out of your face. Junior, act like you're surrounded by a ton of gorgeous women."

Everybody laughed except him. Maybe he wasn't feeling well. Bianca clicked a few pictures. "Need more smiles. Junior, I'm talking to you."

"Everybody smile this time." Walt glared at Junior, who seemed to deflate like a popped blow-up doll, and as soon as Junior smiled, Bianca took her pictures. He was probably annoyed his drug problems would be all over the internet.

"All done." She stuck her phone into her pocket, and everybody slid into their movie-watching spots.

Junior was slinking away, but Walt seized his shoulder. "We don't get enough father-son time. How about you sit by me." It wasn't a request, and Junior shuffled back to the sofa by Walt.

Instead of sitting by Walt, Belle slid into the spot next to Junior. At least we wouldn't have to see her and Walt getting it on. Junior slumped down onto the sofa, and I made myself cozy with Ari.

Tonight's show was a romantic comedy full of laughs, but I couldn't help but notice the one person who wasn't enjoying it… Junior. Maybe next time he'd make better choices.

Chapter Thirty-Two
House of Disillusion

"Can't you give me the name?" I asked Walt a few days later as I sat on the sofa in his office. This was the third time I'd questioned him on the name of the guy he wanted to use for Ari's renewal.

He pursed his lips. "Are you going to keep asking me every day?"

"Yes." I wouldn't let it go this time. I wanted to see who this guy was. Even though Walt had done some amazing things lately, I couldn't rid myself of those little thoughts about what Jaslyn and Ari had told me.

"His name is Nicholas Ward, and I'm sure you'll find him to be an acceptable choice. I'd considered keeping him for my renewal, but Ari's is first, so I'll have time to find another."

"Your renewal?" Walt wasn't due to renew for years.

"Walt," Belle's syrupy voice interrupted us. I turned around to see her standing in the doorway. "Your two o'clock is here, and she's ready for us. Waiting downstairs."

He chuckled. "You'll have to excuse me, Lil. I've got a beauty to attend to in the dungeon."

"Is this that Leigh girl again?" I asked.

Belle smirked at me. "No, Leigh's been too busy. This is Brinn. But she's as much fun as Leigh." Walt wrapped his arms around Belle and kissed her, a long, sensuous kiss. Before they'd pulled apart, his hand was up her shirt.

"Have fun." I didn't need to see this. I used to love watching Walt have sex with his girls, but it wasn't the same anymore.

"I have a file on Nicholas. Just search for his name." He patted Belle on the butt, and she giggled. Then they were gone.

I could go back to my own office, but I went to his computer and searched for Nicholas. Sure enough, it was there: Nicholas Ward. I read all the pages of police reports and court records showing what kind of despicable human he was. Then I jumped onto the internet too.

Nicholas Ward's name brought up many articles on the outrage over the technicality that got him off on his charge of manslaughter of his young wife. He'd had so many calls to 911 for domestic abuse, but her actual death was accidental—so he claimed. I stared at the picture of the smiling, happy guy who looked nothing like an abuser. That picture didn't tell how he'd been convicted of assault of some other guy when he was in college or of his multiple drug arrests or domestic abuse calls with previous women. Neither did it reveal anything about his dead wife killed by his hand.

A thought passed through my head. *Look up some of the old girls*. Girls who'd *retired*. But I couldn't do that. This was Walt's computer.

My mind went back to him and Belle, and curiosity took hold. I'd seen that damn video with Leigh, and it had disgusted me, so why did I suddenly want to see them and the new girl now? Walt would get a kick out of it if he knew I'd been watching.

I went into the video room and closed the door behind me. It took a minute to get the live feed of the dungeon, but there they all were. Walt, Belle, and Brinn, a long-legged blonde.

And holy was she flexible. She stood with her legs apart, bent over, her butt sticking up in the air, with her wrists tied to the bed and ankles attached to the spreader bar. Belle was on the bed, and Brinn's head was at her crotch. Every once in a while, Belle would smack Brinn's butt with a paddle.

That's what Junior needed. A good paddling.

But not from me.

I watched for about fifteen more minutes until they released Brinn and hooked her up to some other restraints. Walt retrieved some tools out of his closet. I didn't need to see any more.

I clicked off the video. This one would probably go into the *Special* folder with Leigh's. I went to the directory and made my way to that folder. There was an additional video there. From a few days ago when Junior came home from rehab. How often were Belle and Walt doing this?

I opened the video. It was the dungeon again, but Junior was in the video, sitting naked. His head tilted down, and the room was quiet, which lasted another minute. The mic picked up voices, but I didn't see who it was until they came through the door.

Belle, dressed in only a robe and accompanied by another woman, swept into the room. "This is Junior. Smile for the pretty lady." Belle pranced over to him, and he looked up at her, but he didn't smile. She spun around to the girl. "He likes to play the cranky old man. He's very good at it. Aren't you, baby?"

Belle leaned over and kissed Junior's cheek. The woman behind her couldn't see, but I could. Junior didn't respond at all, barely even moved his head. His arms stayed on the chair, his feet seemingly glued to the floor.

Belle clapped her hands. "Now, this is Junior's first time in the dungeon, so he doesn't know the rules. We always have a safe word." She turned to Junior. "That means to stop." She grinned before turning back to the girl. "What's your safe word, Mindy?"

"Arrêtez." She laughed. "I've been known to yell *don't stop* before, so I figured saying it in another language would be a good way to make sure we don't accidentally stop."

"Awesome. Now get undressed. We're about to start."

"Yes, ma'am."

Before my eyes, the woman transformed from regular girl to sub, and Belle was the dom. They got on with their little scene, but I focused on Junior. He kept shifting around like he wanted to leave. And why was he naked? Had Belle shared this video with Walt? It was weird that none of the girls had ever mentioned Junior's attraction to BDSM.

He sat, back straight in the chair with a furrowed brow. His eyes kept drifting toward the door, and several times Belle yelled at him.

Mindy's beatings got progressively worse, mixed in with her pleasuring Belle. I should've shut it off, but I didn't. They took a few minutes break to set up something new. Some chains were hanging from the ceiling, and Belle handcuffed Mindy about ten feet in front of Junior's chair, Mindy's ankles chained to a spreader bar on the floor. Junior still hadn't said a word. Maybe now he'd get some action.

"What do you think of my girl?" Belle asked Junior, running her hand down Mindy's naked body. "Doesn't she turn you on?"

Junior gritted his teeth, and his face contorted. Finally he spoke, but I couldn't hear the words because no sounds came out of his mouth. His eyes flickered away from Mindy, but he didn't turn away.

"Mindy, do you like my man?" Belle sing-songed.

"Yes, ma'am."

"Would you like to see him hard?"

"Yes, I would, ma'am."

I rolled my eyes at the annoying talk.

Belle rounded the back of Junior's chair and leaned over his shoulders. She grabbed his dick, but he didn't smile. Ewww.

Shut the video off, a voice in my head said, but morbid curiosity kept me in my seat. Junior's face scrunched up, but not in a good way. And wait. Walt had left with Belle, but he wouldn't be down in the dungeon with his son. Although Junior sometimes slept with some of the women, it was never at the same time as Walt.

Belle continued to play with a now-hard Junior, kissing his neck.

"Are you ready to fuck Mindy?" Belle said. Junior mouthed something inaudible again, but it damn well looked like a no, and he shook his head.

"Well then, I know somebody who does." She beamed. "Eyes on me, Mindy."

Walt's naked gray body filled the side of the screen. Oh my god, no. I jumped to my feet and backed away until I slammed into the wall.

Shut off the video. Shut off the video.

But I couldn't, and the terror reflected on Junior's face at the sight in front of him.

"Look at me," Belle yelled to Mindy's face. The poor girl didn't see Walt looming toward her. Six and a half foot tall Walt with his gray skin, his bone-crushing shoulders, and his bald head. She didn't see his glowing green eyes or his thick red dick.

He wouldn't do this to her… he couldn't.

"No!" I said aloud, the same word Junior was mouthing. He struggled against his restraints, his eyes wide. Mindy followed his gaze and turned her head. Walt towered over her, a beast about to take his prey. She shrieked, a high-pitch, painful sound. He seized her shoulders, and she wiggled and squirmed, trying to get away, but her feet and hands were fastened.

"This is my Walt. Isn't he amazing?" Belle said in a calm voice, her hand running up and down Junior's stiffie.

Walt's sinister smile seemed to cement the girl to the spot, the thrill in his eyes showcasing his horrifying intent. His dick was red like molten lava.

My head was about to explode.

He grappled at Mindy's breasts, tugged her back into his body, and kissed her neck. Her body trembled, her face white. "Please. Please, let me go," she whimpered.

"It's too late for that, my dear," Walt growled. Junior's head fell forward, and Belle jerked it back up.

"Don't want you to miss the show," she said seductively. He closed his eyes. "Walt…" Belle motioned toward Junior.

Walt swept his hand through the air, and Junior's eyes opened wide. He didn't blink. He didn't move a muscle. Almost as if he was frozen in place.

I fell to my knees and grabbed my queasy stomach.

Walt poked around Mindy's backside, and she kept trying to move away, begging for him to stop. "Arrêtez," she cried, the tears falling down her cheek. "Arrêtez! Arrêtez! Arrêtez!"

"Stop!" I screamed at the screen, but my yelling was just as useless as her safe word.

He clutched at her hips, and with a hard thrust, he rammed inside her. An earth-shattering howl pierced the room, and I covered my ears.

He pumped into her over and over, ignoring the wailing coming from her mouth, the pleadings to stop. He was a monster. He'd always been one. They tried to tell me, and I ignored them.

Oh god, what had I done?

I slumped down on the floor, my head pounding from the filth and depravity on the screen. The torture. Finally the screams ended, and I dared look again. A shaking Mindy was sobbing, her knees smashed together. Junior sat limp, his own eyes wet with tears.

I shut off the video.

I'd devoted my life to this man; I'd forced him on Ari. She was going to mother the baby of a demon, a monster.

I gasped. This was my fault. All my fault.

Ari was right. We had to get out of there.

Chapter Thirty-Three
House of Dismay

I stayed on Walt's floor for another fifteen minutes before I shuffled back to my office and fired up my computer. I'd only torture myself by doing this, but I deserved every painful bit. The directory with all our employee information was where I headed.

Walt started the House of Desire before we had computers, but at some point, one of his assistants had copied all their personnel records to digital files. It didn't take long, and now I had an amazing list in front of me, showing when each girl first arrived, their dates of renewal, and when they left and were replaced. He had been doing this for thirty-some years, and so many girls had passed through the doors.

I searched for the girls who had retired. I had their names and social security numbers, but there was no trace of any of them after they left the house. No work records, no death records, no criminal records, nothing.

Not a one.

I shut off my computer and leaned back, rubbing my temples to lessen the building pressure. I didn't want to tell Ari, didn't want to admit that she'd been right.

The only consolation was that at least she'd be safe. Walt would treat her well.

I had to tell her, but I needed to get away from the filth that I'd found. I left my office and headed down the hall, not wanting to talk about everything I'd seen. I found an empty room and sat down.

Mindy's screams rang through my head. Walt had done this the day they brought Junior home from rehab. It was how he was keeping Junior in line, and it also explained why Junior roamed the house with a blank look on his face, hardly speaking to anybody.

Tears stung my eyes as I sat down in a chair. Walt was a monster, and I'd sent the one I loved straight to him. I flicked on my phone to the tabloid report of Ari and Junior as they exited the rehab. It had another picture from another date, of Junior with his arm around Ari.

I checked all our sites, finding one picture after another of the pair.

"Um, Lil?" Cindie nudged me on the shoulder, and I glanced around the room, to the open bottle of wine in front of me. "You okay?" she asked.

No, I'm not okay. Walt raped a woman in his demon form. I'd never be able to look him in the eye without thinking of that vicious act.

I stared down at the other pictures of Junior and Ari. Too many pictures. I shoved my phone in Cindie's face. "Why are they posting all these pictures of Junior with Ari?"

I needed to ask Bianca.

Cindie slid out the bar stool next to me and sat down. "I have no clue."

Oh crap. Ari renewing instead of Walt.

"He's not having a baby with Ari," I choked out. "I mean, he is, but it'll be Junior's body. He's renewing himself soon and…" Ari and Junior would start their happy life together. It made so much more sense than an older Walt getting her pregnant and then dying not long after that.

My forehead thunked on the bar, and I ignored the throbbing pain. Cindie didn't say anything to the loony woman next to her, just sat there quietly.

I needed confirmation about those other girls despite my heart already knowing. I raised my head to face the woman who would hopefully tell me the truth. "What happens to girls who *retire*?"

Her expression held so much pain and sorrow. "They're gone."

Dead. Gone. Never to be seen again. He'd been lying this whole time. All along he'd hurt the ones he claimed to love, pretending they went on to new and better things.

I studied Cindie's weary face as she stared at the wine bottle in front of her. He'd hurt her too. I took a big sip of wine and passed the bottle to her. She did the same.

"Do you remember the night of the bonfire party?" I asked. A stupid question. I'd heard her cries and pleadings for Walt to stop.

"How could I forget?" She shivered, then ran her hand up and down the smooth edge of the chair, her eyes closed and her body stiff. Her screams replaced the ones belonging to Mindy that were running through my head.

"What did Walt do to you when Junior and I left?" It was a question I never wanted to face… until now.

I watched her clench and unclench her hands several times until she opened her eyes. Her gaze fell on the bottle, and she gripped the neck tightly and took a big gulp. Then a second.

"He forced me to kneel in front of him," she whispered, her voice shaky. "I couldn't move. Nothing except my mouth and tongue. He jammed himself inside me." Her face was chalk white. "He was… you know, turned. It was red. My lips barely fit around him, and it burned like a bitch. Like he was continuously shocking me with a cattle prod. My throat hurt so bad, but it was nothing like when he came. It felt like he dumped acid down my throat. I wanted to die. And he wanted me to feel the pain. I didn't know how I'd make it through the party, but he gave me something that soothed my throat, and he warned me that next time he wouldn't give it to me."

The poor girl. I pressed my thighs together. "I'm sorry."

"It's not your fault. It's—"

"No. I mean, I'm sorry for all the things I've thought about you and said about you. You don't deserve that. Nobody does."

She smiled wryly. "I had a bad sore throat for the next few weeks. It finally went away, but every time I look at him, or Junior, I get this stinging in here." She placed her hand on her neck.

Cindie took another swig of wine and faced me. "When I told you about Briar's car accident, I didn't quite tell you the whole truth."

"What is it?" This day couldn't get worse, and I almost shut her up. Almost.

"She was leaving. She took Junior and ran. She swerved on the highway for something. The sheriff figured an animal ran out in front of her. That's what sent her vehicle rolling. I don't know how he did it, but he's responsible."

I gulped. "Then why did you… why did you want to be his girl?"

"Because I thought it would keep me safe." She covered my hand, holding me still, and frowned. "That baby isn't going to keep Ari safe."

The tears burned my eyes. Cindie was right.

I'd sent Ari straight to the devil.

Chapter Thirty-Four
House of Duplicity

Walt joked and laughed with the girls in the dining room, but it took all the strength inside me to act normal around him. I couldn't let him think anything was up. Ari was with a client, but that didn't matter because I didn't have the guts to face her yet. I didn't have the guts to tell her she'd be birthing the son of a monster. She'd be off in three hours, and then we'd talk.

"Walt, stop." Tia slapped his hand away with a giggle.

"Arrêtez," Mindy had said, but he hadn't stopped then. Walt stole another chip from Tia's plate and popped it into his mouth. This was such a normal night, him sitting between Tia and Mulan.

I studied Walt's forty-six-year-old face. He hadn't planned on doing his renewal for a few years, but he'd changed his mind for some reason.

A chip hit me in the forehead, and I looked up at the trio.

"Why so serious tonight, Lil?" Walt asked. "I think we need to get that girl some ice cream. She needs a little sugar."

"Homemade potato chips, great." Jaslyn slid up to the table and nabbed a plate.

"Have a seat," Walt told her, and she plopped down next to me with a hello. "We were asking Lil why she was so quiet tonight."

Thank goodness Jaslyn had given me a moment to think. "Actually, I was thinking about family night. We've done a few movie nights now, so I was trying to figure out something different."

"You should build a bowling alley," Mulan blurted. "Like maybe two or three alleys. Wouldn't that be cool?"

"Naked bowling night?" Tia winked at Walt.

"That's not such a bad idea." He grinned.

"It would be another fantastic option to add to our special packages," I said. Not long ago I would've been excited by this idea, but now the numbness held me in its tight grip. "The men would love that. You could take out some of the parking garage. It's never more than half full. I can get a rough estimate on the costs."

Walt gave me an appreciative look and nodded before turning to Mulan. "Thanks, my dear. You are a smart one. I'll take your idea under consideration." He patted Mulan on the shoulder, and she beamed.

I used to crave his compliments and attention, but now it made my stomach turn.

"Let's talk after dinner, Lil," he said.

I forced a smile, pretending there was nothing I'd like better. Somehow I got through the rest of dinner, spending most of the time lost in my head.

Instead of meeting in his office, he brought me to one of the lounges and poured us more drinks. Just hours before, I sat here with Cindie, my whole life falling apart.

Walt led me to the sofa. *Move away,* my body screamed, but I remained still. He laid an arm on my shoulders, and I forced back the revulsion flowing through me.

"We haven't had much alone time." His breath sizzled my ear, and the goosebumps rose, although not from desire this time.

"You've been busy, and let's not forget the extra time you're spending with Belle." I faked my enthusiasm. "It makes us all jealous."

He smiled. *Stupid,* I told myself. I shouldn't be saying things that might turn him on even more.

"You've been hesitant around me lately."

I had to throw him off track. "I'm just thinking about Ari and everything. I'm excited for her, but it'll bring some big changes."

He set his arm on my shoulder and pulled me close. "Life is always changing, Lil. It's why we do what we do."

But life wasn't always changing for him. Not like the rest of the world. He should've been seventy-one years old, and I should've been too, but here he was running his business in a younger body.

"Some of us are getting older," he continued, his voice forlorn. He had it all, confidence, money, and power, and it was nice to see he worried about what others thought too sometimes.

"You're as good as you were nine years ago."

A low rumble escaped his throat. "I can always count on you to say the right thing." He ran his fingers down the side of my face and jaw. "You never disappoint me."

He straightened up with renewed vigor. "It's part of the reason why I moved up my renewal. Junior is ruining his body, and I'm worried that if I wait too long, he might accidentally kill himself. Or the drugs will ravage his body."

"It's all perfect," he continued. "We'll do Ari's renewal, and her body will be ready for a baby. Then as soon as Ari is pregnant, I'll die. It'll be sad because I won't get to meet my first grandson. Tragic, really." He chuckled.

"How will you die?" This discussion felt so surreal, like we were talking about dinner and not poor Junior's demise. Walt's death would make news, and the world would grieve for him, yet nobody would cry for his son, the man who would actually die.

"I haven't worked out all the details. Ari is my priority. Put her renewal on the calendar for four days from now."

I opened my mouth to protest but slammed it shut. I was supposed to be happy about Ari's renewal and pregnancy. We needed time to make our plan, to make our escape, but I wouldn't worry about that until after her renewal. We had to get through this first.

*

I paced around Ari's room, waiting for her to get off work. We had to talk, but of course she had clients staying until the very end of her shift. Finally, she padded into her room. Her smile lit up the place, but it wouldn't last long.

"What are you doing here?" she asked.

I stared at her belly. In a few months she'd have a child in there. Walt's child. I pictured a creature with glowing eyes and gray skin and a dark heart with no soul. Both of Walt's sons had been born normal, and I hoped my imagination would not become reality.

Ari touched her flat belly and frowned. "What's wrong?"

"Everything." My body drooped.

She shuffled over and wrapped her arms around me. I wanted reassurance in her hug, but none was there. We'd never make it out of here alive. We'd both end up dead.

I pulled back and took a deep breath. "Walt's doing your renewal in four nights."

"I know."

"You do?"

She shrugged. "He warned me. Told me that everything *would* go smoothly."

His threat.

Ari squeezed my hand. "I have a favor to ask. A big favor."

"I'll do anything for you." I hadn't been willing before, and forcing her to stay had been the biggest mistake of my life.

"Will you stay with me that night? At my renewal. I'm afraid I'll tell the guy to run away when he has a chance, and then we'll both end up dead." Her chin quivered.

"I will. I'll have to think of a reason to convince Walt." I pushed a few strands of hair behind her ear. "I bet he'll let me though."

I dropped my hand and stared at her pale face, neither of us speaking. This was all my fault… everything.

"You were right about leaving," I said. "We should've left when there wasn't so much at stake. I'm sorry for making you stay."

"I made my choices, just like you." She smiled half-heartedly.

"If we leave when you're pregnant, he might let us go."

She shook her head sadly. "That won't stop him from hunting us down. He can always find another girl to have a baby. I'm disposable. All of us are." She rubbed her forehead, her brown eyes weary. "What made you change your mind?"

Her voice held a tempered hope, which reflected in her eyes. Hope that we could be free. Hope that we'd grow old together. It was a hope I didn't have.

For a moment I debated not telling her the truth. I didn't want to scare her any more than she already was, but I couldn't lie to her, and she probably knew way more than I thought. All the girls knew what Walt was at some level, but not all knew the depth of his depravity. We had only seen him during renewals, and we all excused it because the men Walt killed were scum themselves.

We looked the other way while those men died, and all because we wanted to be beautiful. But then again, some, like Jaslyn and Cindie, saw the truth. Maybe there were more.

"I have a lot to tell you. We need to figure out what to do and make plans. Walt will want to impregnate you soon after your renewal."

And that meant our time was limited.

Chapter Thirty-Five
House of Doom

Nico stared up in awe through the tinted window as the car drove up to the castle. Not many guys his age got to spend a night in a place like this. Sure, it was a castle full of hookers, but that didn't bother him one bit.

When the guy approached him, Walter Marceline the III, who'd asked to be called Junior, Nico had thought it was a joke, but he looked the guy up on his phone. This guy was the real deal. Nico had to sign that disclosure agreement, but all that said was he couldn't tell anybody about it until the night was over.

They were gonna be blown away when they found out. They might be annoyed at first because he didn't show up at the club tonight, but they'd understand.

It was for sex with drop-dead gorgeous women after all. The girls at the castle were like celebrities, and men paid thousands of dollars to be with them. Junior didn't look all that happy though. A guy living in this kind of place should have a permanent smile glued to his face. Naked women running around, sex for free. Walt's son probably had the run of the castle.

The driver pulled the town car around back and parked. They got out, and Nico rushed after Junior, their steps echoing in the garage. Luxury car after luxury car was lined up in a row.

"I'll bring you up to meet Ari. She's your host girl." It was the first time Junior had spoken since they left Vegas. He was a weird guy. Nico had played on his phone for most of the drive, but Junior had stared out the window the whole way, saying nothing.

They entered the secured doors and went down a bunch of hallways and up some stairs. Nico got a peek into a few rooms and saw a few girls in lingerie, but Junior shuffled down the hallway and led him out to the patio where two women were sitting.

The redhead jumped to her feet and waited for Nico and Junior to reach her. She wore a long slim skirt that had a slit up to her thigh, high-ass heels peeking out from below. Her green halter-top clung to her tits.

"Are you Nico?" she asked. Damn, those big brown eyes suckered him in. He nodded, and she continued. "I'm Ari. It's great to meet you. And this is Lillian."

Lillian smiled and said hello with her full red lips. She was hot with her curly black hair and big tits, and her shirt clung to her body, but it covered too much skin.

He rubbed his hands, imagining them together. He'd never been in a threesome and hadn't even seen two girls go at it—live at least.

Lillian linked her arm through his. "Welcome to the House of Desire. You'll love it here." She led him to a couch and sat down, then pointed for him to join her.

He nodded. Unable to take his eyes off her sexy lips and her sparkling eyes.

Ari perched on one chair, and her skirt slid so that the slit was exposing her leg. A few inches farther and he'd see her panties… If she was wearing any.

"So, um, do you really dress like the mermaid?" he asked.

"Her costume is stunning, and best of all, there's a flap you can open to reach her. Front and back."

The anticipation ran through Nico again.

"And you? What costume do you wear?"

"Well," Lillian said, tugging on his arm. "I've got some silky lingerie … or I can go in nothing. Whatever you prefer."

"I…"

Shit, his head was mush, and he couldn't get a word out.

"We'll figure that all out later. In a few minutes, it'll be time to eat dinner. You need to have your energy for tonight."

*

Nico's body didn't stop buzzing since he'd entered the castle, hormone overload. First a tour, where he met a ton of semi-naked women. He wasn't familiar with all their names, but Lillian took pictures of him with them on his phone.

"So where's Walt?" Nico asked on the way to his next stop. He needed to get a picture of himself with that guy. Part of the coolness of this was the sex, but there were other things too. He'd get to tell his friends about how he hung out with an amazing entrepreneur and businessman.

"You'll see him later. He's a very busy man, I'm sure you know." Ari excused herself and left him alone with Lillian, who led him into a room with several couches and TVs. A sexy-hot Chinese girl uncrossed her legs and stood. Her two braids led his eyes down, her eye-popping tits about ready to jump out of her wispy red and gold outfit.

Lillian introduced the girl, but he didn't catch her name. All he saw was boobs. Not that she could blame him for staring. That jade necklace drew his eyes down like a flashing arrow.

Time passed quickly as they talked, and Nico looked up to see Ari standing in the doorway. Holy fucking hottie. Her soft red hair was pulled back from her face, and a gold necklace with a purple gem hung around her neck.

Her tits were awesome, and he licked his lips in anticipation of seeing more skin.

"Are you ready?" Ari stepped forward, the clear jewels hanging off her skimpy bikini top clinking together. The same gems lined the top of her skirt, which hung low below her belly.

He jumped up and took her hand, almost jerking her to her knees. "I'm sorry." He grimaced and slapped his forehead, but she chuckled as she straightened, and stepped forward. The emerald mermaid skirt shined in the light of the lounge, and the bottom of the skirt dragged on the floor.

"No worries," she said. "This outfit isn't the easiest to move in."

"Um, can we take a picture together?" He held out his phone to Ari, even though it was her he wanted the picture of. "I mean, can she take a picture of us." He pointed to the other girl.

"We'll be going back to my room, and Lil will take all the pictures you want."

Oh yeah, Lillian. How dumb was he?

"Um, sorry. I forgot. I can wait." He had the rest of the night and the next day to take pictures with them.

Lillian had said no nude shots, but with the amount of clothing these girls wore, they'd about qualify as naked, and he was ready to get on with the show.

Inside the door of Ari's room, Nico stopped, his eyes splitting wide open. The blues and greens and purple accents were so cool, and the bed had a sand-colored comforter and sat next to a wall painted with breaking waves. The white froth, the scarred brown rock, even the sun setting on the horizon was all so real.

"I feel like I'm at the ocean." He gaped at the room, wondering if all the others were works of art like this one.

"Hey, again." Lillian shuffled forward, tucking her curls back with her black-gloved hand. Nico gulped. Her breasts spilled out of a silver and black bustier, and her matching panties drew his eyes to her crotch, then down to her black fishnet stockings and silver heels.

He swung his head toward Ari and ran his eyes up and down her body again.

Ha cha cha.

"So what do we do? How does this work?" Nico started unbuttoning his shirt; he couldn't get it off fast enough. The two girls looked at each other, amused, but he didn't care.

Lillian waved a gloved finger at him to follow her to the bed. He hopped over. Why were these damn jeans so hard to get out of? Nico fell over onto the bed, and she laughed lightly.

"Why don't you scoot up there once you're ready." Lillian pointed to the headboard, and he seated himself on all the pillows at the top of the king-sized bed; the two girls went to opposite corners.

Ari reached behind her back. *Zzziiiiip*. Her lustrous emerald skirt slipped to the floor to reveal a matching g-string. Then she and Lil got on at the foot of the bed and crawled toward each other on their hands and knees. They met in the middle for a steamy kiss. It was more than Nico could take, and he stuck his hand down his boxers and got ready for the show of his life.

He watched the hottest girl-on-girl action he'd ever seen, and then they moved over to him and made him a happy man. Sex with one woman would never be enough after this.

A short time later, they were sitting in Ari's funky shell chair with champagne glasses in hand. A Nico sandwich between two naked ladies. He glanced at the phone sitting across the room.

"I suppose you won't reconsider the whole naked picture thing." He slid his hand up Lillian's thigh, and she giggled, but it sounded forced.

"It's not my rule. It's Walt's. He doesn't want any nudes released. If people want a taste of this, then they can pay like everybody else."

"I suppose. What's he like? Do you guys… you know…" He waved his hand to get his point across. He didn't want to say *fuck* to them—that sounded terribly crude. But what a dumb thought to have in a brothel.

"Walt is the best lover I've ever had. Well, the best man." Lil glanced at Ari, who smiled softly.

Holy shit. He'd thought they were just both into girls with the way they'd touched each other, but it was more. "Are you two together?"

Ari looked like she'd say no, but a *yes* popped out of her mouth. "Lil's actually my girlfriend, but nobody knows that outside of the house. Walt's girls can't be having relationships when they're supposed to be fucking guys. It wrecks the fantasy."

He stared at her for a moment, feeling like he was just seeing her for the first time. She was a woman working a job just like anybody else. She wasn't some sex robot without feelings or hopes and dreams.

"And it doesn't bother you when she's with others? Men or women?" he asked Lil.

"I only work with men," Ari answered. "Others will work with women, but we don't get too many around here. Lil can probably tell you the exact percentage." Ari laughed. "But no, it doesn't bother her, and she knows it's my job."

"It's not the type of relationship most people could handle," Lil added, running her hand on Ari's arm, "but we make it work."

Lil glanced toward the empty champagne bottle and crawled out of the chair. "I think we need more drinks."

Ari watched her cross the room to a small fridge hidden in the corner. Her gaze dropped to her blanket, and she traced a circle in the fabric with her finger. "I'm probably the lucky one here," she said in a low voice. "She only sleeps with two people. Me and Walt. And we're all expected to sleep with him, so we're even on that."

"Even the cook who served dinner?" Nico gaped at her; he'd never heard about Walt being into men.

"No." Ari giggled. "He's only into women, and mostly just his girls. Well, I don't know what he does outside of the castle walls, but we don't see him often with other women."

"Guys, I need to get a different bottle of champagne. I'll be right back." Lil slipped on a robe and left the room.

For a few seconds, Nico thought about having Ari all to himself, but a part of him wanted to talk to her and find out what type of woman wanted to work in a place like this.

"How long have you been here?"

"Too long." She smiled wearily.

"You ready to retire?" This whole setup was fascinating really. It'd be awesome to see how everything worked. "I mean, when do you guys quit? I suppose when you start getting older."

The frown on Ari's face deepened. Oh boy, that was insulting.

"Yes, I'm thinking about it. It's a tough choice. I'd have to give up a lot." She motioned to her fancy room. "But enough about me. Let's talk about you."

Lillian was taking forever, and they had a long talk. Exes, friends, and what he'd do after finishing his graduate degree next year. In a half hour, they seemed to hit it all, but then Lillian returned.

"So this is the deal." She sat on the chair next to Ari with another bottle of champagne. "I got permission from Walt. Just for you." She paused, a twinkle in her eye. "I have a special room down in the basement that we can go to. Would you like to check it out?" Lillian leaned forward, her robe opening to show her boobs.

"I was thinking about the tower actually," Ari said.

Lillian gave her a questioning look. "Don't you want—"

"No, let's go to the tower first." She turned to Nico. "It's got an amazing view."

"Sounds awesome. I'm ready," Nico said.

Lillian shrugged but agreed. Ari handed him a robe, and the threesome took off down the hallway.

Chapter Thirty-Six
House of Depravity

For everything I'd read about Nicholas Ward online, he was different. Way different. He had seemed like a creep, but in fact he was a decent guy, and I was surprised his rough life hadn't aged him. He was almost thirty years old, according to Walt's file, but he looked to be in his low twenties. Maybe that was part of his charm.

I had to remind myself about what he'd done to his wife and all the others he'd hurt. It made things easier. And now I understood why Jaslyn had spent that extra time with Georges when she could've brought him to the basement more quickly. She, like Ari, was trying to make his last hours better. Not all girls were willing to do that with the guys Walt brought home.

I glanced at my watch. Walt wanted the renewal done by one a.m. I crawled over to a naked Nico and slid my body next to his.

"You ready to head on to our next stop?" I asked.

"Let's hang out here a while longer," Ari said.

I stared hard at her. Walt would get pissed if we kept putting this off, and we had to stay in his good graces until we could figure out a plan to get out of here.

"A change of scenery would be great. Wouldn't it, Nico?" I motioned to the door. "If we want to break that record of sex in the most rooms in one night, we'd better get moving."

We'd never break that record, even if Nico wasn't meant to die. Cindie and Walt set it years ago, and out of respect for Walt, nobody attempted to beat it. Well, Belle probably would.

Ari glared at me, but Nico didn't see it.

"What do you say?" I prodded. "By the time we reach the basement room, you'll be all ready to go."

Nico put on his robe, and we did the same. I led them down to the renewal room. The setup was similar to that of Georges when we had Jaslyn's renewal. The drugged beer I'd brought down and set here earlier was missing. Where had it gone? I'd measured out the drugs myself so that the Georges mistake wouldn't happen again.

"Cool room," Nico said. Original paintings adorned the wall, joined by a few expensive sculptures. He studied the artwork intently, his hand poised over the top but never touching it. I never had imagined Nicolas Ward would be an art lover.

Ari hunched over on the sofa. "What's wrong?" I asked although those tiny prickles of doubt were building inside me.

"I don't think I can do it," she whispered. "We were talking, and he's really cool. The sort of guy I'd be friends with. That you'd be friends with."

"He killed his wife. He got off on a technicality."

"I don't think it's him. It can't be the same guy. Not the one you told me about."

I turned toward Nico, but he wasn't watching us. I studied his face more closely. He looked similar to the guy in the mug shot—well, not too similar. His chin seemed more square, and now that I thought about it, Nicholas Ward had been six-four, described as a hulk, but this guy, Nico, barely reached six feet.

"It's not him," I gasped.

"What?" Nico strode over, and I tried to cover my whoops with a smile. Walt lied to me again. The disappointment soared inside, one more lie among so many others from the man standing behind the curtain.

My body tensed. Walt was so close he might hear us.

"Why don't you make yourself comfortable on the sofa. Ari and I have things to discuss." I gave him a flirty smile, and he turned away to go back to the sofa. "We don't have a choice. It's too late now," I whispered to Ari. I didn't want to tell her about the beer. Walt had messed up on Georges's drink, and now Nico's was missing. Ari would never go through with the renewal if she knew Nico would be awake, but we didn't have a choice now.

"No, it's not. We can…" Ari stared up at the ceiling as soft music wafted in.

Walt's cue.

Nico looked around, confused, trying to find the source of the music.

"Maybe you can do it for me?" Ari's eyes darted from me to the hidden door where Walt waited, her hands stuffed into the pockets of her silk robe.

"I can't. This is your renewal. You have to do this." I glanced at Nico. He watched us curiously, and any moment he'd realize something was wrong. Walt was waiting, and it didn't matter if this was the wrong guy. She had to do it.

"What are you guys planning?" Nico stood in front of us now, and out of the corner of my eye, I saw the closet door swing open. Walt's eyes burned green, and the room heated up. I had to get this going.

I kissed Nico on the lips to distract him and then motioned to Walt. Ari's eyes flew open, her head shaking violently.

"It's time for the blow job of your life." I led Nico to the sofa. What was she doing? Why was she hesitating? "Sit back and close your eyes."

Ari sulked over, a frown covering her face. I'd step in for her if I could, but it didn't work that way, and Walt would be furious.

She took Nico in her hands and started servicing him. She wasn't putting much effort into it, and after a few minutes, a hiss came from the back of the room. Ari's head snapped up, and we both stared at Walt, who stepped out of the doorway.

His motley skin lit up that side of the room, and his green eyes blazed. His bone-crushing arms crossed, and he pursed his lips. My blood ran cold.

He remained where he was as Ari continued servicing Nico, who slumped down on the sofa, his eyes closed and a grin on his face. He didn't see Walt towering over him. As the moans spilled out of Nico, Ari upped her speed. Never had I seen her so forlorn, so passionless.

But Nico was so close. Everything would be done soon, and I just wanted it over.

Ari dropped Nico's from her mouth and leaned back. "I can't do this. Not anymore," she choked out.

Nico opened his eyes, and his head whipped back and forth between me and Ari. He blinked like he was trying to clear a fuzziness.

"You will do it!" Walt thundered. Nico's head whirled around, his eyes wide with fear. Walt stalked around the sofa toward us, arms outstretched. His beastly stench overwhelmed the room.

Nico's face turned white, and he fell off the sofa in a rush to get away. He scrambled on his hands and knees, whimpering incoherently.

Strong hands clamped onto Nico's arms and held him. He stared up at the raging demon above him, his body trembling. "No, no, no!" he yelled.

"Now, Ari!" Walt's bare chest heaved.

I wanted to run, to escape from the terror surrounding me, but I was stuck in my spot. Walt placed Nico back onto the sofa, and Nico sat completely still, his eyes glazed over as if he'd gone to a better place. A place where no creatures of hell existed.

Ari took him back into her mouth, and a shriek pierced the room. Nico's body thrashed, scream after scream coming from his mouth. Ari lost her hold on him, and I clamped my hands over my ears.

Suddenly Nico's body stilled. The howling continued, his eyes frantic, but he appeared frozen in place. Ari mouthed him stiffly and mechanically, a marionette ignoring the earth-shattering wails. Nico released his load into Ari, and Walt severed his neck with one smooth stroke, saying the words to make Ari young again.

Nico's cries turned to gurgling. Then nothing, and he lay motionless. The blood poured from his neck, dripping down his chest to the sofa, and the sickly-sweet scent reached my nose. Ari huddled before him, her face and robe drenched with blood.

She trembled, staring up at Walt's hulking form. He sailed around the sofa and tossed Nico's body to the side. Nico slammed into the wall, leaving a big red splotch.

He yanked Ari up to the sofa with the same force. She screamed and tried curling into a ball, but Walt unrolled her with no effort, captured her wrists, and held them above her head.

He released her arms, but some unseen force held them tight. He was about to kill her. Oh my god, no! I rushed forward.

"Walt, don't!" I grappled for his arm. A piercing shock flowed up my hand and to my shoulder, and I lurched away.

"Get back into your fucking corner!" he yelled, and even though I wanted to stop him, to plead for Ari's life, my legs would only move backwards.

My back banged into the wall, and I gasped. Walt's fiery-red dick pointed at Ari. Every part of his beastly body was charged, his enormous shoulders, his trunk-like legs, and his thick hands.

I clenched my thighs. He was huge… unnatural. Ari had been with all types of men, had used all types of toys, but nothing could prepare her for Walt's size.

He ripped off her robe.

"No!" Ari screamed, tears streaming down her face. "Please, Walt, no!" She sobbed, her chest heaving. He waved his hand over her face, quieting her, but not the tears.

"Back up," he growled. He touched her chest to move her toward the sofa, and she jerked back. She looked at his hand as she backed away, and stumbled. She fell onto the sofa, her hands still remaining above her head.

"Walt?" I begged. "Don't do this."

He scowled at me with hate-filled eyes. I opened my mouth to speak but couldn't. Oh god, what had he done to my lips? I couldn't open them. I couldn't breathe. I clawed at my mouth with my fingers, and finally my lips parted, allowing in deep gasps of air.

Walt smirked and turned back to a quivering Ari. He settled on top of her, driving deep inside. Ari shrieked, but the noise cut off mid-stream. Her chest heaved, and her mouth was wide open, but no noise came out as he pounded into her.

Tears flooded her eyes, and I tried to shut mine, but my lids wouldn't close. My eyes were frozen open.

Walt slammed into her over and over. His grunts grew more intense, almost deafening, and with a bellow that resonated deep within my soul, he filled her full with his demon seed.

He pulled out of her and smashed her legs shut. Then waved a hand over her face. The screaming pierced me to the core, a torturous pain I'd never heard before. She howled as if she was burning from the inside. I finally was able to close my eyes tight, but the pictures were seared in my head.

The man I'd once loved and admired nudged me with his foot. The gray skin was gone, and his green eyes were back to normal, but the fury remained.

"Take care of her," he growled, then stomped off. As soon as the door slammed, I scrambled over to Ari and held her fragile body tight in my arms, rocked her, and cried with her until her wailing finally abated. Over and over, I said her name, telling her I loved her, telling her I was sorry, telling her everything would be okay. Her body was a limp doll in my arms, and she never said a word. Not one.

We didn't move for what felt like hours. At last she looked up at me, wiping her bloody damp hair out of her face. Blank, lifeless eyes stared at me and scared me more than anything. She was alive but not with me. Slowly she crawled to her feet and trudged toward the door. She was halfway out before I stopped her.

She stood motionless and stared at me. "Wait here," I said and ran back to the room to get her robe. The silky-smooth fabric was soaked in blood, but it was all I had. I stuffed her arms in the robe and tied it around her waist.

Somehow I got her up to my room, and I sat her on the toilet. She didn't say a word as I wiped her face free of blood. I ran the washcloth under the running water, the blood draining down the sink. If only the pain would disappear so easily.

I took out an oversized t-shirt for her. "Raise your hands," I said. She did as I asked, and an image flashed in my head: her hands suspended in the air with Walt in front of her. I gasped, turning away so she didn't see my emotions.

She didn't move, her arms stiff, and I stood behind her fighting the tears as I tugged the t-shirt over her head. Then she went over to my bed and crawled under the covers.

I lay with her, not knowing what to do. Not knowing what would happen. And even though Ari's tears were depleted, I cried and cried, so scared I'd just lost the woman I loved.

Chapter Thirty-Seven
House of Disfavor

I jolted awake to Ari's cries for the second time that night. The sunlight peeking through my shades gave little comfort, and I cuddled up behind Ari, trying to wake her up with a gentle touch. The wailing stopped, and I burrowed into her scorching back.

I didn't know what to say... what to do. The man I'd loved and respected raped the woman I loved.

Ari slid her legs off the bed and to the floor, slowly sitting up. Nico's blood was crusted in her hair; I should've gotten her into the shower like I had Jaslyn. She hunched over, and I placed my hand on her shoulder to rub away the tension.

Her whole body shuddered, and she pulled away and shuffled to the bathroom like an old woman. The toilet flushed, the shower ran, and I waited for the door to open.

The crumpled white towel from last night lay on the floor, stained red, and my sheets would need a good washing. Why had Walt done this to her? She didn't deserve any of this. Nobody did.

The bathroom door swung open, and Ari trudged out as she stuffed her hair into a loose ponytail. She dressed in fuzzy pajamas from my drawer and sat at the vanity table, staring into the mirror.

"Are you okay?" I asked, immediately kicking myself. "Can I get you anything?"

She opened a drawer, took out a brush, and brushed her hair. Except it was still in the ponytail. Her face contorted, and she took out the band before resuming the brushing.

I got up to go to her and caught my reflection in the mirror. I needed to get rid of my blood-stained clothes. She continued to stare into the mirror while I slipped on a pair of pajamas. I stepped behind her and took her damp hair in my hands. She didn't flinch, didn't even look at me.

"Can I get you something to eat?" I tried again. She smelled so fresh and clean, but her eyes showed her pain.

"I'm pregnant."

My gut wrenched, and I swallowed hard to keep the vomit from rising.

"You don't know that. It was one time."

"Yes, I do." A tear slid down her cheek onto the tabletop, but her face remained void of emotion.

I reached my arms around her chest to hug her, but she collapsed onto the vanity, sobbing. I held her once more because that's all I could do.

*

All morning we stayed in her room. Bianca stopped by and tried to get the story out of us, but I didn't say a word, and Ari hadn't spoken since her breakdown that morning.

Now Judith had appeared with a beer cheese soup specially made by Kyle and a glass of apple juice. Ari whispered a soft thank you and crunched up the saltines. Her first words for hours.

"There was a lot of blood this time." Judith studied Ari's morose face. She meant the room, which she probably cleaned up this morning. Judith settled on the bed next to Ari, who put the spoon to her lips and blew. Neither said a word, but Judith stroked Ari's knee lightly as Ari stared at the spoon.

"There was," I finally replied. Judith regarded me now, understanding in her eyes.

How many other girls had he done this to? Cindie, down on her knees as punishment for that night with Junior. Jaslyn, when she'd gone through that rough spot with her renewal. He'd been kind, giving her that spa day and money for a new dress, but I'd left the room. What had he done to her once I was gone? Why did everybody else seem to know what was going on, but I didn't?

"I'm pregnant," Ari said, the spoon poised in front of her mouth. "And after the baby is born, he'll get rid of me."

"No, that's not true," I assured her, but the panic deep within told me otherwise. Ari was a means to an end like every other girl here, and when he tired of us, we would disappear.

Judith and I exchanged glances. "You don't know that, dear," she said. "He'll—"

Ari whipped out her free hand to silence Judith. "I'm not an idiot. We all know what'll happen."

"You have nine months. A lot can change in nine months." Judith tried, but Ari wasn't having any of it.

"Yeah. I'll talk to him. It'll be okay." I couldn't even convince myself that was true, so I doubted Ari would believe me either. There was no denying that once Walt had that baby, Ari would be dead. Died in birth, they would say.

Ari smiled wearily. "Kyle has outdone himself. Please tell him thank you."

"You can tell him." I nudged her foot.

She reached over to the nightstand and grabbed the remote control, then settled back on the pillows. She flipped the TV on and skipped through a few channels until she hit a re-run of some baseball game.

"San Francisco didn't make the playoffs. Maybe next year." She shrugged at the TV.

"Who's playing in the World Series? Is it coming soon?" Judith asked.

"Boston. And either St. Louis or Colorado." She lifted her arm toward the TV and turned up the volume. Not super loud, but loud enough to send me and Judith the message.

We sat together watching the game, but if anyone would've quizzed me on the score or who was winning, I'd never be able to say.

Halfway through the sixth inning, the door flew open, and Walt stormed in. Ari shrunk back, and I stood, getting in between them.

"Judith, you have work to do. You are excused," he said. She took the tray with the empty soup bowl and scuttled out the door.

"Lil, it's time for you to go back to work too, but first, you need to pack a bag for Ari."

Wait, what? Ari's face contorted, and she clutched my arm, her nails digging into my skin.

"Ari is moving to my room until we are assured a pregnancy. She won't be working anymore until my child is born."

"No, Walt." Oh my god. He raped her and would continue raping her until she was pregnant. I couldn't let him take her.

I suddenly couldn't breathe and clawed at my throat. Walt stood ten feet away from me, but it was like he was choking me with his hands.

The pressure eased, and I gasped for breath.

"I gave you my orders." He folded his arms, and his eyes glared green. "Now, go."

I didn't want to leave my room, leave him alone with her, but I had no choice. He followed me out the door and watched me pack her bag without a word. I included some of her favorite comfy pajamas, several yoga pants and tees, and a few other things.

"I'm waiting," Walt growled from across the room.

"Don't you think it'd be easier—"

My throat constricted again, and I clutched at my neck. The pressure released, and I breathed normally.

"Let's go." He spun around and stormed toward the door.

Back at my room, he jerked the bag from my hands. "Say goodbye to Ari."

Goodbye sounded so permanent. He couldn't mean that. I reached for her, to hug her and hold her tight, but Ari crept around me without a second glance and went out the door, taking my heart with her.

My door slammed, and I collapsed on my bed, the baseball game playing in the background covering the sounds of my sobs.

He'd taken away my Ari, and I'd never been more alone in my life.

Chapter Thirty-Eight
House of Disenchantment

I didn't get a damn thing done yesterday, and today wasn't much better.

My computer screen displayed the report I sent Walt. I didn't know what to say to him or how to talk to him, and I stayed away from his office most of the day, and he hadn't come to me. I did the bare minimum, the things that had to get done, and now I had to go talk to him to discuss which vendor I was recommending for something. I'd been putting it off, but he'd be calling me soon since the day was coming to an end.

I needed to know how Ari was doing and how he was treating her. What if it took months for her to get pregnant?

I finished my cup of coffee and flung open my door, ready to face Walt. I about jumped into the doorframe. Bianca was standing in front of me, her hand poised to knock and a surprised look on her face. She laughed, placing her hand on her chest.

"Whoa," she gasped. "You scared the bejeesus outta me."

"I just about had a heart attack, so we're even." I chuckled along with her, backing up and shutting the door behind her, thankful for being able to put off seeing Walt for a short time. "What can I do for you?"

"The website has been updated with the new header. Did you see it yet?" She sat down tentatively, and I retreated behind my desk.

"I've been busy, but I'll check it out later. I'm sure you did an awesome job."

"Thanks. But… I heard a rumor. Well, see… I've been posting all these pictures of Ari and Junior, and we both know she's not crazy about him. And then I overheard Meri talking to Mulan about Walt moving Ari into his room. What's that about?"

The tears welled up in my eyes, and I turned away. I couldn't tell her what happened to Ari without breaking down, and as soon as she left, I had to go see Walt. I opened a drawer in the filing cabinet to give me some time to compose myself.

"Walt is having another baby."

"With Ari?" She didn't hide the surprise in her voice.

Focus on the baby thing. Walt hadn't announced to anyone his baby plans, but Bianca could keep a secret. I blinked back the wetness in my eyes.

"Yes, I guess so. Don't tell anyone yet." I removed a folder and slammed the drawer shut. "I have to go see Walt. I'm already late. I'll catch up with you later." I stood, folder in hand, and avoided her face as I shuffled around her. She could let herself out.

I took each agonizing step toward Walt's office and stepped inside to find him clicking away at his computer.

"Are you ready to discuss my recommendation?" I didn't bother trying to fake it with him. He knew how I felt.

He motioned to take a seat. "No. We need to talk about other things first. I'm sorry for what happened at the renewal, but I had little choice. I can't allow any disobedience from my girls. Not on this level."

My chin trembled, and I swallowed back the lump. He didn't have to rape her.

"You had no problem when I disciplined Junior and Cindie. You approved."

I hung my head. I'd been wrong then, wrong about so many things.

"I want you to understand how things will proceed. Ari is in my room, and she will remain so until she is pregnant. I don't want to hear you asking every hour when you get to see her again. You'll see her when I decide you see her. That's it."

My throat tingled, but I wasn't sure if it was him doing it or my reaction to him.

"Yes, sir." I had no fight left in me. My love was his prisoner, and I couldn't do a damn thing about it. I thought about Bianca and the questions she asked. "What will you tell the other girls? They might wonder why Ari is with you when she's supposed to be with Junior."

"Don't worry about that." He clicked open the calendar on his computer. "Now Halloween is almost here. We have the trick-or-treat charity event. I expect you to be there with a smile on your face. You still represent the House of Desire, and you'll do so properly. Unless…" He paused, narrowing his gaze. "You feel like your time here has come to an end."

I sat up. "No. I'm fine." I'd never see Ari again. I bit back the tears forming in my eyes. "I'll give a hundred and ten percent like always. I promise."

"I expect no less," he said sternly. "Now tell Jaslyn she's taking Ari's place at the Halloween event."

"I will." I jumped to my feet and rushed to the door.

"And, Lil," Walt huffed. I slowly turned around. "The rest of the girls don't need to know what happened. We don't need lots of gossip running around the house, so you'll update them on how Ari is doing. How she's enjoying her time off and is relaxing."

"I hear you loud and clear." I shot out the door, wishing I'd never have to see his evil face again.

I checked the schedule. Jaslyn should be finishing with a client soon, so I headed to the welcoming room, which was empty since all clients were being serviced and no others were on the schedule for another few hours. I slumped down on the sofa and rubbed my temples. I didn't want to consider how long Ari might be with Walt if she had trouble getting pregnant.

She was scared and alone in his room. At least he'd be feeding her, caring for her physically, but at the same time he'd be raping her. I cleared the images from my head before they overwhelmed me.

I would keep going for Ari; she needed me to be strong, and I needed her.

Jaslyn showed up fifteen minutes later and saw me sitting on the sofa. She nudged her client to the door. It took a few minutes for her to escort him out, but soon she was back.

"Lil, what's wrong?" She wrapped an arm around my shoulders. I tipped my head up and peered into the mirror on the opposite wall. I studied what she saw. My messy hair was in chaos, and I wasn't wearing makeup. My t-shirt was one I would've reprimanded other girls for wearing in public, and I had on yoga pants and high heels. I'd been wearing these clothes all day, yet Walt said nothing.

My throat thickened, and I bit back the tears. "Can we go to your room?"

She led me to her bedroom in silence. I plunked down on the love seat and kicked off the stupid high heels that didn't even match my sweats. I was a mess, and I didn't know where to start. She plopped down beside me and waited. I still didn't speak, afraid that the tears would flood my eyes once I started.

"Do you want me to get Potsie?" She nudged my shoulder and smiled. "He always makes me feel better."

I glanced over at the guinea pig but couldn't afford a smile. It was then I noticed the whole room was decorated for Halloween. Cottony white spider web stretched across the corners, and cardboard ghosts lined the walls. Halloween was one of Ari's favorites, and she'd miss out on the trick-or-treating party. But really, a minor trick-or-treat party was nothing compared to what Walt was doing to her.

"Ari's renewal…" A few tears slid down my cheeks. She was alone in the room with a monster. A monster I'd loved and trusted. A monster I'd dedicated my life to.

Jaslyn squeezed my hand. "What happened, Lil?" I heard the trepidation in her voice. I wasn't sure how much Ari had talked to her or if she knew Ari wanted to leave. I should've encouraged Ari to go when she had the chance. It was too late now.

"Do you remember after your renewal when Walt and I had that talk with you?"

"I'll never forget it." She grimaced.

"What did he do after I left?" I'd been stupidly jealous that he was giving her his special attention.

She rubbed her temples and frowned. It was bad but hopefully not as bad as what happened to Ari.

"He told me to give him a blow job. I was holding his dick, and he turned… well, you know." She gulped, her face pale. "It was like touching a hot burner. He went back to normal and warned me that if I didn't shape up, then I could blow him when he was red hot. I had to finish it, but at least I didn't scorch my mouth."

"I'm sorry."

"It's not your fault." She scooted closer and patted my knee. "He fooled you. You're not the only one. Not every girl here has done something to earn his wrath, but those who have would never admit it."

"They're good actors."

"Well, when it's your life on the line, you do what you have to."

Stay with Walt or lose their lives: it wasn't much of a choice.

"What happened at the renewal?" she asked.

The deep breath I took did little to steady my nerves. Jaslyn deserved the truth, no matter how hard the words would be. She'd understand, and she'd give me a shoulder to cry on.

I opened my mouth and began my story.

Chapter Thirty-Nine
House of Discontent

Belle glared at me during cocktail time before dinner as if it was my fault Walt had moved Ari into his room for the past two weeks. The worst two weeks of my life. Thirteen days I'd gone without seeing Ari. Thirteen heart-wrenching days of being on auto-pilot: doing my job but feeling nothing but pain and loss. Thirteen days of faking that things were okay. Of trying to plan how Ari and I would escape.

Thirteen days of knowing we'd never escape.

Belle stood in the corner talking to Meri, not even bothering to lower her voice. She swiped her brown bangs off her forehead and huffed. "I told him he doesn't have to have sex with her *every* night, but he still goes into the sitting room with her."

When Belle had told me the same thing, I'd wanted to correct her with the word rape, but she'd never see it that way; she was as vicious and vile as him.

"Wait, what?" Meri's nose wrinkled up. "Why's she in the sitting room?"

"Because I am in his bed. He only chose her to be the mom because her numbers are down. He wouldn't lose much by having her off work for nine months. If he'd taken me out of commission, he'd take a big hit."

I rolled my eyes at Belle. She was too big for her britches, and I would love to see someone put her in her place, but nobody would attempt to take out Walt's new favorite. They never tried with Cindie either.

"I don't get it," Belle continued. "Sometimes she acts like she doesn't even want to have sex. She should be grateful he chose her."

Grateful he raped her? I gripped the sides of my chair to keep from getting up to yell at Belle. I didn't understand why she was complaining because she still spent most nights in his bed.

My heart ached for what Ari went through. I imagined slicing open Walt's neck with his dagger, and I kept my mouth shut, scared to talk to anyone. Jaslyn was the only one I'd ever shared with.

Bianca knew the truth about Walt. Cindie too. But who else? I was convinced Briar was a great faker like the rest of us, pretending to love her life. She was one of the few who didn't pester me about Ari, who hadn't shown at least a smidgen of jealousy that Ari didn't have to work. All the other girls had bitched at one time or another that it wasn't fair.

Yeah, well, it wasn't fair my girlfriend was locked up being raped by a monster. It wasn't fair she'd lose her life after giving life. Every time I heard one of the girls complain about Ari and all her free time, I wanted to slap them.

I didn't. I held back for Ari's sake.

Jaslyn and Bianca brought me a glass of wine, and I realized I'd been sitting at the end of the table alone with no drink in my hand. I was like Junior. Although he was surrounded by a few girls right now, he was isolating himself and not speaking to anyone. I'd told Walt I'd give a hundred and ten percent at my job, and I was failing. I had to be better for Ari, and that meant socializing with the girls like I used to do.

"Still haven't seen her?" Jaslyn whispered. I shook my head. Despite him warning me not to ask, I begged him every day to let me see her. He'd say no, and I'd do my job and push through the day, working hard to keep her screams from echoing in my head. And I'd tell others that I was talking to her and making sure she was feeling okay.

Keeping the pain off my face was difficult, but I spoke in a normal voice for anyone close enough to hear. "She's been trying really hard to get pregnant."

Walt clapped his hands and called out to everyone.

"Thank you, ladies, for all joining me." He smiled broadly, taking his seat at the head of the table. Belle sat to his right, and Cindie was relegated to the farthest seat, next to Junior. Not that she seemed to mind.

"So as you all know, Ari and I have been trying to have a baby."

I almost snorted.

"And I'm pleased to announce that Ari is pregnant."

My stomach dropped. Ari had said the same thing the morning after the rape, but I figured it was her emotions speaking. But wait. If she was pregnant, now she'd return to her room. I'd see her once again.

The chatter grew louder, a mix of jealousy and excitement and confusion. Some of them didn't know what happened to Walt's sons because they hadn't been around when Walt got rid of the last one. Maybe he was planning on sharing that with them. He had to be because everyone questioned Ari and Junior's relationship. They all thought it was an unexpected and weird love triangle, but they didn't know Junior would soon be dead and that Walt would take over his body.

It hit me then, and I fought the rising tears as Ari's words replayed in my head. "Think of what I'll lose."

She'd been troubled upon finding out Walt picked her to have his child. I thought she meant losing her freedom, losing her body, or replacing her dead son with a new one, but I was wrong.

Ari knew what I hadn't. That baby was only a vessel that one day Walt would assume.

Ari would lose her son.

Again.

Walt smiled fondly at the girls. "This is such an exciting time, and we have many big changes coming. No word to anyone outside of the house though. Not until I say so."

Before the tears dripped down my cheeks, I slid my napkin under my eyes. Cindie's face mirrored my own sadness.

I faked my way through the rest of dinner, drinking wine and pretending to be happy, except I was anything but. Walt was preparing to leave the dining room, and I stopped him, plastering a smile on my face. "Should I help Ari move her things back to her room?"

"That won't be necessary. She'll spend her pregnancy in my quarters."

My mouth fell open with a silent no. Walt frowned, setting his hand on my shoulder and squeezing.

"Lil, Ari has a new job now, and she won't have time for other relationships. You need to think about moving on. Her time here is limited," he whispered.

I almost dropped to the floor; his words confirmed that Ari had been right about everything.

He brushed past me and out the door. A warm hand grasped my arm, and I found Cindie's caring eyes. "I'm sorry," she said.

I replied with a thank you because that's all I could handle.

Chapter Forty
House of Despondency

Three days later, Walt called me into his office. He tossed his pen onto the desk and grumped, "Did you see what he's done now?"

He picked up a printout from a gossip website and threw it in front of me. I scanned the pictures of Junior and some skanky girl. The first few lines talking about how he was caught with a backstreet hooker.

It was the picture that got me: Junior's sunken eyes and the added thirty pounds. The photographs were taken through the window of the car, and the girl's head was in his lap.

The reporter got to her after it happened, and she'd spilled her story. I'd be willing to guess she added her own details about the event for extra cash.

"How the hell am I supposed to make it look like he and Ari are together when he's pulling this shit?" Walt snatched the paper back before I'd had time to finish the article. "Hmm. This can work out for us. Maybe he and Ari took a break. Which makes sense since she's not working. He was devastated over losing her."

Walt dug in his drawer and took out a phone I'd never seen. He clicked through his contacts and held the phone to his ear.

"Hey, I've got some news for you," he said after a few moments. I about fell out of my seat. He sounded like a woman, soft and mysterious.

"No," he giggled. "Did you see the news about Junior? He's all torn up about Ari. That's why he went to the prostitute... I know. And he's got any of us here to choose from." He acted all offended.

They spoke a bit longer, and Walt hung up the phone. "There, that should take care of the problem."

"What was that?" I asked, unable to hide the incredulity in my voice.

Walt smirked. "Damage control."

He had sat there for years and bitched about the media leaks, but he'd probably been doing this all along.

"But why?"

Lil," he sighed. "You've been in this business long enough to understand the realities of public life and how we must direct the narrative. Now we'll need Bianca to post about their making up. Please tell her to do that in a few days."

He was the master manipulator.

"How will she know what to post? They're not in a relationship."

He eyed me for a few moments before speaking. "Lil, your work has gone downhill. You haven't been paying attention to our social media sites. This is becoming a problem."

I squeezed the pencil in my hand. He could do to me what he'd done to all the others, make me disappear.

"I'm sorry."

"I've realized my mistake in all of this and have decided to let you and Ari see each other again. As friends. She's been awfully mopey, and I'm tired of it. Starting in a few days, you may see her."

I could barely contain my excitement, but I didn't want to let on to Walt how much it meant. I wiped my sweaty palms on my skirt. "Thank you so much. I've missed her a lot, and I promise I'll do better."

He smirked at me like he saw into my head. "I talked at dinner about how we'd be seeing changes around here. A minor shakeup, if you will. It's time for Cindie to retire. She hasn't been performing very well lately."

It was like he'd dropped the curtain, and now I was able to see exactly what was going on behind the scenes, each and every horrible deed. Part of me wished to go back and become the ignorant girl again, but that was impossible.

"But she still does better than some of the other girls." The numbness I'd been feeling for so long over not seeing Ari was being replaced by anger and disgust.

He waved me off. "No, she's on a downward trend. Her bad attitude has spilled over into her work, and she has the gall to gripe to others about me after all I've given her." He leaned back in the chair, his face tight.

"I'm considering suicide. Off-site. The police will want to investigate, and we'll let them into her room where there'll be a note, but we'll make sure they find nothing else. We'll need to procure a gun."

"That's too messy," I blurted. *God, what am I doing?* I didn't want to be a part of her fake suicide, but I'd be involved no matter what. I should warn her.

He grinned. "That's why I pay you the big bucks."

Cindie had never given a damn about me, but that didn't mean she should die. But if Walt discovered I ratted him out, he'd be scheduling my suicide too. My stomach twisted in knots. He was planning so many deaths.

"I'll consider this further," he said. "The best thing is to do it after I die. She killed herself out of grief since she discovered my dead body. She couldn't live without me. Everybody would believe that."

Cindie had been on his arms for years, and nobody would question her suicide.

"But how will you die?"

"Heart attack." He patted his chest. "By the time they find me, I'll be dead."

Walt had it all worked out. It was so easy for him to fool everybody, but then again, this wasn't his first time.

"It's time to celebrate." He sat next to me and tossed my notebook to the side. His hand slid up my thigh, and I shivered with revulsion.

"I expect more out of you, Lil. Don't disappoint me like Ari did."

His threat chilled me, and I remained still.

"Get your clothes off and get on the desk," he growled. I shot out of my seat and jumped out of my clothes, remembering the tightness on my throat and the way he could squeeze the life out of me without touching my body. What was better, a slow death, wasting away day by day or quick and painful at Walt's hands?

I faked enthusiasm, doing it for Ari. Although he wouldn't harm her physically, I didn't doubt he enjoyed torturing her mind, and I'd rather he have sex with me than raping her.

"Touch me. It's been too long since we've made love." His arms pulled me into him. Walt had no heart, no soul, and I'd been so blind, but now I couldn't refuse him.

He shoved me to my knees. For years we'd been equals, but now he was putting me back into place. He was in control. I tried to think about other things, happy things, but I didn't picture Ari because no matter how I tried to see my beautiful girl, all that entered my mind was her screaming in pain. I allowed the emptiness to take over my mind as my body performed the motions.

He placed a hand on my head to stop me and carried me to his sofa. I put my faking skill to good use, the many tricks I'd learned over the years. He didn't seem to notice, or maybe he didn't care.

When he collapsed into me, my arms welcomed him, but my head screamed no. When he told me he loved me, and I whispered those words back, I died a little more inside.

"It's nice to have you back." He patted me on the shoulder, and I stayed on the sofa as he dressed and strutted toward the office door. "I've got a few things to check on. I'll see you later."

I scrambled back to my office and allowed the emotions to fill me again. Disgust, pain, horror. All at once it overtook my heart and body, and I crumpled onto the sofa.

The worst part was that I was trapped here forever, and in no time, my Ari would be gone.

Chapter Forty-One
House of Duress

Another two days passed, and Walt still wouldn't let me see Ari. Finally he'd told me I could visit her today. He was out of the house for a short time, so now would be perfect.

I slid my finger on the scanner, hoping he'd allowed me access again. I wanted to see her on my terms, not in front of him.

The door clicked, and I sighed a breath of relief and stepped inside.

"Lil," Belle said, coming around the corner.

Please go away.

"Where's Walt? I need to talk to him about something."

He had said I could see Ari, so there was no need to lie, but I didn't want Belle around either. I headed to his bathroom to check there first, so she'd think I was looking for Walt and not Ari.

"Do you think I'm dumb?" Belle stood there with her hands on her hips, a stupid pout on her face. "She's not here. She's out with Walt and Junior."

Oh no. Walt kept holding that carrot out, and then he denied me again.

"When will he be back?"

"Why don't you give me a message, and I'll get it to him when he returns."

"No, this is business. When he makes you his partner, then I'll discuss business things with you."

"We've been having fun." Belle turned around, heading for the sitting room, also known as Ari's prison. "Every night we celebrate. It almost makes me jealous the way that Walt makes love to her." She grinned. "Of course, she's invited me in on that action too."

"What are you talking about?" I stomped after her. Ari wasn't in the room, but I smelled her scent.

"Me and Ari. I don't know why I turned her down when I first moved in. She's got a spectacular tongue."

"She wouldn't touch you with a hundred-foot pole," I spat.

Ari might not have had a choice with Walt, but she'd never choose to be with Belle. I spun around to get out of the room and ran into a solid mass in the hallway. Cindie stumbled backwards.

"I'm sorry," I said as she righted herself. I had to tell her about Walt's plan. I'd done so many wrong things in my life, but this was a time where I could do the right thing.

"Did you see her?" Cindie asked.

"No. She's out with Walt. He told me I'd be allowed to see her again, but he screwed me over again."

Cindie frowned, her head cast down. "I watch her from my window when she sits on the balcony. For hours and hours. She stares off into the hills while rubbing her belly." Cindie patted her stomach absentmindedly and then clenched her fists.

"Does Walt touch—"

No, I don't want to know.

Cindie relaxed her hands and waved me to follow as she started walking. I didn't ask where we were going, and she led me to her room, to her balcony. She closed the doors behind us, and I looked over at her perfect view of Walt's room.

"You're welcome to use this anytime." Cindie laid her hand on my shoulder.

"Thank you. I…" The tears slid down my cheeks again. I had to hide them away when I was working, but alone I'd cried more tears this last month than I had my whole life.

I faced Cindie. "We need to talk."

We sat down on the chairs, and I tried to think of the way to soften what I was about to say, but there was no way to do so.

"Walt is going to kill you."

Her face didn't change, no shock, no sadness, so I continued. "He'll be taking over Junior's body soon, and *he* will die. And then you're next. You'll commit suicide because of your grief."

"I'll probably be better off." Her voice held no emotion, and she stared over the grounds. "We all agreed to this, even begged for it. We made a deal with the devil, and at some point we all have to pay."

"But we didn't know, not until it was too late."

Her head flicked back toward me, and she studied my face. "Yeah, the first time, but every time after that, we knew exactly what we were doing. I suspected years ago his stories were bullshit, and one night he admitted it all to me. In that moment, I knew my fate was sealed."

Ignorance was so much easier than the truth. He would kill us all someday. Invisible hands squeezed my throat.

We sat, sharing no more words.

"Will you ever choose the route of Belle?" she finally asked.

The old Belle, the one whose body had joined so many other girls who disappeared at Walt's hands. Maybe death would be welcomed, but the thing that scared me the most was where I went after death.

"I don't know." I didn't think I could live without Ari, but I had months to change his mind about her. There was a chance, but my heart didn't believe that.

A hard resignation crossed Cindie's face. "I know that day is getting closer. I'm just…"

Scared to death.

"I am too," I finished for us both.

Chapter Forty-Two
House of Defeat

A few days later, Walt strode into my office. "Ari is feeling better and will be joining us again. Tell Kyle to prepare lasagna tonight so we can welcome her back."

I tried to temper my excitement, but it was threatening to spill out. After he returned to the house with Junior and Ari the other day, he once again denied me access to her, claiming she wasn't feeling well.

Walt sat down and slid the chair closer to my desk. "She had been unable to accept this pregnancy but has finally done so. She's chosen to move on. You may go get her and bring her back to her room to shower and dress, but Lil…" He clutched my hand, his skin unnaturally hot but not scorching. Or maybe it was because my hands were clammy.

He flashed his green eyes at me. "You and Ari are done. I trust you. Don't disappoint me."

This was a test, and if we didn't pass, Ari would be stuck in Walt's room until the baby was born.

I unclenched my teeth, my jaw aching. "You can trust me."

I worried he'd follow me, but he returned to his office while I went to see Ari in his bedroom. Thank goodness Belle wasn't around. Ari lay on a lounge chair on the balcony where Cindie said she usually was. Her once curvaceous body was skin and bones, and her lustrous hair now limp.

I wiped the silent tears off my face. "Ari?"

She spun around, a smile lighting up her face. Until she looked back at the door and tensed. Terror paled her skin.

"He told me I could visit." I hugged her tightly, but she was a stiff board, her arms at her sides. "Kyle is making lasagna for you tonight."

She shrugged and pulled away. "I heard the trick-or-treat party went well. I probably didn't miss much. I didn't have a costume yet anyway." Her voice was so flat and unnatural.

"It was..." Depressing without her. "Okay."

"I've been busy. Walt gave me a camera, and I've been taking pictures out here." She waved her hand at the hills. "It's the same scene basically, but I've captured it in all sorts of different light." Her voice remained emotionless. "You'd be amazed at the wildlife you see when you sit quietly and watch."

I rubbed my arms, my body chilled. He'd changed her; she was no longer the girl she used to be.

"I'm sorry." I blinked away the tears. "I never imagined things would turn out this way. Please believe me." I gripped her hand, but it remained limp.

"It's okay. Belle told me what you said."

"What did I say?"

"That you'd moved on and refused to come see me because I refused him. That's why nobody came to see me."

I swallowed hard. All this time she thought I didn't love her anymore, that nobody cared about her. "Did Walt say that too?"

"He doesn't talk about you unless it has something to do with business." Her chin trembled lightly, and I reached for her, but she pulled away. "Or when he tells me about all the times you two are together."

"Oh god, Ari. That's not true. These last few weeks have been horrible, and he—"

"It doesn't matter, really. Life goes on. I'm stuck in here, but you..." Her voice cracked, and a tear slid down her cheek. "How can you keep having sex with him? And Belle? How can you tell him you love him after what he did to me?"

Ari hid her face in her hands, the sobs rolling through her. I'd never felt so low. I should've broken down his door to see her. I should've fought harder against Walt. They'd lied to her and told her she meant nothing to me.

I tugged her wet hands away from her face. Despite her sallow skin and bruised eyes, she was beautiful. She was my world, the only thing that mattered, and they'd made her feel like trash.

"I never slept with Belle. I—"

"But, she said—"

"And she told me you invited her into your bed too."

"I didn't," she said. "We haven't ever been together."

"I know." I put my finger to her lips. "She's a liar. I would never touch her either, and Walt, it's not my choice."

She shook her head violently. "I saw the video. You went to him, Lil. In his office. In the tower. In your room. You were the one in control."

"He showed you videos of us?" Impossible. I never willingly went to Walt.

"Belle did."

"They're fake. They—"

"They're not fake. I saw it with my own eyes."

"No." I dropped my head and tried to figure this out. Old videos most likely. "They're real, but they're not recent. I swear, the only place we've had sex is in his office one time, and I didn't want to." I tilted her chin so she was looking at me. "He hurt you. He raped you. And I could never willingly be with him again. Every day I have to face him and what he did to you, and it takes all my strength to keep going."

I fought the tears. He'd violated her in the worst way, and I couldn't erase that.

"I love you so much," I said. "I'm so scared because he told me we couldn't be together, and I'm scared for you and this baby. I don't know what to do, but we have to do something. We have to try."

"Oh, Lil!" She threw her arms around me, and we cried together. So many things were going through my head, so many questions, and I wanted to stay here on this balcony.

I forced myself to pull away. "I'm supposed to bring you back to your room and get you ready for dinner."

"He's really letting me out of here?" She leaned back toward me and grasped my hands.

"Yes." The reality that Ari would join us again began to sink in. "But it's a test. We have to do what he wants; otherwise, he'll stick you away again."

She shrunk back and glanced toward his room. "I never considered this place a prison, not until now. How many people would give anything to be here, and I just want to get out."

"It is a prison." These stone walls kept us captive, but there had to be a way out. "What will we do?"

She shrugged, her face lined with defeat. "There's nothing we can do. We can't run. Can't hide. He's got more power than I ever imagined, and there's no way to kill him. I've thought about a hundred ways, but I don't think anything would work. He'd stop us first."

There had to be something. He wasn't immortal. He required the renewals like we did.

Except for one small detail: he needed the body and blood of his son. He didn't want to start over in a new person's body. He wanted his current life to keep rolling.

"I know what he'll do after my baby is born, and I'm okay." Ari's voice was so forlorn, so empty. "It'll save me the pain of losing another boy. I've accepted that."

But I wouldn't. I couldn't.

Chapter Forty-Three
House of Dysfunction

Ari and I only talked of trivial things on our walk back to her room. While she was getting ready, I scanned our social media accounts. There was nothing new about Ari or Junior, but a search of the internet showed the *rumors* about how Ari might take him back, that she loved him despite his drug problem and would do anything she could to help him. Walt must've made more calls to his reporter friend.

His master plan included a death for Ari in childbirth, which would create the least amount of questions, especially so few months after Walt's own death. And "Junior" would mourn his beloved Ari so soon after his "father."

And he was adding Cindie's suicide to that too. It was one more reason why I should lobby to keep Ari alive. Too many suspicious deaths were not a good thing, but he'd never go along with it.

After a good shower, some makeup, and a bright purple dress, Ari was back to her normal self, at least on the outside.

"You look amazing." My whole body wanted to jump out of this chair and run to her, to take her in my arms and kiss and hug her and never let go, but Walt might be watching.

I accompanied her to the dining room, and other girls quickly swarmed her, wanting to know how she was doing since Walt had told them she'd been feeling ill.

I heard a gasp behind me and turned to find Jaslyn staring at Ari. "She's back. Did you talk to her yet?" she whispered, leading me away from the others.

"Yes, he finally allowed me to see her. But we can't have a relationship." I watched as Walt brought Ari and Junior together for a picture. It took some urging from Walt, but Junior forced a smile. The light had extinguished in his eyes that day in the dungeon, and it still hadn't come back.

Depression, that's how they'd spin it. Until Walt took over his body and things returned to normal. The world wouldn't even question how he'd quit using heroin cold turkey. His pregnant girlfriend and the death of his father would drive him to clean himself up.

Tia stomped up to us. "Okay, what the fuck is going on. Walt's got Ari pregnant, but I keep seeing pictures of her and Junior all over the place."

Jaslyn and I exchanged glances. Tia wasn't here the last time Walt renewed himself, and I wasn't about to explain it all to her.

"You should ask Walt," I said.

Her hands flew to her hips, and she glared at me. "You're his assistant."

"Wouldn't that be weird if Walt got her pregnant, and she was in love with Junior?" Jaslyn played up the situation to a girl who loved drama. "What do you think Walt would do?"

Tia's face lit up. "He'd kick her out. I don't get why he wants a baby in the first place."

"I think he misses having a child around. Junior being an adult and all." Jaslyn motioned to get my butt out of there as she continued with her theories on why Walt wanted kids.

I slipped away. Tia would learn about Walt's renewal soon enough. Unfortunately, I ran into a pouting Belle, and she grabbed my wrist and scowled, her eyes following Ari and Walt.

"Did she move back into her own room yet?" Her dark face reminded me of that night with Junior in the dungeon. How excited she'd been to see Walt rape Mindy. She was insane like Walt.

"She's gone."

Belle had brought all those other girls to the house. Leigh, Mindy, and Brinn. She had a vicious streak, and maybe she was stupid enough to screw Walt in his demon form. This was as good a time as ever to ask. I lowered my voice. "Did you ever have sex with Walt when he was…" I paused. "Different."

Belle snorted. "Are you fucking kidding? That dick is red hot. I don't know how Ari survived. Nobody else has. Maybe he can control it though. Not like I'm gonna try it." She shivered.

I zeroed in on her words. *Nobody else has.* I'd shut off the video before the end of Mindy's rape, but Leigh… Her body had seemed so limp after Walt finished with her. It'd looked like she and Belle were kissing, but I'd never seen her move. Only Belle.

And the voice. When Walt asked if it was the best sex she'd ever had, it was only one word, but that could've been Belle.

The skin on the back of my neck prickled. She was evil, pure evil, and I couldn't deny what I knew deep down: those girls never left the dungeon alive.

Walt had killed those women with no remorse, and now he'd move on to Junior and Cindie and Ari.

I wanted to stay as far away from Belle and Walt as possible, but I wouldn't be able to keep that up. I still had to work with Walt and convince him everything was okay.

Dinner ended, and Ari and I were ready to leave, but Walt waved us over to him and Junior standing in the corner.

"Ari, you're looking marvelous tonight." His gray eyes studied her.

"Thank you," she murmured, her head tilted down.

"I wanted to inform the two of you about the party next week." He set his hands on Ari's and Junior's shoulders. "I expect you to keep Ari company."

Junior's head flew up, and he opened his mouth, but Walt frowned, and Junior's head nodded in obedience.

"All night long. Do you understand," Walt added, squeezing both of their shoulders.

"Yes, Walt," Ari said at the same time Junior said, "Yes, sir."

Walt probably had a few more of those phone calls in his fake voice lined up to make.

"Good." Walt removed his hands and strode back to the girls who hadn't left, and Ari and I slipped away to my room.

"I guess this is the start of the end." She settled onto my bed.

I didn't say it, but the end had started as soon as I talked Walt into making Ari the mother of his baby.

"No, we're making a plan," I said. "It'll take a lot of preparation, and we'd better look at everything from every angle." Our lives were at stake, and we couldn't make stupid mistakes

Ari shook her head. "You have your life. You can't give that up for me."

"Ari." I clasped her hands. "My life is nothing without you. I won't leave you here to get killed. We are going to make a plan."

We'd have to make sure we did our research on where to go on outside computers. We'd have to stash money away and have every detail mapped out. Our lives depended on it.

She blinked away her tears and hugged me. "Tell me what you were thinking."

We were in this together until the very end.

Chapter Forty-Four
House of Deception

Walt threw one last party before his fake heart attack, surrounding himself with all his friends. Their Walt wouldn't be dead, but poor Junior would be. We'd all mourn the man we loved, and then Walt would start a new, fresh life.

Everybody would be none the wiser.

This party was small, only fifty of his closest friends and business partners, and informal. No princess dresses or tiaras. I stared across the room where Ari was chatting with others, no sign of a baby bump, but she was only about a month along. It was the first time all evening that Junior wasn't by her side.

I slipped over and led her off to the side to get drinks and some privacy. "Did Junior give you a little breathing room?"

"Ugh, he's been like a leach all night." Ari rubbed her temples. "I try to back away from him, just to get a few inches of space, but he always crowds back around me. He's certainly playing things up for the guests. Did you see his tie?"

I shook my head and glanced at Junior to see a tie that matched Ari's teal cocktail dress. The teal handkerchief peeked out of his front pocket. "Nice," I commented. "Did you two plan that?"

Ari huffed. "I wondered why Walt asked me the other day what I was wearing."

Walt motioned to the two of us, and I nodded to him. "Paste that fake smile back on," I said, and we headed over to Walt and

Junior. We'd followed his rules and kept our distance from each other for the most part.

"Ari," Junior said. "Where did you run off to?" He tugged on her hand and pulled her to him. She kept the smile on her face the whole time.

"Sorry." She laughed.

"New love is so sweet," one of Walt's friends swooned. She was a respectable old lady who'd been a friend of Walt when he was in his original body, and as far as I knew, she, nor anybody else, ever suspected who they were really talking to.

When Junior died, and Walt took over his body, it would be like Junior did a complete one-eighty with his personality. He'd become responsible and stop all his childish actions.

"I'm so glad these two found each other," Walt said to his circle of guests, his arm hanging over Junior's shoulders. "I'm so proud of my son."

Before everything went down, Junior would've been beaming, but now he wore a tight smile. He'd become an emotionless puppet, no joy and enthusiasm, no challenges or defiance of Walt's commands.

Walt waved his hand and turned to his son. "Junior is starting to settle down now. He's found a good woman." Walt glanced at Ari and smiled. "I'm so proud to have him on board with me, learning the ropes. One day he'll take over my empire. Right, son."

"Right, Father." Junior nodded mechanically.

"A toast is in order. Lil?" Walt swung his head around until he spotted me, and I stepped forward to stand shoulder-to-shoulder with my torturer, pretending this was a joyous occasion. I had Walt fooled. Sure, he knew I was sad about the Ari thing, but I submitted to him blindly without opposition. She submitted to him too, and he wouldn't expect that we were planning an escape before the baby was born.

Walt held his crystal wineglass in the air. "To my son, Junior, the most important person in my life. And to our new venture."

"Here, here," the crowd said, and we all clinked glasses.

"Congratulations, Junior." I leaned over and kissed his cheek. If only he wasn't here, Walt couldn't take his life next week. Then Walt would have to wait longer until Ari's baby was old enough.

I excused myself so it didn't look like I was hanging around Ari too much.

Later, as the party was wrapping up, Walt cornered me, sliding his strong arms around my waist.

"Tonight has been a success, Lil." His fiery breath assaulted my ear, and I held back my cringe. It took everything inside me to turn and face him with a smile.

"You deserve it. It's a special night for you." I patted his arm encouragingly. "The world will miss you."

His lips brushed mine, a move that used to make me soar inside, but now I fought the urge to throw up.

"After my renewal, you'll be my first to experience my new virile body. I know why you've been pulling away from me lately."

A wave of nausea swept through me. He'd seen through our ruse. I'd been so dumb to think we could fool him that easily. He hadn't announced the baby to the world, so he could get rid of her right now and find another girl.

"Cindie told me the truth." Walt tucked a few strands of hair behind my ear. "My body has slowed down, but after another week, I'll have that all back."

"What did Cindie say?" My heart thumped against my chest.

He ran his finger down my nose. "Just that I wasn't making you *happy* like I used to. But don't worry. I understand I'm not the virile man I once was."

I wanted to shake Cindie. She'd created doubt in Walt's head over my loyalty, and now she stood there talking to someone like my whole world wasn't about to crash down.

Oh, but wait.

He thought I was losing attraction to him because he was aging, which meant he was giving me a reprieve until he made himself young again. She got me that reprieve, as short as it was, but next week all that would return to normal. I couldn't handle having sex with him all the time. Not anymore.

But I wouldn't have a choice.

"Thank you for understanding," I said.

"Well, I should. Remember our first night together before I renewed you? You were the first woman over forty I'd slept with. I still remember your sagging skin and chubby legs. How tired you got. It was so hard to hold back my revulsion and get through that night. I don't want you to feel the disgust like I did back then."

He gazed off over my shoulder, and I swallowed down the shock. He'd told me I was beautiful, that the sex was amazing. He'd been manipulating me since the first day I saw him. By now, his betrayal shouldn't hurt, but it did.

I forced a laugh. "I'm sorry. I shouldn't be so superficial." I actually never once noticed that he was losing his steam.

"It's an internal reaction. We can't change how we feel. But I appreciate you putting up with me."

"Think about when you have your new body. I can't wait to christen the house with you." I choked back the bile in my throat. Junior looked nothing like the previous Walt, and he had his mother's looks, and now Walt would expect me to have sex with the body of his son, a man I first met when he was thirteen. It felt incestuous.

I was taking one hit after another, and it would never end.

Chapter Forty-Five
House of Death

Tonight Walt was dying. Or rather Walt Junior.

The calendar was cleared for the evening so all the girls could be a part of this night. Walt had even sent home all the other employees. Kyle and the kitchen crew were gone now, and even our security was excused. To the outside world, it was another family night where Walt and the girls had some innocent fun. What happened in the basement would be nothing close to innocent.

Junior slumped in his seat at the table. I was the official babysitter tonight, keeping him occupied and stopping him from leaving early.

"I'll be back." I took out a bottle and headed into the kitchen. I opened the wine and poured only a bit more into the glass, then diluted it with water.

Bianca stepped in behind me. "What are you doing?"

"It's for Junior. Walt wants him semi-sober. Will you do me a favor, please?" She nodded, and I continued. "When he remarks that it's off, will you take a drink and pretend it's fine?"

We headed back out, and I gave Junior the glass. He took a sip and wrinkled up his nose. "This tastes funny."

I didn't say a word, but Bianca reached out. "Let me try it." She took a drink and laughed. "Tastes good to me."

Junior took another drink, stared at the glass, and shrugged.

After eating, we gathered in the theater room to watch a show. The action movie started, and Junior perked up. At least he'd enjoy his last few hours of life watching one of his favorite movies.

Walt wedged himself between me and Cindie, and we posed for pictures that Bianca would post on our social media pages. One big happy family. The last night of Walt's life would be spent with those he loved.

I focused on the screen, trying to forget what was coming, until Walt nudged me.

"Why don't you get things ready," he said.

I retreated down to the renewal room before everyone else arrived. We had set up the room earlier, so there wasn't much to do. I closed my eyes in the silence. In no time there'd be a very different scene going on in here. Walt wanted everyone there to be a part of the ceremony. Those who didn't know the full story about Walt would find out now.

After the movie ended, the girls slowly filtered in, that nervous energy back, and chatted quietly, but the buzz filled the air.

Walt marched in with Junior at his side.

"What are we doing down here?" Junior's head swung left and right, taking in the room decorated in a way he'd never seen it. He spotted the table draped in black, the dagger shining underneath the light in the box, the crystal chalice. He stepped back, his face ashen and his eyes wide and blinking, and grasped the arm of the sofa and held on tight.

"Just a celebration. Come with me, my son." Walt tugged on Junior's wrist and led him to the table. Junior moved as if trudging through concrete. He grimaced at his feet but didn't stop.

"Why don't you lie down," Walt ordered, pointing to the table. "Lil, get my tools."

I scuttled over and grabbed the glass and dagger case.

"No, I don't think so. I, um…" Junior looked toward the door, then to his feet, and his shoulders leaned forward like they were trying to move his body. His voice quivered. "What's going on? What are you doing to me?" Junior grunted, his face red.

"It's simple. My body is getting old, and you…" Walt scowled. "Are killing yours. So it's time for me to take over." He nudged Junior.

"No. No. I'll stop. I won't touch heroin ever again." His face contorted, and he seemed to struggle against the unseen force that was commanding his body to crawl onto the table. "Don't do this. Please."

All of Walt's girls formed a circle around the table. Princesses dressed in their finest lingerie, here to witness another death. Ari, Jaslyn, Cindie, and all the rest. Some were clearly disturbed by the scene, but all remained motionless.

I stood at the head of the table with Walt's special case in my hand. Nobody said a word, the air so heavy and thick.

"Don't do this. Please." The pitiful noises spilling from Junior's mouth didn't even sound like him anymore.

Walt smirked, and his face changed, dark marks speckling his gray face, green eyes flaring. Pure evil. The dread swept through me. How long would he continue hurting people? His sons. Ari's son. All of us.

"It must be done. Unfortunately, I can't wave a magic wand and make myself immortal." Walt moved forward and stroked Junior's head with the black fingernails on his wrinkly gray hand. "You are special, my son. Only you can provide me with a new life."

Only Junior.

"I don't want to be special," he whimpered, tears gathering in his eyes. "Please, Father. I promise I'll do what you want."

"Oh, now you call me Father. Always when you want something." Walt scowled once again.

"Hand me my dagger, Lil?"

Junior is the only one who could provide Walt another life. The words repeated in my head as sobs shook Junior's body. The timing of this ceremony was so important. Walt had to collect some of Junior's blood and drink it before he died.

"Lil!" Walt growled, and I opened the black case in my hands. Purple velvet cradled the silver dagger, clean now but soon to be covered in blood.

I held forth the case for Walt, and he removed the blade, sliding his finger along the sharp edge. A thin red line appeared, and he licked it.

All eyes fixed on Walt—except mine. I studied every girl in the circle. Many emotions played across their faces: fear, revulsion, and curiosity, but the sparkle shone in Belle's eyes, the way she leaned forward with a satisfied smile. She wanted this as much as Walt, and she scared me the most.

And Ari.... The baby boy inside her bred to lose his life in twenty-some years.

Things could be different. Maybe... possibly...

For now, all Walt had was Junior, but if Junior wasn't here, Walt would need a new son who was old enough to take the helm, and by that time, Walt would be around seventy. His body wouldn't be as strong as he was now. Ari's son might have a fighting chance if he knew what was coming.

Walt grasped the dagger and traced it around Junior's neck, pressing only lightly to create a chain of blood not deep enough to cause his death. The pain flashed in Junior's eyes, and his screams rang out.

Several of the girls shifted or looked away, and Jaslyn covered her ears. Belle's small grin grew.

"For pete's sakes. Shut the hell up." Walt waved his hand in front of Junior's face, and the noise disappeared. Junior's head stilled, but his mouth remained wide open in that silent scream.

I stared at the thin red necklace on Junior's neck. Then Walt. Then Ari's tummy.

"Prepare the chalice," Walt demanded, and I set the crystal goblet that would catch Junior's blood next to his arm.

Walt took Junior's hand and felt for a pulse. His heart must have been flying by now, although he'd stopped screaming. A heart attack would end it all, if only Junior would be so lucky to die before Walt gathered and drank the blood. Walt would be stuck waiting another twenty years for Ari's baby to grow up.

Holy Shit.

My body fired up as Walt held the steel blade to Junior's wrist, ready to create a better blood source. "Don't worry," he said. "You'll pass out from pain before I collect what I need."

Junior's eyes darted between his wrist and his father. I couldn't comprehend the terror inside him, to witness his own death at the hands of the man who was supposed to love him.

Walt carved deep into the artery on Junior's wrist. Junior's face scrunched in pain, and Walt handed the blade back to me and twisted Junior's arm so that the blood would drip into the cup. Only a sip or so was needed to transfer Junior's life force, a few drips not enough. Walt could've used an IV and put Junior out. It could've been clean, but he preferred to terrorize his son.

That slit in Junior's wrist wouldn't matter because it would heal in the renewal process, and we all would stand here and wait until there was enough blood to complete the ceremony.

If Junior were dead, Walt couldn't do the renewal. Junior needed to be alive when Walt drank the blood and said his dark words.

The red-stained dagger rested in my hands. Only this might stop Walt from taking Ari's baby. I'd do it for the life inside her even though I'd die. I pressed my eyes shut for a moment, gathering the courage. This was the only way to gain more time.

"I'm sorry, Junior," I whispered.

Walt swung his head toward me, and I shoved him as hard as I could. He stumbled and fell backwards to the floor, and I slashed the blade across Junior's neck. Hard and deep. I had to sever his artery immediately. He needed to die.

Junior's head fell back, blood spurted out onto my face, and the dagger felt so heavy in my hands. Screams erupted around the room as Junior cough and gasped for air, but he'd never breathe again. And I couldn't bear to look into his eyes and see his life drain away.

"No!" Walt roared, and Belle scrambled to help him up, but she got in his way and slowed him down. He pushed her aside and darted over. Walt clutched at Junior's free arm, holding a thumb over his wrist, but the blood was no longer spurting from Junior's neck. The room buzzed with motion, bodies moving everywhere, but all I saw was Walt's green eyes and the fury born from the depths of hell.

Junior was dead, and Walt would have to wait to renew his life. Walt seized Junior's body and flung it across the room.

He leapt over and smacked my face. "What have you done?"

My head exploded in pain, and the dagger flew to the ground. He smacked me again and again until he finally leaned back.

Tears flowed down my cheeks, and I scratched at my throat as it constricted, but no release would come. Screams echoed around me, and bodies rushed around. I heard banging and other loud noises. Darkness clouded my vision, and peace settled over me. I didn't feel any pain.

With my death, Ari's baby would have a better chance, and that's all I wanted.

Chapter Forty-Six
House of Deliverance

I coughed violently, sucking in a deep lungful of air. My throat burned, and my eyes were fuzzy. I scratched at my neck. Walt's hands were still choking me.

"Relax, Lil. Settle down." Ari's sweet voice cut through the chaos in my mind. "You're okay. You're alive."

Something wet dampened my cheek, and I squinted up to see the most beautiful woman in the world crying.

"You're okay," she repeated as she hugged me to her chest.

But for how long? Walt would…

My eyes flew open, and I tried to sit up. Oh my god. The room was bathed in blood. Red everywhere. The floor, the ceiling, the walls. Junior's body lay crumpled on the slick floor with Belle a few feet away. The dagger I'd used to kill Junior stuck out of her chest, her once-white skin now stained as red as my heart and soul.

"You safe." Arial stroked my forehead.

But we weren't. Walt would kill us all.

"Where's Walt?" I whispered, my voice hoarse. Cindie sat on the floor covered in blood, and Bianca cried in the corner. She looked up, and our eyes met. She ran over and knelt beside us. Everyone else was gone.

Ari helped me sit up, and then I saw Walt face down in a pool of blood. Shards of mirror surrounded him and reflected the light from above. Ari hugged me tightly, hurting my chest, but I didn't tell her that. I never wanted her to let go.

"Cindie stopped him. He was killing you." Ari sniffed and leaned back, still holding onto my arms. "She smashed it over his head. He fell to the floor, and she cut his neck before he got up. Belle tried to stop her."

"Belle was in a rage." Bianca's blood-spattered chin quivered. "She was going to kill Cindie." Her eyes filled with tears, and we all looked toward Cindie, her blonde hair stained with blood, her clothes red. She trudged over, and Bianca embraced her.

"Cindie saved your life," Ari said, and Cindie leaned down and grasped my arm.

"I'm so glad you're okay." Her voice faltered. "I thought we lost you too."

I flung my arms around her and locked them around her neck. The tears welled up once again for the girl I'd once despised. I'd never be able to repay her.

"Thank you." Emotion choked my voice.

"No, thank you." She released me and turned to Junior's bloody body. "But what do we do now?"

*

The house was eerily silent. I showered quickly to wash off the blood and gathered my wet hair in a ponytail. It didn't take long to pack my bag with a few clothes and important items: my favorite pictures of Ari and me, a few mementos from the last two years, and all the cash and expensive jewelry I owned.

Ari trudged into the bedroom, suitcase in hand. "Good, you're out of the shower. The girls are preparing the house."

I stared at her, so many memories flashing through my mind. I'd never see my beautiful girl in a gorgeous gown again. I'd never stroll these hills again with my love. We'd never share an ice cream sundae on the balcony while arguing over chocolate versus vanilla. My throat tightened, and the tears spilled out.

"Oh, Lil." Ari ran to me and squeezed me tightly. She'd been through hell and back, and I didn't think I could explain to her that although I never wanted to see this house again, I'd miss it so much.

"I'll just… This place…"

She kissed me on the forehead. "I'll miss this room most of all." She glanced around my bedroom. "This was the one place I felt most comfortable, the one place where I could be myself. Our whole lives have been one big act, but with you, I feel real. I'm afraid of what's to come, but I know that as long as you're with me, I'll be fine. I love you, Lil."

"I love you too." I hugged her again and set my hand on her belly. "This is our new life, and it'll be okay too."

We pulled apart, picked up our bags, and headed into the hallway. On the second floor, we ran into Cindie, gas can in hand. "Bianca and I found all the cans. She's filling them up outside, and I've started down this hallway. Why don't you drop your bags off and go get a can?"

Ari brought our bags to the waiting car in the front drive while I went into Walt's office to retrieve more money. Luckily, with all the cash and valuables he had in his safe, we'd all be able to start our new lives again.

I stared at Walt's desk and around his office. So many memories were tied up in this room, in this whole house, but I couldn't let them slow me down. I gathered all the money and stuffed it into my bag. He'd betrayed us all, and I wouldn't waste any more tears on him.

Downstairs, the girls were dousing the walls, floors, and furniture with gasoline. We needed the fire to spread fast so that the sprinklers didn't put the flames out. I grabbed a can and went down the hall to another studio, worrying that a spark might set the whole house ablaze before we escaped.

It took us a while because we'd quickly empty a gas can and had to run down and get more, but we soaked the whole floor, the smell of gasoline overwhelming everything.

"Let's get some of the first floor too," Bianca suggested, and despite my aching body, I agreed. We drenched a few strategic rooms and gathered in the welcoming room.

We hadn't talked about who would light the fire, but no way would I let Ari be in the house with all that gasoline. The fumes might cause an explosion, or she might not get out before it spread.

"Give me the matches," I said. "We need to get out of here."

"No," Ari cried, the fear in her eyes.

"I'll do it," Cindie said. "You all stay here. Only one of us should go."

I needed to finish what I'd started. I grabbed her arm. "No, I can—"

"Lil." Cindie put her hand on my arm. "You need to stay here with Ari. She's going to need help with that baby, and you can't get caught in the fire." She stared at the room behind her. "It's too dangerous."

I steadied my voice. "You be careful." I reached out to hug her, not knowing how I hadn't seen the good inside her all those years.

Cindie's chin quivered. "This isn't goodbye, okay. Don't you dare tell me goodbye. You guys go to the car and wait for me."

"We'll see you in a few minutes." I patted her back, and the three of us trudged out the front door. The bright lights from the castle lit up the night, and we lumbered to the waiting car, nobody saying a word.

The front door lay open, and I held my breath, praying she'd make it out alive. Only a minute or two had passed, but it seemed like forever.

"What's that?" Bianca pointed up to the castle. Belle's bedroom light was on. "What's she doing in there?"

"I don't know. I shouldn't have let her go by herself." If she didn't make it out, I'd never live down the guilt.

The light remained on, and we waited.

And waited.

The three of us stared up at the castle we used to love.

Ari held tightly to my hand. "I see flames." She pointed. "Second floor."

"You're right," Bianca said, and Ari clenched my hand even tighter.

Finally Cindie burst through the front door, and I allowed myself to relax. She met us at the car, and we all surrounded her in a big hug.

"Why were you on the third floor, and in Belle's room?" Ari scolded.

"I'm sorry. I stopped to spit on her memory." She grinned, but then her head fell, her eyes full of a weary sadness. "I wanted to start the fire in my room. Cindie is dead, and I wanted to make sure that room went up in flames."

I stepped back, the guilt and shock flooding me. I was the only one with my original first name. "I don't know any of your real names. Not even you." I squeezed Ari's hand.

"My name is Lauren. It's nice to meet you." Cindie offered her hand with a smile. I shook her hand, and we all laughed.

"Bianca?" I said.

"Marcia is my name, but I might pick something more modern." She shrugged. "And how about you, Ari?"

She looked between the three of us and smiled softly. "You know what? I'm just Ari. It's who I want to be."

"Uh, girls, we'd better get away from the house. It's about to get hot." Cindie pointed. No, Lauren—I'd have to get that right.

Flames licked up the sides of the walls from the second-floor windows. We crawled into the car and drove down the long driveway. Once we were a safe distance away, Cindie stopped and got out of the car. We all joined her.

"Thank goodness the sprinklers didn't put out the flames," I said.

"Oh, I shut off the main valve to the house," Cindie said, and I laughed. I never would've imagined she even knew where it was. "My father was a plumber." She grinned.

The orange flames danced, the thick black smoke floating to the sky as the fire engulfed the house. We'd have to leave soon because someone would notice the smoke and call the Pahrump fire department. Not that they could do much.

"Are you sure you don't want to stay with us?" I asked Bianca. She was traveling with us to Denver but would then leave us.

"No. I want to catch a flight to Berlin right away, so I'll at least get out of the country before they come looking for us. From there, I'm not sure."

"We'll have to figure out our plan too, so when things die down, you know how to find us."

"Definitely." Bianca set her arm on my shoulder and squeezed. She glanced down the highway in the direction of town. "We'd better get going."

Bianca and Cindie crawled into the car, but I stayed outside with Ari for a few more moments. We stared up at the burning castle.

Ari gripped my hand. "I'm going to like growing old with you."

"Me too. And no matter how old and gray you get, I'll still love you." We hugged, and I pulled away, but she halted me.

"One thing, Lil." Her voice chilled me inside, and I wasn't sure I wanted to hear her words. Ari set her hand on her belly. "Promise me that if the baby is anything like his father… and I mean anything… you have to take care of him. Because I don't think I could."

I laid my hands on her warm tummy. He couldn't be evil like his father.

Images of all the pain and suffering Walt caused flowed through my head. Every life stolen. Every body harmed.

"Yes, I promise."

She leaned her forehead into mine, our wet cheeks touching. That time would never come, I knew it. He'd be a normal, beautiful baby, and he'd grow up to be nothing like his father.

I felt it in my heart.

We took one last look at the castle walls and crawled into the car that would lead us to our new life.

Acknowledgments

House of Desire was my first stab at a horror story even though I actually published Shallow Depths first. This story started out as a novella, but I decided to develop it into novel length, and it's been many years since I first began writing it.

Thank you to Judy L Mohr for helping me with my story, and thank you to my Book Beta Peeps for being the best writer friends around.

Thank you to Amanda Walker for working with me to get a cool castle picture on the cover. In case anyone is wondering, it's Corvin Castle in Romania, and one day I can maybe visit it.

Thank you also to my readers. Not all my horror writing will be as dark as this one, buy I guess I started off with a bang.

About the Author

Reading has always been a big part of Suzi's life. She even won the most-pages-read award a few times in her junior high English class many, many years ago. She started many writing projects as a kid but never actually finished anything, and then she took a big break from writing that lasted well into adulthood.

She's written in a variety of genres, including horror, suspense and thriller, and has even dipped into fantasy slightly with her fairytale retellings. She's also published contemporary young adult novels under the name Suzi Drew.

In addition to writing, she works as a freelance editor, which means she gets to read at work too. Outside of the writing world, she enjoys spending time with her family and friends and her sweet and fluffy dog.

To find out more about Suzi,
go to SuziWieland.com.

Other Stories by Suzi

<u>Thriller Novels</u>
Black Diamond Dogs

<u>Horror Novels</u>
House of Desire

<u>Horror and Suspense Novellas/Short Stories</u>
Shallow Depths
(Un)lucky Thirteen
Long-Term Effects
The Silent Treatment
A Story to Tell
Panne Dora Pass

Twisted Twins Series
Glenda and Gus
Two for the Price of One
A Hard Split

<u>Fairy Tale Novellas</u>
The Down the Twisted Path Series
The Whole Story
An Unwanted Life
Killing Rosie
The Perfect Meal
When the Forest Cries
In the Queen's Dark Light

Please visit SuziWieland.com
for more information.